Merlin and the Dragons of Atlantis

By Rita and Tim Hildebrandt

The Bobbs-Merrill Company, Inc.
Indianapolis/New York

Published by The Bobbs-Merrill Co., Inc.
Indianapolis/New York
Manufactured in the United States of America
First Printing
Designed by Delgado Design, Inc.
Library of Congress Cataloging in Publication Data
Hildebrandt, Rita.
    Merlin and the dragons of Atlantis

    I. Hildebrandt, Tim. II. Title.
PS3558.I38435M4 1984   813'.54   83-15566
ISBN 0-672-52704-9

A special thank-you to Jim Lawrence for sharing his expert method of
outlining a book.

Sincere thanks to Sue Oster for typing the manuscript, to Lorraine
Lenches for transcribing the tapes, and also to Charlotte Wieland for her
research.

Our appreciation to our agent, Adele Leone, for her interest and support.
And, finally, to our editor, Barbara Lagowski, for her encouragement
with this book and for her special friendship — thank you.

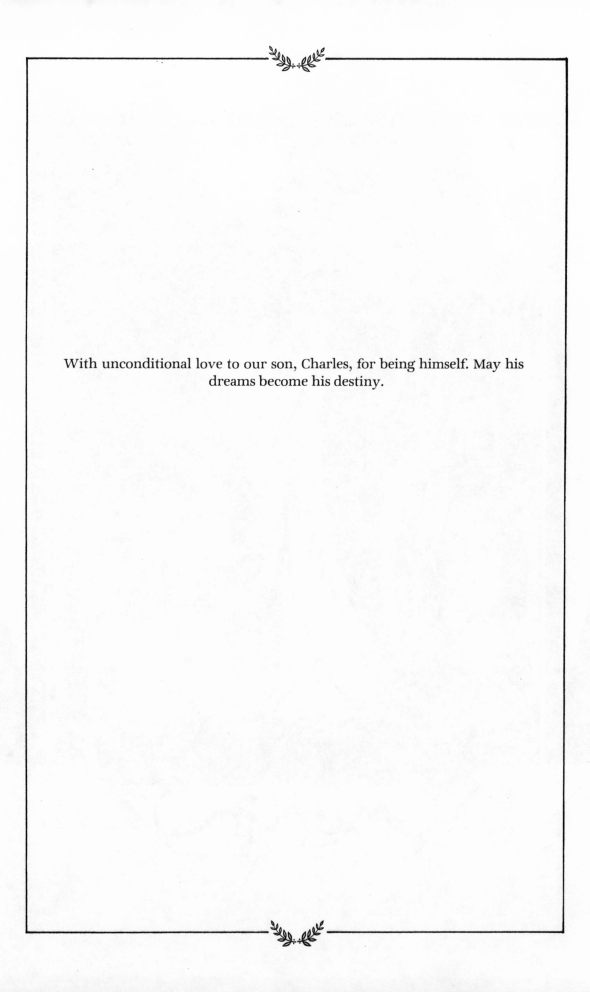

With unconditional love to our son, Charles, for being himself. May his
dreams become his destiny.

Merlin

Prologue

Under the deep midnight sky, filled with flickering stars, the great monolithic circle casts no shadow on the windy plain that juts out to meet the bay. The gray clouds that curtain the moon's illumination gradually part, flooding the ground with the light that spills from the full orb of night. Suddenly the monolith comes alive, lit as if it were a stage, ready for a performance.

Filing in around the circle, each stone's shadow marches to different lengths until they meet converging on the circle's entrance. There they stop. Then a single rank of stones advances forward, in the direction of a large mound. This grassy knoll gapes open as if awaiting cargo. Now veiled in moonlight, the strange site exudes its powerful force, nature touching nature, its energy felt equally by each blade of grass, every wildflower, all living things.

From the mound, a rutted path leads a far distance away from the plain and toward a small settlement. In that special village live the architect and the builders. For them, the circle of stone with its power provides much of their uniqueness.

So it was that, at a time in history when most of humanity was suffering the trials of primitive existence, the people of one small pocket of civilization lived in a relatively advanced state of technology.

Secluded in a hidden glen near the mountain ridge that bounded their land, the unusual Druid village existed in peace for more than two–hundred years. Under the leadership of a chief and council, the Druids developed — and took pride in — a working knowledge of water–power systems, blacksmithing, beekeeping, mining, and crafts. The villagers grouped the round, stone houses with thatched, conical roofs they built along the energy fields they called earth lines. While in fact the Druids were gifted with psychic powers and an innate understanding of fellow creatures and plant life, these earth lines were thought to enhance their superior mental agility. Because they believed that each individual provided a vital link in that power they considered each equal and special.

Set apart from the village and nestled within a group of trees stood a slightly larger house, inviting and friendly as if waiting for visitors. In this house dwelt not only the reason for the villagers' technological superiority but the inspiration of their peaceful philosophy: a man, old beyond reckoning. Because he chose not to be, he was not their governing chief — instead, he was their guide and their teacher.

1
The Darkness Comes

The biting winds of December calmed to a whisper as fiery sunlight began to break the black of night. The old man, wrapped in a shabby fur cape, was bent as if he carried a heavy burden. Slowly he trudged up the rutted, timeworn path that led to his secluded house in the woods. Unexpectedly he stopped and deliberately looked up. His breath smoked in the cold while he considered his ancient stone dwelling as it stood alone in the frosted clearing. He studied it as if it were the first time he had seen that beloved site — or as if this would be the last time he was ever to see it. Then he continued haltingly up the path. He had not yet reached his home when its heavy, wooden door was flung open. A young servant, his vigil now ended, rushed out to help his venerable master into a warm bed.

"Go tell the chief that it is now time," he feebly ordered the servant, who was helping him out of his heavy clothing. He was wet with perspiration. Then he collapsed against the soft mattress and closed his clear, but age-old blue eyes.

"Oh, no! No! No!" Overcome with grief, the young servant nonetheless ran frantically out, and down the path toward the sleeping village in an effort to fulfill his master's wish. "He is dying!" Sobbing and crying aloud, the servant made his way toward the center of the peaceful settlement.

"He is dying! The Great One is dying!" At last the stumbling messenger reached the Druid chieftain's house. While anguished villagers gathered outside, the weeping servant knelt before the astonished ruler.

"How can this be?", the chieftain lamented, his face twisted with heart-break. Hurriedly, the leader threw on his furs and raced along the old familiar path toward his friend's house. "He has been part of this village as far back as the old lore can be sung. Why now? We need to learn so much. What will I do without him?" The brooding leader's sorrow was heavy. He looked back at the village. "What will they do without him?" He reviewed the turn of events with disbelief while the entire village paraded behind him to the old man's house.

In the room where the ancient sage lay, a blazing fire welcomed the elders. They knelt respectfully before his bed, but he would have none of that.

"Get up! Get up! You must never kneel before me." He had lost count of the times he had admonished them for their deference. "I have told you my time was near. Now it has come. Prepare to take me to my tomb. I must die alone." His voice was now strong, and the anguished chief obeyed his words without question.

As he was placed on a fur–lined litter, the villagers surrounded him with bouquets of dried flowers and summer herbs. The Great One, who always loved to hear his people in song, ordered the mourners to join in happy melodies while they carried him to the top of the hill. There, the opening to the grave led down a flight of steps to a doorway that opened out into a large room. Except for the high, stone bier, the tomb was empty; the painted walls, which depicted scenes of the village's history, were its only ornamentation. When the prone body of the Great One was set in place it seemed lonely against the stark barrenness of the tomb, and the grieving chieftain became reluctant to leave his teacher.

"How can we abandon you like this?" he sobbed. "You are so alone."

"That is the way it must be. Hurry and say your farewells. The parting will be less painful for both of us if you go quickly." The aged, worn man then embraced the chief and some of the others in the main party. Tears were shed by everyone; then, finally, the last words of love were spoken. "I have given you all the advice and knowledge you will need to remain a good people. Go in peace and remember all that I have taught you." Thus, with one loud, scraping, thunderous sound, the chamber was closed. Immediately, the villagers began the Herculean task of covering the burial place with the mounds of dirt that would, in future generations, hide even the Druids' memory of him.

But within the darkened vault, the old master lay very quietly, as if to gather his strength. Abruptly, with his energy all but gone, he struggled to his feet. He lit a torch.

Now he must ready his tomb, in case one day it would be opened. In his place on the bier, he laid the body of a man he had found dead of overexposure earlier that night in the forest. Though exhausted by the transfer, the Great One pressed on; time grew short. Holding a torch, he threw himself against the door to a passageway that he alone knew, then sealed it carefully behind him. Hastening along the dark corridors, he paused to pull down the ingeniously placed beams that totally concealed each segment of his dark route as he passed. No one must find him in his secret resting place.

The unknown room lay beneath a time–honored ritual place of the Druids. There, above his tomb, his people would light the funereal fires that would burn for two turns of the moon. Simultaneously, he would begin his own ritual below; a rite whose origins were set in motion nearly ten thousand years before. He removed the precious vial from his pouch. Once, it had been filled to the brim, but now there would be serum for just three more times, and only if he conserved it very carefully. As he contemplated his fate, his thoughts became somber, and he interrupted his rite.

"Why continue this charade?" The same all–too–familiar question. "I am so tired of it. After all, what have I really accomplished in all these centuries?" He closed his eyes, sighed, only to again start the ritual. His answer was always the same — life was always too precious to let go. "Next time, I'll see a different mankind." His spirits lifted a little at the thought. "These people have learned so much from my teachings, and this time the savage beasts have not found me." He spoke aloud, in satisfaction that he had had an opportunity to work with his people, undisturbed, for many years. And, for the first time, the teacher was convinced that they would do well. He found his comfort in that knowledge.

The moment had come. He prepared himself for the serum. First, he took out his box and filled the syringe with the precious fluid. The Great One then shot it into his veins. While he waited for it to take action in his weary body, he carefully arranged his clothing and lay down. A hypnotic trance washed over him, soothing him. This trance state would last for several weeks before he would actually drop off into the deep sleep — the sleep of centuries.

"How long will it last this time?" he questioned himself. "And how much of my knowledge will be left, if any, when I wake?" He closed his eyes as if to dream. The last sound the Great One heard as he drifted into unconsciousness was the soft rustle of feathers in the darkness. That muted sound soothed him for he knew that he would not awake to loneliness.

Above the Great One's tomb, the villagers had finished covering the burial site. At the ritual stone's circle, the fires had been burning for many days. These fires heated the ground so intensely that the warmth penetrated through to the stones of their master's secret grave. The heat would aid in the working of the serum, but the Druids knew nothing of that. They only followed the old man's orders and burned the ground within the stone ring.

When the smoke and light from the fires had been raging for a full week, as if desperately signaling some unknown rescuer, a villager tending the fire noticed two black spots against the face of the rising sun. With every passing moment, they loomed larger, moving steadily closer to the village, until they obscured the sunlight with their awesome size. Terrified, the villagers shrieked and scattered as the bestial flying creatures began to strafe the village with bursts of flame. The settlement was dwarfed by the horrid, plated, swooping things that incinerated houses and humans alike. They grabbed at the screaming, vainly fleeing villagers and crushed them in their blood–dripping claws. From every direction, the victims were being surrounded, then slaughtered instantly as if by rows of automatic scythes. It was futile to attempt escape. The few survivors, like paralyzed prey, watched, frozen with fear as the two immense flying monsters landed with ease in their once peacefully flowering field. On the ground, they commenced touching off violent whirlwinds with every motion of their wings, while the earth shuddered from the grotesque stamping of their talon–tipped feet. By the unearthly whirring sounds and grotesquely massive movements, the stunned villagers understood that these two colossal horrors were communicating with each other. All at once, the pair turned toward their prey — and, to the villagers' astonishment, began to speak.

"Take — us — to — Merlin!" demanded the larger monster. Its voice, if it could be called a voice, rang like a steel sword striking an anvil. The sound was deafeningly mechanical. But no one seemed to know to whom the awful voice was referring. Nor did the "speaker" wait long for its answer before crushing one of the mute villagers in steel–like claws. Several others were squashed or shredded alive before the chief realized it was their Great One who was being sought.

"He is dead," the chieftain replied.

"You — lie!" The monster's scraping voice showed a slight sign of frustration.

"But we buried him many days ago." Although fear–ridden, the chieftain still stood his ground.

"Take — us — to — his — place!" commanded the smaller of the two, making sounds in a higher-pitched but equally grating voice.

Why are they looking for the Great One? the villagers wondered; what has he done that they seek to destroy us? But no one voiced these thoughts; all were too petrified to do anything but obey. The monsters were led to the burial site. To the horror of the villagers, they began to claw away the dirt as if a thousand years of frustration, anger, and hatred were being released with each frantic flinging of earth and gravel. When, at last, they struck solid rock, they suddenly stopped. Now, overcome with fury, the monsters ripped away the doorway with the ease of a man picking up a pebble and throwing it into the air. The open door released the pungent odor of decaying flesh. One of the beasts opened the roof of the tomb.

"No!" the elders cried out. "He is dead!"

The lead creature replied by seizing the chieftain and chewing him alive with his spike-lined mouth. The pair now extracted the putrefying cadaver from its bier, then — realizing they had not found the body they sought — released an earth-rending cry of thwarted vengeance. Their talons, like razor-sharp plows, dug deep furrows as the beasts tore furiously into the ground. Many other burial mounds were dug up. Now the fires at the circle reminded the pair of their own incendiary power, and they blasted the few remaining survivors and their homes. When they had finished, the village and its people were no more.

2
Excalibur

While the beasts were devastating the once–peaceful village above, the Great One lay safe deep within his secret tomb. He slept deeply, secure in the awareness of having left the village safe, and having concealed himself from the beasts. What would he have done if he had known of the destruction going on above? But he would not know, for, though his mind was very restless, his body was slowly reaching the deep–sleep state.

As he sank gradually into unconsciousness, many images flickered and flashed before him — all ultimately converging and turning back . . . back to a time long ago when he was young. Was he ever truly young? In his sleep he sighed and the dreams solidified . . . Yes, he was young, and coming home, after being away on a long journey . . .

"Five years . . . has it really been that long?" he asked himself as he watched from the window of his transport. As his silent craft hovered over the sparkling clear bay waters of the port of Alta, there, beneath him, lay the land he knew so well. At this time in its history, the concentrically ringed Alta was a bustling metropolis of pyramidical buildings, lush parks, and mirrorlike waterways. With its neatly arranged residential areas, it remained the queen city and capital of the island continent the traveler called his motherland — Atlantis.

Not much had changed in the five years of his absence. Citizens and motorized vehicles still flowed like tides through the immaculately clean streets and walkways. Plants and trees lined even some of the major thoroughfares. Still under construction when the traveler left, the central plaza was now completed. The massive pillars of the colonnade were evident even from the height of his ship.

"Ahh" he sighed, staring through the window at the scene before him. Yet, he did not truly absorb the view, engrossed instead in a more social issue: "I wonder how changed I'll seem to them after all this time in that northern wasteland . . . I . . . ."

A whining noise was his answer as a wet nose was pushed up against his cheek. "Oh, Mupi! Listen, you pest. Aren't you glad to be coming home?" the young man questioned as he stroked his pet's back.

Mupi had been a gift from his best friend. The creature was a product of bio–engineering, one of the many experiments being conducted by Atlantian scientists. Mupi turned out to be a pet instead of a working model. "Just too friendly" was the prognosis. He might have been destroyed, but he and Mupi became fast friends while he was working at the lab.

Mupi could not talk, but was intelligent and made his wishes known in

Mupi

various ways. He even learned to speak telepathically to those with whom he wished to communicate.

"Well, you feathered, feline lizard," he said, "do you think she'll be at the base to meet us? . . . Well, I guess not. But she did promise to be at the ceremonies. So let's both take a deep breath and calm down. Right?" Since the young man directed his conversation more to himself than to his companion, Mupi didn't bother to answer. He only snuggled up against his master and prepared himself for the landing. He much preferred doing his own flying to riding along as a passenger in some metallic aircraft.

Now approaching the base, the ship began its landing procedures. The tropical vegetation loomed gigantically. Here, at the southernmost part of Atlantis, the sun warmed the land all year round; for those aboard the transport climate was a complete change from the north, where winter held the land in its iron grip for half the year.

The pilot checked his position, contacted ground control, and gently set down. No sooner had the airship landed than anxious officials whisked the two passengers off to a waiting ceremonial boat. From the bow of this graceful craft, Mupi's much-loved master would make his grand entrance, welcomed by the citizens of Alta as one of the State's great heroes. Lining the canal banks, the people threw flowers and shouted, "Hail, Prince Merlin!" Oh, yes, he was indeed a prince! Merlin was proud of the honorary title he had so recently won. Reserved for Atlantian intellectuals and artists, it was a carryover from the country's long-abolished monarchy — yet Merlin felt every inch a prince.

"Hail, Prince Zaran!", again the crowd called out. Merlin turned to see his

Merlin and Zaran

closest friend, who was dressed as he was, in the formal, red uniform of Atlantis. Zaran rode through the canals in a separate vessel. As his boat came alongside Merlin's, the two waved and greeted each other.

"Well! You finally came home, you rascal," Zaran called out laughingly. "And you don't look too abused by the northerners either."

"Thank you," Merlin laughed. "But of course I could never look as dashing as you do in that outfit," he mocked.

"I see you still have that mistake with you," said Zaran. "How is it going, Mupi?"

Mupi whined and looked up at Merlin. "We're doing just fine!" Merlin answered. "It's great seeing you, my friend. We'll catch up on news after this circus is over."

They had been close since childhood, especially after Zaran's mother died. Merlin's mother, Kara, became a surrogate and the two were seemingly inseparable. Now they were both en route to a national celebration in their honor. The two had made astounding scientific achievements for the State and were today to receive the Platinum Hawk, the State's highest honor. Along with the award came a new prototype hand weapon, Excalibur, a deadly combination of firepower and a protruding blade.

At the gaily decorated docks trimmed in the State's colors of silver and red, the princes were escorted to the open, silver ceremonial carriage and were then paraded through the broad avenues. Lining both sides of the confetti-filled streets were cheering and flag-waving crowds who had been waiting for hours. As the two rode together in the silver carriage, Merlin sat erect. He was never more proud of Zaran, the true boyhood friend who had grown into a great mind. They shared glances and smiled the knowing smiles of kindred spirits. Seemingly Zaran had everything — looks, brains, personality; as well as artistic, musical, and diplomatic talents. He was the perfect "star" to which the State could look for its image of the ideal Atlantian.

Merlin waved to the crowds absent-mindedly and put on his public smile. It pleased him to see Zaran revel in the glory. Merlin was always more reserved, single-minded, and not quite as good looking as his friend. Though he also possessed talents in art and music, he left the diplomacy to the more flamboyant Zaran. Even with his great intellect, Merlin always thought that he did not equal Zaran's standard, so he spent more time in study and research.

After hours of greeting the waiting people along the parade route, Merlin and Zaran finally arrived at the central tier of Alta — a great plaza dominated by a crystalline, transparent, stepped pyramid, topped with an enormous silver statue of a grotesquely winged beast, the stylized symbol of Atlantis. Halfway up the pyramid was a large platform that encircled the structure. Merlin and Zaran ascended to the platform and the red chair on which Syus, the ruler, was seated. White baskets of red and white flowers lined the steps until they arrayed the statue at the top with great bouquets. The ruler rose to greet them.

He began in a loud and solemn voice, "Today we honor our two special scientists, Prince Zaran and Prince Merlin. They have proven their loyalty to the State through their great discoveries in the fields of scientific research. Merlin, through his life extension studies, and Zaran, for his magnificent war machines." Turning toward them and holding up the Platinum Hawks he said, "All Atlantis is grateful and we hail you as stars over us. Today you are the two most loved and honored people on the continent." The crowds cheered wildly.

The leader then handed each his award. The cheers were deafening. The Atlantians were very proud of their heroes, even when they were not soldiers. After the thunderous crowd became quiet, Syus unexpectedly announced the decision of the Community Committee For Scientific Studies. "Merlin is to conduct his life extension experiments on the genetically engineered war machines that Zaran has introduced into our forces." Merlin was thrilled to hear that he would be working with his friend, and turned to smile at Zaran. He saw none of that joy reflected in his friend's strained face. Merlin leaned toward Zaran.

"Hey, Zaran, it'll be great working together again — and now, as a team! Don't you think?"

"NO! I do not! Those creatures are mine! I don't need any help from you or anyone else." Crushed and startled, Merlin couldn't imagine what had gotten into his friend. Zaran continued. "A team — ha! You came back just to meddle in my experiments."

Now, Syus encouraged the young scientists to hold their statuettes high over their heads to exhibit the Platinum Hawks to the adoring crowds. Each also fired his Excalibur weapon into the air, thus showing its power. They descended the edifice to tumultuous applause, Syus walking between the two waving "friends," and the three mounted the glittering silver coach that would drive them home. As the ceremonial coach with its "cargo" of the three most important people of Atlantis rolled along the streets of Alta, Syus talked continuously about their new project. Zaran's brooding silence disturbed Merlin, but the exuberant Syus filled the gaps until the coach reached its first destination, Zaran's house. After a quick goodbye, Syus continued his chatter and Merlin tried to remain enthusiastic but finally withdrew. Syus, remembering Merlin's quiet nature, continued the one–way conversation until Merlin was at his own front door. Once home, he was so inundated with well–wishers, visitors, families, and doting officials that there was no time for him to consider the turn of events.

That evening, dignitaries and their families assembled in formal attire for the celebratory state banquet and party. Younger men wore their summer whites — loose–fitting short–sleeved silk gauze shirts, embellished with colorful embroidery at the shoulders, neck, and front. The elder statesmen wore longer versions of the richly embroidered shirts; some to the ankles, cinched at the waist with a wide sash or belt. The Atlantian women adorned themselves in long white silk gauze dresses, also richly embroidered. For state occasions, only silver jewelry was used, and an array of gleaming ornaments — from hair clips to anklets — abounded on everyone, men and women alike.

The vast banquet room easily accommodated the nearly five–hundred people being served. This room, on the top floor of the highest pyramidical structure in Alta, had windows that opened out to a magnificent view of the city, with its dancing, glowing, multicolored lights. The white room, trimmed in pale blue, had a gray–blue stone floor, which was polished to a mirror finish. The main table sat on a central dais with smaller tables circling it. Each table was decorated with the State colors. The sixty–foot ceilings were pierced with skylights. Hidden illumination flooded the festivities. As with all banquets, there was too much food and an overabundance of drink. Of course, there were also speeches and toasts to the new honoraries. The two smiled politely and thanked everyone for the great opportunity to work for the State Of Atlantis.

After dinner the hall was cleared for music and dancing and the central dais became the band stand. As was his manner, as soon as the formalities were over, Merlin was the first to step out of the spotlight, much preferring to watch the festivities from somewhere other than center stage. On these occasions, Merlin could always be found in the corner of a room talking with two or three friends. But tonight the scientist took time out of his conversation to scan the crowd, until, at last, he saw her glide through the great, carved silver doors. Though he had seen her earlier at the banquet, he hadn't had an opportunity to talk with her.

Dressed in her flowing, white gauze with its silver embroidery, MaReenie, the alabaster beauty, with long, raven curls, gracefully made her way toward Merlin with her arms outstretched, a signal for him to approach. The prince rushed out to greet her with a tender kiss. She had been the love of his life ever since his childhood; he would be or do anything to please her. "Congratulations, my shy prince," she smiled lovingly. "I saw you out there today. You looked wonderful surrounded by all that glory and adoration of the State. I told you, it was going to happen to you. Oh Merlin, I'm so happy for you!" Her congratulations were warm

Merlin and MaReenie

and genuine, underscored by an extra hug. "I know you hate all the formality and publicity, but I'm afraid it's part of being so good at what you do. But I must say, you received your honors more gracefully than I." Merlin acknowledged MaReenie's status for she, the artist of the friendly triad, had already won two Platinum Hawks for her contributions to the State's educational policies.

Merlin looked into her eyes, then stepped away and bowed slightly from the waist in a formal manner. "Thank you, my beautiful princess." She giggled quietly and curtsied. Even on this important occasion they played out a part of their childhood, re-enacting a time when both only dreamed of becoming members of the Atlantian royalty. Now they both had been so honored. He looked up and broadly smiled back at her. Then he changed his manner. "I hoped I would have seen you sooner," he said anxiously.

"Oh, so you missed me," she teased. "Well, I have been working very hard on a surprise for you and one for Zaran, too, but you will have to wait until tomorrow to see it. Be ready, because I'll be over early," she said. Then MaReenie interrupted herself. "And speaking of Zaran, have you seen the prince of the social whirl?" She looked around at the crowd.

Merlin's thoughts were suddenly stabbed by the mention of Zaran's name. "Oh, he's around," he replied reluctantly. Though he feared losing his cherished companion, he answered her question. "The last time I noticed, he had a group around him over at the far end of the hall." He emphasized "group" and pointed across the room.

"Well Merlin, I shall find him, and the three of us will sneak out of here. We three have been separated much too long. We have to celebrate in peace, don't we?"

Thus abandoned, Merlin watched as MaReenie crossed the hall. "She'll get us all together again," he said hopefully to himself. "She always says the right thing."

But when MaReenie found Zaran in the center of a group, telling stories and jokes, she was quickly caught up in the excitement and swept away in the laughing and the dancing. She simply forgot about the patiently waiting Merlin.

Only when she rounded the floor with another of her many suitors did MaReenie catch a glimpse of Merlin, in conversation with his parents, and remembering her mission she immediately went over to Zaran. But despite her attempts to coax him away, he would not leave the party.

"This is my night, MaReenie. Go with Merlin if you want to, but I'm staying." Zaran was adamant, and MaReenie reluctantly returned to the waiting Merlin to apologize.

"Where did your parents go?" she asked first.

"Oh, they've stepped out in the reception area. They were supposed to meet some friends there."

"Merlin, I'm so sorry for neglecting you. I'm just as bad as Zaran. It seems we both always have to be in the thick of the party." She was obviously contrite. "Anyway, he won't come."

"Don't worry about it, MaReenie. Besides, you know I will forgive you anything." He smiled.

"You're right — let's forget about him." Then she asked, "Aren't you going to ask me to dance?"

"Okay, but remember you asked for it," he teased, with a smile and a mock bow. They both knew that dancing was not one of his strong points.

But Merlin was completely happy to have MaReenie in his arms even if she did not give him her total attention. The pair happily greeted the gathered well-wishers as they circled the hall even calling out to the self-absorbed Zaran while sweeping past. He looked up just in time to see MaReenie blow him a kiss — which he returned, then continued with his conversation. The threesome were together again; to reveling observers it looked as though their friendship would last forever.

3

Atlantis: The Nation

Alta

Many days passed, during which the harried Merlin rested and pondered Zaran's behavior at the honors ceremony. Technically, he was still on leave from his State duties; during this time his equipment was being set up at the "Old Labs" building located at the intersection of Third Canal and Fifth Bridge. He was staying with his parents in a small apartment attached to their country home outside the Alta city limits. Now Merlin sat staring at his Platinum Hawk trophy. Mupi lay on the floor, dozing in a spot of late afternoon sunlight that streamed magenta into the spacious but spartanly decorated living room. In the corner of the room was MaReenie's gift — a bust of Merlin that she had sculpted. Merlin pulled back the white drapery to allow the greatest amount of fuschia sunlight to enter the wall of clear windows. He turned to look out at the view and began to question Mupi — and himself — about Zaran.

"What do you think happened to him, Mupi?" Mupi knew an answer was not needed. "And what *is* it about his project that has made him so agitated?"

Here Mupi thought he knew the answer, since he was one of Zaran's genetic mistakes. But the flying creature silenced his thoughts, lest Merlin pick up on them. He knew Merlin was blind to everyone's faults, especially when friendship was involved. So Mupi would not help sort out the puzzle. But Merlin persisted.

"What's happening here, do you think?" He did not wait for an answer. "And I wonder why they want to involve me in Zaran's security project." Mupi had dozed off again; he was too sleepy to use his telepathy. There was no use in "talking" to his worried friend — Merlin would soon have the answers to all his questions.

Providing state security had always been the purpose of certain scientists' jobs, but recently it had become Syus's passion. More and more scientists were performing all types of very strange experiments in the name of security. Syus spared no means to achieve this "needed" security, but Atlantis had not always been so dominated by fear. Merlin remembered his mother telling him the stories of the old days when life had been much freer, especially in Alta.

The ringed, canal city of Alta was certainly the largest but by no means the only city in Atlantis. The vast continent boasted many such bustling metropolises of modern technology. In the northeast was Meza, the mining city. Turron was the manufacturing city in the center and Xuacar, mainly a military operation, was in the west. All of Atlantis's urban areas had been designed as modern, functional cities with minimal consideration to the aesthetic. Alta, though, as the capital, was not only the most technologically advanced, but also the most beautifully designed.

Alta's construction began with the diverting of the great river, Nabix–Alesia, which flowed north to south into the sea. Seven circular canals were formed and filled with its water. The immense city's size was staggering, even as compared with those of the twentieth century. The center wheel or plaza served as a ceremonial focal point of Alta. Here stood the great glassine pyramid that housed all of Atlantis's government offices, and where, in its penthouse, Syus kept his office and home. This building, larger than the largest pyramid of Egypt, contained a massive fountain, whose ballet of water and lights joyfully soothed all its visitors. The fountain also encircled a beam of light that shot up to power the gigantic crystal at the pyramid's pinnacle. At the top of the pyramid, a stylized statue of the beast of Atlantis stood impregnated with the cyclopean crystal. Serving as the flaming nerve of Alta, the imposing structure dwarfed all of the capital city with its lighted presence. The other buildings surrounding Syus's home housed Alta's leisure and propaganda activities. These included the arts of dance, music, and painting.

The next circle was occupied by educational facilities, the third devoted to research. The fourth and fifth contained business and military buildings, while the residential areas — largest of all — were sixth and seventh.

Over the centuries, Alta had gradually been rebuilt and the newer buildings were of pyramidical design. Some were flattened at the top; others held gigantic crystals at their pinnacles. All of Alta, as well as all of Atlantis, was connected by an elaborate system of roads, rails, and bridges, part of a most effective public transportation network. The citizenry relied upon public transit, while private vehicles, a type of hovercraft, belonged to governmental and rural residents. However, public transport, even in the outlying areas, was so efficient that only a few even considered owning hovercraft.

All Atlantian cities were new, crime–free, clean, and untouched by pollution. Even living in those cities whose main industries were manufacturing and mining was a pleasure. The cities had a crystalline power source that not only stored energy but was used for power transmission. In this way, Atlantians enjoyed a life filled with every conceivable comfort.

The Atlantians had not always known such an existence. Their development had taken many centuries. The old records of Atlantis described the original inhabitants of their continent as an intelligent but primitive people living in a virgin land: a land with a natural wealth of rare mineral deposits and lush vegetation. The ancient records also indicated that these people welcomed a superior race to their continent. It was this race, then, with its great knowledge, that began Atlantian development. Through their scientific efforts, the newer arrivals enhanced the already intelligent race and gave them vast amounts of knowledge by which they could become an advanced civilization — socially and technogically progressive. From these, then, all Atlantians were descended.

While the first southern areas were settled and governed by individual chiefs, they were later united under one ruler who was called a king. By this time, experimentation was in full flower, yet a mortal weakness showed itself. The king became greedy. More power and wealth were needed to satisfy his desires. So the people built warships and flying machines for the conquest of the northern coastlines and eventually the whole interior. The king then crowned himself emperor of all Atlantis, but as evil follows evil, the Empire fell into the trap of corruption that comes with too much power and wealth for too few. Yet even when the Empire was overthrown, Atlantis became a totalitarian, militaristic state. It was this efficient regime that completed the modernization and rebuilding of the continent.

Atlantis was a continent out of time, unparalleled in advances that made life on this earth nearly perfect for its people. The State's scientists had conquered disease; life expectancy was 250 years. Poverty had been eliminated. New buildings and housing went up everywhere. Roads and public transportation were unmatched in their efficiency. Every citizen of Atlantis was healthy, well fed, clothed, and educated — and every citizen of Atlantis worked for the good of the State. There was no need for money, for the government provided everything.

Yet the leadership also made demands on its people — ever-increasing demands until the State became an agency of suspicion, a government by fear. The State was swift to control the lives, even the very thoughts of the individual. Along with poverty, freedom was abolished. Every moment and element of a person's life was monitored. State spies were legion. However, even with each citizen's total indoctrination from birth, Atlantis still — inevitably — had trouble with a handful of dissident thinkers. These were usually pronounced insane or mentally deficient and executed. Certainly the government was not perfect, but the citizens endured its faults in favor of a life of comfort and security.

At the same time that Atlantis was enjoying its golden age, the rest of the world, except for one other continent, crept into the Stone Age. Alone in its development, Atlantis did not share its progress with the rest of the world. Isolationist policies were passed and even the few Atlantian outposts located on the coastal areas of the nearby continents were not given any more aid than was deemed necessary for Atlantis's good. Syus, in his greed and paranoia, feared competition — he would not boost a neighboring nation's technology with his secrets, only to have it grow up and attempt conquest. The State had developed an arrogant, nationalistic, paranoia toward the rest of mankind. Nevertheless, the world would soon know the power of Atlantis.

It was into this Atlantis that Merlin had been born.

A Lemurian in Atlantis

The month had passed too quickly and only two days of Merlin's leave remained. Naturally, the entertainment provided by family and friends made it a month of relaxing and partying. He had also seen a great deal of MaReenie. All this celebrating aided him in putting aside his problem with Zaran, but now, unfortunately, he would have to begin thinking about his new work.

"My new work . . ." It was ironic. Merlin couldn't begin any work at all. First, he needed data that only Zaran could provide, and his childhood friend was still not speaking to him; and second, the brooding Merlin didn't feel much like working. Depression had set into his very bones. He felt physically and emotionally paralyzed.

In the early morning sunlight that warmed the vivid, bursting flowers in Merlin's secluded garden, the busy butterflies flitted from one floral profusion to another. Merlin sat mesmerized, watching the scene of Mupi's continual flapping and chasing of anything in sight. Amused by Mupi's game, he finally began to laugh. So when he heard his name, he was taken by surprise.

"Merlin? I hope I'm not interrupting anything." His mother, Kara, although almost 175 years old, was still lovely. Her long, once dark hair, now mostly gray, was worn up in the style of the old Empire.

"Oh no, I was just laughing at crazy Mupi."

"I'm so glad you have him, my dear. You always were a collector of strays, and he, by far, is your most interesting one." Merlin knew his mother remembered the many homeless creatures brought to the house for safekeeping, They both laughed at the thought of it.

Without any warning, she abruptly changed her tone. "You've been a little moody, my son. I know you're troubled by your incident with Zaran and I hoped that he would call or eventually come to his senses. However, you know how he can be." She did not wait for Merlin's reply. "Is there any way I can help you, Merlin?" Her concern was evident by the strained tone in her voice and the look on her face.

"No, Mother. No one but Zaran can help," he replied dejectedly.

"I'm not so sure of that, Merlin; perhaps we should have a talk. I would like to say something to you about Zaran, that, well . . . I should have said long ago."

"Oh, Mother, please! I don't want to hear anything bad about Zaran. After all, you know he *is* my best friend. I am certain I can resolve the whole thing by talking to the Committee."

"What are you saying? No one goes against the Committee! To do that courts danger, my son."

" It will be all right, Mother. It *will* be all right. I won't go against the Committee; I just want to talk to them about this project."

"Perhaps you should wait. Speak to Zaran first, before you do anything rash!" It was obvious that she remained unconvinced of Merlin's intentions. Merlin continued his attempt to soothe her, but his efforts were futile. Kara understood better than he the dangerous ground her son treaded. Unlike Merlin, who had lived his entire life in a protected environment, Kara knew how the government handled its people . . . even its princes. Hurriedly she left. Merlin remained in the garden, smiling. "Oh, if she isn't a typical mother!" he said to himself. "Always trying to treat me like a child. After all, I *am* a grown man!" Then he clapped his hands and called out to Mupi. "Come on, Mup! Time to go and see one of your favorite people."

To Mupi that could only mean MaReenie. He knew very well that she was Merlin's favorite person, too. Excitedly, he zoomed into Merlin, nearly knocking him down; Merlin burst out laughing. "Okay! Okay! We're off to see her, you idiot! Come on, we'd better look our best if we want to win her heart."

Having left Merlin in the garden, Kara hurried along the veranda that joined her son's apartment to the main house. Her single thought was that she must, without delay, talk to her husband. He would know what to do.

The regal Kara Gwen Yonaja was not native to Atlantis. She had immigrated to the continent long ago, before the creation of the despotic state. At that time, the emperor wielded the power; the overthrow of the Empire was still only a glimmer in the eye of the now–assassinated Vumis, Syus's predecessor. Instead, Kara was born in the faraway and obscure land known as Lemuria, an island–continent located in the ocean now called the Pacific. But to the Lemurians, its name was Quiro. Originally true Atlantians, Kara's ancestors — some time between the uniting of the chieftains and the rule of one of the first kings — separated from the continent to form a different kind of a society. They were a spiritually oriented group who abhorred the greed and power that became the basis of their nation's materialistic lifestyle. Leaving their homeland, they migrated west over the sea across the land now known as the Americas. Aside from relinquishing all that was familiar to them, these people endured countless hardships in the world outside their native continent. It was a completely barbaric region, the habitat of enormous, primitive beasts, — mammals and insects that preyed upon them. Though they were totally unprepared to cope with what they found, more than 150 stout-hearted souls dauntlessly forged on, farther and farther from Atlantis.

After crossing the savage continent and two hostile oceans, the exhausted travelers were warmly welcomed by the peaceful shores of Lemuria. The happy, preliterate natives generously opened their hearts and homes to the weary strangers who gratefully accepted the hospitality. They ate and rested as they had not in their two years of hardship. At last strong and refreshed, they took turns recounting their adventures. When their tale was told, the eldest Lemurian, an ancient but vital woman, offered the strangers their homeland in which to settle and live in peace. The refugee Atlantians attempted to thank the Lemurians by giving them gifts — pieces of clothing or jewelry that had survived the journey — but the natives refused. No thanks needed to be given; only the promise that the new arrivals would live peacefully with all who inhabited the land. This the vagabond Atlantians promised.

In a short time, the two groups became one. At first, the new settlers attempted to build homes like those in their native country, but these projects were soon abandoned. As they became immersed in the Lemurian way of life, the style of their architecture began to take on a more organic look. They became as happy and carefree as their hosts, while living in harmony with the other creatures of the land. When, like the natives, they abandoned a diet of meat, the island animals, no longer fearing them, became their companions. At last a paradise was theirs. But more was to come — more than they could have ever imagined.

While they toiled in their new homes, a great, unseen force increasingly made itself felt among the Atlantians. Soon they became so totally a part of their newfound culture that in the end they abandoned their earlier technological strivings altogether. For now, their yearning for scientific advancement was replaced by a new knowledge — a knowledge of the power of the mind. It was not like the Atlantian mental prowess, a process of the mind bending outwards to subdue the forces of nature. Instead, the Lemurian mind recognized the strength that comes from communion with nature. The islanders' sensitivity reached out to all creatures — they became one with every wild beast and colorful bird that inhabited that placid land. When they had lived in Lemuria for three years, the settlers began to intermarry with the primitives.

Shortly thereafter, the eldest woman suggested that the new Lemurians walk with her to the interior of their ocean-girded homeland. They followed through dense vegetation, far beyond their settlement until they

Lemuria

reached a clearing. There they found a natural, circular stone wall formation in which the natives had carved out an entrance. In this spot, in accordance with a Lemurian traditional rite, all ate of a bright, red fruit of the refa tree, found only in this part of Lemuria. Following that ceremony, all began to feel the force of their minds swing out wide towards each other and grow stronger. Now, they understood the power that ruled this land. They saw the futility of the singleminded striving for scientific and technological knowledge that characterized their homeland: real learning, they saw, came from nature's energy, the universal forces that surged through them in the stone circle. Now they could read each other's thoughts; they even communicated with the creatures of the field. Together they truly became one with each other. This newly awakened knowledge, each realized, was true power.

By the time Kara was born, the Lemurians had truly established paradise. Along with their incredible telepathy, they had mastered mental communication with nature to such a great degree that plants began growing to enormous size and even to specification, so that homes were made of living plants and trees without damage to the organisms.

They also developed long–distance telepathy so that no technology was needed to send personal messages.

Yet as the Lemurians' psychic ability increased, with it came a premonition of evil tides flowing towards their land. Though they sensed that the coming difficulties were inevitable, they joined their considerable forces to develop a mental barrier, which they aimed toward the east — and Atlantis.

Kara, like all Lemurian children, was trained to use her mind. She learned games to develop certain techniques such as a type of psychic hide–and–seek. She also practiced limited movement of objects. At the age of fifteen, along with others of her age, she was taken to a stone circle located on one of the lieu lines, or earth power routes. The Lemurians had discovered these earth lines all over the continent. There were even some leading into and across the oceans. Along with their circles of monoliths, the lieu lines were used to increase their mental capabilities. All children were taken periodically to these circles to meditate, to gain strength but primarily to achieve peace of mind.

The day of Kara's twenty–third birthday marked the first official expedition of Atlantian scientists and soldiers to the shores of Lemuria. They landed with pomp and fanfare, bearing gifts for the leaders. Though many Lemurians sensed some type of peril with the Atlantians' coming, their premonitions eventually gave way to curiosity. After all, some of their own ancestors had come from the strange and distant continent, and they wanted to know more about these handsome, fair–haired people. In command of the cavalcade was a young, handsome soldier/scientist named Arthur Yonaja. It was Kara's father, accompanied by other elders, who went out to greet the travelers. Kara hid in the background, safe behind a small group of people. When at last she peered out, she recognized at first glance that here, in the dashing Arthur Yonaja, she had found her future life's partner.

As an emissary, Arthur told the Lemurians of the Atlantian emperor's desire to trade technology and machines for any knowledge of their special abilities or culture. If allowed to stay, this envoy was to study Lemurian civilization. In the end, however, most of the Atlantians learned little, for these technological people would not or could not relinquish their prejudice and contempt for the machine–poor Lemurians. They had not been able to understand the psychic power of the Lemurian men and women, and regarded their feeling for nature as barbaric. Another stumbling block to the scientists was that the Lemurians would not tell of their secret fruit, for they sensed danger.

However, those few Atlantians who released themselves from technology found that they were reluctant to return to their native land. They had found peace in paradise. Arthur's future hung somewhere in the middle. He learned and appreciated the ways of the Lemurians, but wanted to bring this knowledge to his own people hoping they would profit and become more peaceful. On the other hand, he had also discovered love.

The only child of Lemuria's wisest couple, Kara had been educated to take her place in their special society. But Kara had found Arthur instead, and her parents feared the outcome — both for Kara and for Lemuria. Despite her parents' bitter opposition, Kara and Arthur desperately loved each other, and after some time had passed, they married. The two lovers exchanged their vows in a beautiful and solemn ceremony under one of the many great and colorful toadstools found on Kara's homeland. Arthur promised to care for his wife and never to let any harm come to her, yet he would take his bride far from her Eden, to Atlantis.

As Kara boarded the craft that would carry her to her new home, a fear entered her mind — she sensed destruction and turned white at the cataclysmic vision that formed in her mind's eye. But, responding to Arthur's gentle concern for her, she let those dreadful visions pass from her mind.

They flew to Port Quae, an Atlantian outpost. There Kara and Arthur discovered that the emperor had sent messages of his displeasure with the results of the Lemuria expedition. He had pronounced the Lemurians outcasts, and forbade any relations with its people under pain of death. The two lovers were devastated at the news. Kara feared for Arthur's safety and he for hers. Quickly, Arthur had documents forged so that Kara could be introduced as a native of one of the Atlantian outposts which he had visited on his way to and from Lemuria. She, meanwhile, worked to lose her native accent.

But while the lovers reacted from great fear, the truth was that Arthur was beyond suspicion. He had always returned in glory from his expeditions; and this time he had brought many samples of strange vegetation and even animals not native to Atlantis. As a matter of course he was decorated by the emperor. Later, when they were settled in their home, Kara's ability to read people's minds helped Arthur advance more quickly in diplomatic circles. It appeared that Arthur knew naturally just how to handle everyone; it seemed that he sensed just what was on any person's mind. Kara and Arthur became the toast of the elite. Eventually, Arthur was chosen as confidant to Vumus, then to Syus, with whom he served until his retirement.

But for Kara, life was not completely happy. Many anxious years passed before she bore a child. Then when the long–awaited Merlin was born, she saw in her son many characteristics of her people, which delighted and frightened her. Even though these qualities made the child seem vastly more intelligent and precocious than his peers, he became a favorite of all with whom he came in contact.

When Merlin was very young, Kara would, in secret, play the same little psychic games with him that had sharpened her mental powers as a girl in Lemuria. But these sessions were curtailed when Merlin once forgot his promise to keep their secret and openly read the mind of one of the family's dinner guests. His parents were embarrassed, the guests shocked, and Merlin repentant. He knew he had disobeyed. Though Kara and Arthur assured their guests that Merlin's accurate reading was merely coincidental, the couple sensed some suspicion towards Kara — after all, she was a foreigner. But as dinner resumed, all was soon forgotten, or so it seemed.

Every day, Merlin grew more Atlantian and less Lemurian. Just as children outgrow a second language learned on their grandmother's knee, he forgot how to direct his powers, though he sometimes received vivid mental images while deep in conversation. Even those stopped as he suppressed the power more and more. Kara watched her child become a man, always proud of his accomplishments; yet she worried that Merlin seemed doubtful of his real worth. This insecurity seemed to become more pronounced when her son "adopted" Zaran as a member of the family; but even so, she attempted to love Zaran as a second son.

Now, that "second son" was at the heart of the matter she sought to speak to her husband about — Merlin must be stopped from speaking to the Committee and Arthur would know how to prevent it.

As commander, adventurer, and statesman, Arthur was the epitome of the Atlantian noble citizen. Twelve times he had been decorated by the emperor and then nine times by the rulers of the new order. All of those honors, however, were bestowed in the earlier days, before the new wave of fanaticism and greed for world domination had gripped the State. When Arthur could no longer stomach what was happening, he gradually retired, claiming that he wished to give younger men more opportunity to gain recognition, while he himself supervised his son's education more carefully. Besides, he said, he wanted to write about his campaigns and record the histories of the conquered peoples in the Atlantian Empire. Occasionally, he would be ordered to appear publicly for state celebrations, especially those honoring dead heroes. Although opposed to the corruption and wholesale conquering of weaker nations, Arthur was a survivor. Moreover, he vowed to protect his wife and child. Therefore, he never said anything detrimental publicly, or even privately, about the government. In matters concerning his son, Arthur reluctantly let Merlin go through the public schooling system so as not to arouse suspicion. But that decision took its toll on Merlin and Arthur regretted letting his only son become a pawn of State propaganda.

Kara was burdened by these thoughts as she hurried down the hall to her husband's study. She abruptly opened the door. "Arthur!" Her high-pitched tone betrayed her frantic state of mind. She had not remembered the long–established house rules.

"Oh Kara, darling," Arthur replied eagerly, as if trying to hide his wife's

apparent emotional upset. "You're just the person I want to see. Walk with me out in the gardens, my dear, and look at the glorious blossoms out in the west field. I haven't seen such a summer in years!" He said all this while reading his wife's anxious thoughts. He understood the emergency, but there were spies everywhere; the State had even placed listening devices in their home.

She understood. She had momentarily lost control. But now Kara composed herself. "Oh, Arthur, you're so romantic, even after all these years. What a coincidence! I was coming to tell you about a swarm of butterflies out in the front yard. I didn't want you to miss them."

Excitedly, they hurried out into the gardens, stopping to take in the foliage just beyond the door, then slipping out into the west wildflower field. There they paused, watching the breeze ripple the fields and holding hands. The two aged lovers spoke first with their minds, but when they reached the middle of the field they reverted to the Lemurian language. They discussed the dangers and possibilities of telling their son about Kara, Lemuria, and more important, about Zaran.

From his window, the steward could only see the two aging lovers looking into each other's eyes. He would not learn their secrets, for they were safe from all who would try to listen. In his report he would state that the old statesman must be getting senile after all these years. He and his wife still acted like star-struck lovers even after a century and a half of marriage.

5
MaReenie Always Wins

During the five years that Merlin spent in the northern provinces researching the health of people living and working in the frigid arctic climate, Zaran had undergone some drastic personality changes. More and more he had become obsessed by power and fame, notably political glory. As he left a trail of used people in his wake, Zaran rose to power with amazing speed. Finally, he positioned himself in two important posts, one as advisor to Syus, the other as chief state scientist. At first, no one questioned his prudence as he ruthlessly strove to perfect the genetic engineering design that the brilliant scientist had begun when he and Merlin were still fledglings. As Zaran worked incessantly, even going days without sleep, increasingly some officials feared that the haggard genius would have a mental collapse. For Zaran, though, the perfection of his project meant he would reach his goal, achieving unlimited State glory — and with it, power.

Many years before Merlin's departure to the Northern provinces, Zaran had attempted to develop a prototype. At that time he secretly used human tissue samples, which he crossed with those of other creatures. Then, after hard work and many false starts, he eventually produced a strange–looking crossbreed later known as Mupi. Even though the lovable creature was more feathery than malicious, Mupi certainly was a great accomplishment. However, to Zaran and, more important, to Syus, Mupi exhibited all the wrong qualities. He was friendly, a little clumsy, and would not harm anyone even if provoked. Accordingly, Zaran considered Mupi a failure. He ordered the creature destroyed — but thought again, deciding that Merlin should be the most worthy recipient of this "failure." Thus the devious Zaran gave Mupi as a mock present to Merlin on his twenty–first birthday, secretly hoping to humiliate him. But instead, and much to Zaran's chagrin, Merlin was genuinely thrilled with his present. For Merlin, Mupi became an endless source of companionship. In his naive way, and hoping to aid his friend, Merlin constantly kept Zaran informed of Mupi's progress. Because of Mupi's instant trust of his new master, Merlin immediately discovered the creature's capacity for learning. Unknown to Zaran when he gave Mupi to Merlin, Mupi had a great intelligence. In every report Merlin continued to thank his friend for such a wonderful gift, and although Zaran found these reports an immensely helpful adjunct to his ongoing genetic research, it infuriated him to think that Merlin found Mupi so affable. Every time Merlin would say in his letters, "He doesn't have a mean bone in his body!" Zaran would grit his teeth. Years later — after more experimentation, and using information sent to him in Merlin's reports — Zaran finally evolved exactly what he and Syus wanted. He developed the ultimate creation: living war machines.

Still, the genius was never satisfied with his achievements. Consequently, this day, the day Merlin's work on Zaran's creature would commence, Zaran mulled over Syus's startling announcement at the honors celebration. He felt betrayed. "What could possibly have made him accept Merlin for my project?" he asked himself. Zaran's own thoughts angered him as he paced the quiet laboratory. This immense facility, usually occupied by seventy–five scientists, assistants, secretaries, and workmen, now housed only the skeleton night–shift crew, mostly guards, who patrolled the huge, circular hallway. Zaran had spent many nights in the lab working alone or with his crew of assistants, but with this newest phase of the project completed there was no need for the many helpers who had worked around the clock in the years preceding the breakthrough. Nevertheless, Zaran, as usual, was exhausted by his continual attempt to exist without proper sleep. He worked alone to perfect the already perfected creatures. His lifestyle was draining not only his body, but also his mind. Even logical thinking was straining his sanity. Thus, the more he thought about his project, the more he plotted revenge; first on Merlin, then on Syus.

"I'll show them who's the best scientist for this project," he told himself. "Just because I had one mistake! I'll bet that's why the Committee turned against me. That damn creature. I should have destroyed that fool thing the moment I set eyes on it." Cursing his fate, relentlessly persecuting himself, he paced through the night until he finally collapsed in his chair.

As the sun was just breaking across the dawn horizon, the stylishly dressed MaReenie sped along the canals of Alta. While Merlin had not heard from his partner and friend, he had heard from MaReenie. The night before the artist and the confused Merlin talked into the wee hours.

It was she who finally convinced him to work himself up and attend to his new assignment as if nothing had happened. But in spite of her outward show of optimism, MaReenie was now on her way to the Old Labs, worried about the meeting between the two friends. In her haste she was splashing everything along her route. Normally she would have stopped to admire the rosy hue of the breaking dawn, but not today. Instead her mind was riveted to her destination, her usually sunny disposition chilled by her thoughts of Zaran. "How could he have been so cruel?" she said to herself. "He's obviously pulling one of his malicious tricks to punish everyone. Well, this time he's gone too far!" By the time MaReenie approached the docks, she was fuming aloud. She parked her speedboat and took public transit to the laboratories. When at last she found herself in front of the pyramidical building, most of her fury had been spent.

Though the armed guards — dressed in their red and silver State uniforms — knew her, the dark-haired beauty was asked to present proper identification before entry could be allowed. Once inside the building, MaReenie found the lift systems inoperative; consequently, as she hurried down the dimly lit stairway to the underground floors where Zaran's laboratory was located, the anger began welling up inside her once more. Reaching the first underground level, she found guards again demanding identity prints. The shift had just changed, and the early morning security forces were unfamiliar with Zaran's friend. Her classification had to be checked. She stepped under the violet-colored light and stared into the lens that identified her; then, holding her hand over the brightly lit square in the wall, she triggered the electronic eye. A pair of huge black metallic doors, large enough to accommodate a two-person hovercraft, slid open with a whispering whine.

And there was Zaran — in a horribly agitated state. He was screaming to himself. MaReenie's abrupt appearance startled him.

"What in the hell are you doing here?" he demanded. "Spying on me, no doubt."

Over the years she had had some experience with Zaran's temper. So immediately, she softened her manner completely.

"Zaran, I came to see you. I've been worried about you." The astonished Zaran altered his manner. Smiling at her, he opened his arms as if to receive her. The artist didn't move.

"I'm sorry, MaReenie. I'm sorry. I just haven't slept in days." Now he was relaxing. He dropped his arms, breathed deeply, and rolled his head from side to side, then around — as if to release himself from his debilitating passions. He collapsed into the chair, cradling his head in his hands.

MaReenie looked around. Her artistic sense bristled at the sterile look of the laboratory. How could he stay here night and day? No wonder he had become so pathetic! But at least he was now more composed. MaReenie walked over to him and gently touched his head, then began speaking to him in a soft tone.

"Zaran, everyone has been wondering about you, and why you stay away so long." Her voice reflected her concern. "Then yesterday I saw your father and he told me . . ."

She had hit a nerve. Zaran jumped up. In a raging, defensive manner he said, "Well then, you know!" He turned away, attempting to calm himself and converse in a matter–of–fact manner. MaReenie proceeded cautiously. "Zaran, why did you say you were going on a holiday with your father and uncle when . . ."

"Don't interrogate me, MaReenie. That's my business. I needed to get away." The fair–haired man didn't like this trapped feeling. Then, unexpectedly, he blurted out, "Alright, I lied. I lied."

"Merlin is very upset — and worried," she announced.

"Good!" he gloated as a wide, diabolical smile covered his face.

Shocked, MaReenie faced her longtime friend. She really didn't know him at all.

"Zaran, how can you be so cruel?" She was pleading, but also struggling to control her anger. "He's your friend. He had no more warning about the Committee's decision than you." The argument continued, MaReenie's voice betrayed her feelings — her retorts taking on the high pitch of desperation. But precisely at the moment, when MaReenie accepted the futility of the battle, Zaran abruptly relented.

"All right, all right. I'll talk to Merlin." He added, sarcastically, "Happy?"

Had she won? For the moment had the surprised MaReenie succeeded? She thought she had, but she was wrong. In his exhaustion, Zaran simply did not want to deal with all her arguments. He agreed to talk to Merlin — and to work with him.

"Oh, Zaran! I knew you would understand. We're all such good friends." She flung her arms around Zaran's neck, kissing him on the mouth. Overtaken by the excitement of the moment, he grabbed her at the waist and whirled her around and around in the air. All was forgiven. The two laughed and talked for a while longer. Then MaReenie said her goodbyes. She could hardly contain herself. The series of guards who checked her through the usual security before she could be released from the building seemed unending to the elated artist. She was overjoyed as she ran out into the now-crowded streets of Alta. It was almost nine o'clock and the city was alive with its citizens as they rushed to work and into the many shops and activities that the city offered its people.

Zaran, on the other hand, was left watching his elated childhood friend dart out between the now closing lab doors. Deflated, he turned, looked down at his feet, sighed, and tightly squeezed his eyes shut. Yet there was work to do. He stalked across the empty lab to the immense corridor at its farthest wall. The entrance had been specially adapted for Zaran's purposes. A full sixty-five feet high, only a room of such an exaggerated scale could accommodate the beasts who had consumed his life for the last five years. There the creations that were Zaran's obsession, the objects of a passion that made it impossible for him to lead any semblance of a normal life, patiently waited. He studied their spacious quarters, which resembled an enormous hangar. The sunlight from the single high window beamed at the entrance, and there Zaran stood, as if, at last, he basked in the spotlight he so craved. Yet it was into the darkness that blanketed the rest of the quarters that he stared. There was nothing but silence. Presently, two bright, yellow-green eyes peered back at him through the blackness. A strange voice demanded Zaran's attention.

"Did—she—win—again?"

"No! . . . I don't know!" Zaran replied in confusion.

"Is—Merlin—coming?" A pause.

Zaran was sure now. "Yes."

"Why?" Again the voice questioned.

Zaran slowly and deliberately wiped his forehead, face, and eyes with both hands. He was tired. The questions were draining after his battle with MaReenie. The voice continued, probing needle-like into the subject.

"Will—you—let—Merlin—work—on—us,—your—ultimate—achievement?"

Zaran was slowly losing control. "Don't press me, Rajak! Remember, I'm the creator!" At that, the conversation was finished.

Zaran stepped out of the sunbeam and into the corridor and hurried back to his brightly lit laboratory. It was then that he felt the weight of his overwhelming defeat. He cried out, wildly screaming out his fury and frustration.

"Dammit! *Dammit!* MaReenie always wins!" He threw up his tightly closed fists. "She always knows how to handle everyone." His voice dropped. "Manipulator!"

With all his faults and whether it was good or bad for him, Zaran greatly loved MaReenie. He loved her even more than he realized. For him she was a stabilizing factor, a point of reference in his life. But now he was angry and exhausted, tired of her meddling. At this moment, sapped of the control he so desperately needed, Zaran did not love anyone or anything.

His self–indulgence was abruptly interrupted by a voice calling on the message system. "Prince Zaran, you are to go up to the penthouse office in the Crystal Pyramid for a meeting with Syus. You are to come immediately, Prince Zaran. I am to escort you." The messenger waited for a reply.

"I'll come to the lobby in a moment. Inform the leader I will be there as soon as possible."

6
The Old Labs

Having left Zaran at the Labs, MaReenie hopped onto the public transport system and headed for Merlin's house. Almost from the first moment of her arrival, MaReenie's exhilarating report to her concerned friend about her meeting with Zaran relieved the worried scientist. MaReenie not only exaggerated Zaran's enthusiasms, but purposely omitted the upsetting details of her visit with their friend. Merlin, of course, suspected some intrigue on her part, but MaReenie insisted that her meeting with Zaran was purely coincidental. With the excitement of the previous evening and anticipation of Merlin's exciting new job, she said, she had been unable to sleep. To relieve her tensions she went boat riding, and her trip through the canals unexpectedly ended at the Old Labs. She said she often visited there to see Zaran's creatures, which held some strange fascination for her. Since Zaran was supposedly still away on vacation, she was surprised to find him there.

MaReenie found it painful to lie to Merlin, but she couldn't bear for him to know the truth about his dearest friend's change of heart. Moreover, she was confident that Zaran's pride would never allow him to admit that she possessed any manipulative ability over him, so that he would be the last to relate the truth of the matter to the reassured Merlin. Besides, MaReenie's story was again confirmed when, shortly after she arrived, Merlin received a message from Zaran. Although it had been sent by one of Zaran's assistants, the communication was exactly what Merlin wanted to hear. His old friend would meet with him at the laboratory sometime around three o'clock that afternoon. Zaran was anxious to see him and would provide him with any information needed to begin the new work.

MaReenie was relieved; she left, saying she desperately needed to sleep after her attack of insomnia. Nevertheless, before going, she felt it necessary to issue some words of caution.

"Merlin, you've heard the stories about how hard Zaran's been driving himself, haven't you?" she asked.

"Yes, but I don't think too much about such rumors. After all, MaReenie, to accomplish anything worthwhile, a person must sacrifice and endure hard work. As an artist, you certainly must know that." Merlin understood about hard work — he worked every day of his life just trying to be as good as his friend.

"Well, anyway I want you to understand that he *is* exhausted." MaReenie was emphatic. "So don't . . . I mean . . . Oh Merlin, take care of yourself." With that, she opened the door and left.

Merlin stood in the doorway, completely baffled at her warning. He thought a moment, then sensibly decided he had too many other things to consider — like his work — to be disquieted by the emotional MaReenie. Besides, she had always been a puzzle to him, and if he had not yet resolved the mystery, neither would he resolve it at this moment.

Merlin spent the rest of the morning and early afternoon working in his cluttered room. The news had flipped a switch in his mind. He began to attack his project with a vengeance. Therefore, by the time he was ready to set out for the laboratory — leaving a whining Mupi at the door — Merlin had reams of notes and questions prepared for Zaran.

As he made his way to the meeting, Merlin felt a flush of excitement, the kind one gets when seeing old friends. But his eagerness did not prevent him from exercising care as he maneuvered his silver hovercraft through Alta, above the swarming crowds. Normally, his mind would have been too preoccupied with his work to notice these people; but this afternoon, contented and placid, Merlin felt free to watch the scene below. Though for a fleeting moment, he wondered why Zaran had not contacted him directly, Merlin was carefree for the first time in the month since his return.

Over the years, Merlin had acquired a reputation for always being late or sometimes not even showing up at all. His friends were glad to pardon his tardiness, attributing it to the young scientist's preoccupation with his work. Today, however, was different. He arrived early.

Like MaReenie, Merlin too had to undergo the security checks at the front gates, but he found that once he entered the vast lobby the lift systems were operative. Down he went to the underground levels. The doors of the lifts opened to reveal an alien environment.

All of Alta was a thoroughly modern, technologically based city. But here, under the Old Labs building, Merlin found something so advanced, streamlined, functional, and tremendous in scale that it surprised even the model Atlantian. Clearing another security check, he was greeted by one of Zaran's assistants, an elderly, bearded scientist; the beard was somewhat out of place in the world of clean–shaven, short–haired men. After an exchange of perfunctory greetings — the older man congratulating Merlin on his recent award — the pair proceeded to the conference room, passing through the main corridor, which opened out to the laboratory's many extensive research rooms and offices. On reaching the conference room, the older man departed, leaving Merlin in front of the

closed door. Before Merlin had a chance to knock, the door opened, and he was greeted by Zaran's smiling face and open arms. It was as if nothing had occurred.

"You're early! What's happening to you?" Zaran joked.

"I don't know. Perhaps this is a new phase in my life," Merlin laughed. It was like old times again. Merlin was relieved.

"Well, take a good look! What do you think of the old place? I've made a lot of improvements since you were here last." Zaran proudly waved his arm around with a great, sweeping movement.

"It's great! And so much larger! It looks like you've blasted out half the underground of Alta to get this space," Merlin said in awe. "You must be pretty important to get all this space! Most of us still have to work in cubbyholes." Merlin felt a pang of envy, but he reminded himself that this laboratory was now to be shared by Zaran and himself. "I can't imagine we'll get into each other's way."

Zaran laughed; he made no effort to comment on Merlin's statement about his importance. "Come on. I'll show it all to you, and believe me, there's a lot to see."

The conference room itself was of considerable size. A huge partition could be opened to accommodate larger groups. There were glass screens on every wall, allowing the projection of any visual images needed for seminars, meetings, or briefings. Here Zaran had arranged a whole array of visuals to explain the concept of the project from its conception. Zaran accounted for certain gaps in information, saying, "There is still much data that's classified, even to you." There was a slight tone of sarcasm in his voice, but it went unnoticed by the enthusiastic Merlin.

And when Merlin remarked on the amount of security, Zaran brushed the comment aside by expounding on the importance of maintaining a sterile environment and the new lights developed to ensure its hygienic conditions. "I've perfected the total system," he said, "so that now, when a person clears security they may enter almost any place within the complex and still remain in their street clothes; all this without any danger of contaminating the labs. Though there are still some sensitive areas, as I call them. Extra precautions are taken on these sites by the one or two who are allowed to enter." His pride was obvious as he continued to show his visuals.

"You'll notice that every room and area has its own particular lighting. Each individual color and direction of each light is programmed separately. As a matter of fact, every room is painted the exact color that will encourage the proper work intensity. The lighting system I've devised with my engineering staff shows no outlet or source. The brightness reflects the feeling of nature and in some cases, the ceiling, walls, and even the floors are lit. I've left nothing to chance."

He clarified the function of every room, office, laboratory, and cubbyhole with graphics, maps, drawings, and photos by using the video screens. Then, after the very long talk, he invited Merlin to take a tour that resulted in two hours of walking around the massive underground complex, and finally, the descent to a lower level where the "project" was operational.

Here was Zaran's private world, where he had spent most of the last three years. The door to the lift system opened to a small reception area. Behind it were two bright silver-colored metal doors about thirteen feet high.

Not very impressive, thought Merlin, remembering all he had seen upstairs. Then the doors slid open. The view was breathtaking. With ceilings 100 feet high, the size of the room seemed almost immeasurable. To the left was a section designated as Zaran's sensitive area. There, enclosed in a transparent smoked-glass vault were hundreds of test tubes and lab dishes; each held incubating tissue samples. Zaran explained to Merlin that this was a new project he had recently begun, and that no one was to enter the area. No one — including Merlin.

"I certainly understand," Merlin reassured him. "I'm not here to interfere. Only to help with your existing creatures." Zaran responded with a discerning look.

Along the right wall as he entered the laboratory, Merlin noticed enormous charts, picturing and plotting the transition and mutation of creatures known to the Atlantians as dinosaurs. Long, long ago, Atlantis had been overrun by these horrendous, gigantic lizards — in all their known sizes and shapes. They had inhabited the continent up to the time Alta was first built, and in fact, a few remained, in captivity, in Atlantian zoos. It was upon only one of these reptiles, however, that the charts focused — Tyrannosaurus Emperor — the most fierce and brutal of them all. Zaran seemed pleased when Merlin inquired about the charts.

"Well, I like a man who gets down to business. Good. There's a lot of equipment, especially the older models, that's more or less outdated now. So I don't see any point in giving you a minutely detailed tour of this project if it's not necessary. At any rate, you'll find out best on your own how the material will be useful to you — if it's useful at all — during your stay here." Zaran had apparently been eager to come to the point, and Merlin had just obliged him.

Pointing to the wall, Zaran then began his scenario. Merlin could not believe his use of old charts, when on the upper level there had been every conceivable type of electronic equipment for communication. That matter, however, did not faze Zaran. He obviously wanted to use the charts.

"As you know, this is the first model with which I experimented." He directed Merlin's attention to the second chart. The first was a compilation of all the dinosaurs found on Atlantis; Zaran ignored it.

Actually, the second chart did not show the first creature on which Zaran had tested his theories. The first had been a combination of animals, none of them dinosaurs. These experiments had produced mixed results, most being total failures except for Mupi. But Zaran refused to acknowledge his first experimentations. He continued to explain each chart, telling Merlin of the work done to produce each mutation and progression until he reached the final piece. It was not a chart, but rather a sort of poster with a photograph of the creature and the words blocked out in a line.

"Here are the final products of my work." Zaran's voice was bloated with pride as he pointed to the poster. "They are the perfection of efficiency and self–sufficiency."

"What do you call them?" asked Merlin.

"Dragon," Zaran replied. "Using the first letters of our logo."

Dynamic
Response
Against
Governments,
Organizations and
Nations

7
MaReenie's News

$\mathcal{A}$fter all the excitement of the morning events, first with Zaran then with Merlin, MaReenie found herself outside of Merlin's apartment. Realizing that her boat was docked in the third circle of Alta and her only means of reaching it was through the public "transportubes," she felt too exhausted to contend with the scheduled routes. Besides her dramatic exit — complete with her "Merlin, take care of yourself" speech — the actress–artist could not bear to be so anticlimactic by again ringing the doorbell and asking Merlin for a ride home. Since Kara's house — one of only three antique homes that had not been torn down by the new order — was just next door, she went there, and announced herself to the inter-com. When the door opened, Kara welcomed MaReenie with open arms.

Kara, as always, was happy to see her surrogate daughter, the little girl she never had. Kara had long ago promised MaReenie's mother to care for her daughter if anything were to happen to Raena, and this she did, from a true sense of love rather than duty.

As usual, MaReenie was full of news. But despite her eagerness to hear it, Kara hurried her newly arrived guest out to her greenhouse where she grew her odd–looking trees. From the hothouse they slipped out into the newly added gazebo. MaReenie was too tired to react to the evasion of the house, though she did plead to stay put someplace.

Finally Kara felt safe to hear MaReenie's news. And, unlike her son, she would hear all of it.

No one ever lied to Kara. They simply didn't try. But to MaReenie, that did not matter. She always felt as if she was talking to a soulmate when-ever she confided anything to Kara. A special bond of respect and truth held the two women together. Whatever MaReenie was like to the rest of the world, the act stopped at Kara and Arthur's house. There she could be herself; there she was totally secure.

And now, the lovely young artist revealed to Merlin's mother every detail of her morning adventure with Zaran. Kara expressed concern about the overworked Zaran's health and emotional state.

"He's nearing a breakdown, MaReenie. You shouldn't take such chances, and above all don't count on your friendship to protect you." She warned MaReenie about playing a game with Zaran. "There are rumors about his terrible temper."

"Oh Mama K!" MaReenie pleaded. "He always had a temper. You know that! I just don't want Zaran and Merlin to be at odds. There's no reason for it. It's just a stupid misunderstanding."

But Kara continued carefully questioning MaReenie about even the most minute detail of her conversation with Zaran. After satisfying herself that she had gotten all the facts, she saw that the exhausted MaReenie was beginning to doze off in her chair. But the young woman awoke when Kara told her:

"Don't worry my dear — about anything. I'm sure you only did what you thought was best. And after all, you did manage to get them back together. I do feel, though, that it might have been a mistake not telling my son about Zaran's true feelings. After all, you know he will eventually find that out for himself. But I'm certain everything will be all right. . . . MaReenie, my child, you know that I do think of you as my own." Kara smiled at her and MaReenie felt the love between them rush through her. "My dear, you've always tried to play the pacifier between those two, haven't you? But just remember, at times it has backfired on you and you were caught in the middle. One day you'll have to let them work it out all by themselves. MaReenie, you must understand me. I'm not criticizing you; you see I know exactly how you feel. That's why I can sympathize with your feelings." MaReenie jumped up and went over to Kara. The two women embraced.

"Now, MaReenie," said Kara, "I can see that you're exhausted, so why don't you rest here for a while. I'll take care of getting someone to pick up your boat, and Arthur and I will take you home later. All right?"

Kara's suggestion was exactly what MaReenie wanted to hear. Her mind was blank as she followed Kara to the spare room, and as soon as her head hit the pillow she was asleep.

Kara closed the door to the spare room and went out to the garden. There the tiny hummingbirds were feeding on the many varieties of bright, red flowers that she had planted especially for them. The handsome woman watched them from her white chair, then from the metal lounge. Presently she began mulling over the events of MaReenie's encounter with Zaran.

"He's up to something! I just know it." She shook her head and leaned back. She was resolute — she would not interfere. "I just wish MaReenie would make up her mind which one of the two she really loves. Then she could stop playing games with them." Kara sighed. She knew how much Merlin cared for MaReenie and, above all, she did not want her son to be hurt. But for now she closed her eyes and waited for Arthur to return. Her thoughts drifted to their plan; perhaps it was time to put it into action.

By the time MaReenie awoke, night had spread its heavy veil over Alta. At first, in her drowsiness, she was startled to find herself in the spare room at Kara and Arthur's house. Then she recalled the day's events, stretched her arms over her head, looking around at the familiar room. There, sitting cross–legged in the bed, she began a retrospective of all the wonderful memories that objects in this room stirred in her mind. She smiled, for Kara had decorated the whole place with old toys, pictures, and oddities — mementos of Merlin's childhood, and some of MaReenie's too. On the shelf near the north window were hand–made presents from MaReenie and Zaran to Merlin. She remembered the competition between Zaran and her over who would create the best gift. Then, in order to antagonize Zaran, Merlin always made a bigger fuss over her present. MaReenie laughed when she thought of the look on Zaran's face. Still the same, she thought. Always competing.

Her eyes took in the whole room at once as if she were a camera with a wide–angle lens, seeing it all as if it were yesterday — the three of them playing in MaReenie's yard, she acting out the role of the impish, tiny mother. There was always something about the little girl with the raven curls that instigated activities totally unbecoming the children of honored citizens of Alta. Many a time the three were punished for helping themselves to the prized strawberries in the farmer's field, or for scaring some old lady with their fiendish makeup. Somehow, though, their punishment never seemed too oppressive — the comrades were always comforted by each other.

As they grew into adolescents, their friendship deepened yet so did the competition between Zaran and Merlin. MaReenie sometimes giggled at the two rivals; at other times she ignored them completely. Already creative, she was too busy working at her art to worry about the two antagonists. Her very promise as an artist required discipline and dedication to develop. Thus, much of her time was spent secluded with her tasks, not to mention her schoolwork and a full social calendar. Her two old friends were also developing their own interests and their many separate activities caused each to go his or her own way. However, when they did get together it was as if only a moment had passed since they had last seen each other.

Now in Merlin's old room, a grown woman sat on the bed with her elbows on her knees, hands cradling her chin. Her two childhood friends had become her two suitors. MaReenie knew her fiercely independent streak — she would always need a tremendous amount of freedom. She surveyed the leftover toys, games, and mementos. But she was now grown. Yet, despite the fame her work had brought her, MaReenie still could not release herself from her one childhood obsession. She had to play the peacemaker between Merlin and Zaran. It infuriated her. Why did she always resort to any ridiculous tactic to achieve her end? She couldn't answer. All she knew was that she would sacrifice almost anything to keep them friends. . . .

A knock at the door broke her thoughts.

"Are you awake, my dear?"

"Yes, Mama K. I'm getting up now."

"We're waiting dinner for you."

"I'll be there in a moment." MaReenie's stomach was eagerly answering the call to food.

After a dinner of roasted chicken basted in wine sauce, rice with nuts, and a large salad followed by a cup of mixed fresh fruit, Kara and Arthur drove MaReenie to her home. At dinner, Arthur made no reference to the events Kara had described to him. Instead, he seemed to be much more interested in how MaReenie's father, Zirth, was. And also what new projects the artist had started. As always, they kept the conversation light. MaReenie was certain Arthur knew what had happened but had a feeling she should not bring up the subject now. Kara and Arthur conversed as usual about his day and hers; they both said how happy they were to have MaReenie for dinner. They missed the old days, they said, when the children would all sit at the table and spill out their news, though MaReenie sensed that the two people at the dinner table had other things on their minds, and she couldn't understand the reason for the charade. But, she thought, it must be important, and as a natural–born actress, she played her part.

Later, when she was at her front door, MaReenie invited her two hosts in for a visit. They declined politely, saying it was late, but that they would get together with her and her father later in the week. It was indeed late, but MaReenie was wide awake after her long sleep. She waved goodbye to Kara and Arthur, then entered her house, only to find that her father had already gone to bed. He had left a note for her with her calls and visitors, and a goodnight P.S. saying not to stay up too late working. But that was exactly what MaReenie would do. Her work was her life — and her therapy.

8
The Dragon's Keep

The two colleagues were still studying the charts that hung in the vast laboratory when Zaran cut their conversation short.

"Well, that's it!" He sounded somewhat relieved. "Let's go over to my office and have something to eat. You must be starving. Besides, I need to check on my calls." It was obvious to Merlin that Zaran was attempting to play the gracious host though it was apparent he was becoming increasingly edgy. And Merlin also had a thing or two ticking in his mind.

"What do you mean, that's it? I haven't seen the living specimens yet! After all, that's why I'm here!" After the electronic lecture and after the antiquated charts, Merlin couldn't believe that Zaran would prevent him from seeing the beasts.

"Oh, of course — you'll see my magnificent creations," Zaran replied in a soothing manner. "But I thought we would do that later, after some nourishment. We've been on our feet most of the day, my friend." Clearly Zaran was trying to pacify his future co-worker; no less noticeably, however, the high-strung scientist had lost his easy condescension as he grew tense and tired. Still, Merlin acquiesced to Zaran's suggestion that they eat.

In Zaran's office the two associates chatted innocuously, Zaran carefully steering the conversation away from the new work. When their meal had been served by one of the laboratory assistants, the two ate silently. They had finally run out of useless things to say to each other. After he had taken a few bites of food, Merlin looked up at Zaran, and saw that he was completely absorbed in his own thoughts. Merlin at last began to observe his best friend in a different light. Zaran was no longer the old childhood companion; the person across the table from him was not the same friend that he had left five years before in Alta. Certainly he looked the same; the face was still handsome, though perhaps somewhat thinner. But the set of his jaws was sterner and the look in his eyes had lost that innocent mischief. Instead, Zaran's eyes gleamed with a little too much ambition, maybe even greed. Merlin felt a sadness come upon him. What could have happened to Zaran that caused such a change? Perhaps it was he, Merlin, who was acting immaturely. Was he reading things into his friend's actions out of jealousy or fear of Zaran's success? He tried to put everything out of his head and continue his meal.

Zaran picked and pushed his food around on his plate. Merlin himself was now eating more reluctantly. He studied the lines around Zaran's eyes. They seemed to give him a pinched look.

Yes, thought Merlin, Zaran is as tight as a vault. He generates no feeling of warmth as he once did. Even about the work he's closed and secretive. He's omitted so many of the important details and guarded his project like a jealous lover. Again, Merlin looked down at his plate, only to continue speculating about Zaran's charade. Abruptly Zaran broke the prolonged silence.

"Good, I see you're finished with your meal. Well, don't you think it's about time that you see what a dragon is really like?" Zaran stood up with a start; his whole demeanor changed. He obviously had come to a decision about something and now he was ready. Oddly, whatever made Zaran ready filled Merlin with anxiety.

"I'll show you the keep and introduce you," said Zaran. Merlin's anxiety grew — were Zaran's dragons to be treated as the superiors and he the subordinate? Zaran continued, "Then I'll have to make a few calls but I'll be back to see how you fare. At any rate, I need to finalize the arrangements with security, supply, and the rest of the staff so that you can function as independently as possible. I'm sure that's what you want." The dragons' creator simply seized Merlin by the arm and they were off. "Now come on — I thought you were so anxious to see my beasts." Zaran was smiling and excited, just like a child eager to show off his new toy.

The two scientists hurried through the immense corridor toward the underground holding pen that housed the dragons. When they entered the gigantic area the keep was bathed in a very dim night light. By the shadowy light, Merlin could see that there were no doors or gates; no barriers of any kind to separate the creatures from their visitors. Instead, the vast area was divided into immense stalls, each holding one creature. Zaran, apparently accustomed to the darkness, went off to switch on the lights, leaving Merlin in the dimness. Merlin felt an ominous stillness and marked the yellow–green eyes that peered out at him.

Then, without any warning, the lights blazed on, momentarily blinding all its victims. When Merlin recovered, he found himself standing rigidly, staring into the belly of a monstrous beast. He raised his head. There was the iridescent black, ugly head with a multi–horned frill surrounding the glowing eyes; the same eyes that glared back at him from the darkness. Merlin sensed intelligence in those awesome eyes and drew back at the sight of the jaw, equipped with sharply–pointed, massive teeth that made the dragon look as if he were smiling hideously at some ghastly joke. The head, with its many horns and teeth, was formidable enough, yet the body that supported its weight astounded Merlin — it was composed of

Rajak

pebble–grained armor–like plates that formed the creature's hide. The immense feet were rigged with razor talons that could skewer any victim. To complete this living weapon were massive wings, which unfurled to reveal the tremendous muscles that controlled them in flight. At first glance, the dragon seemed to be of a basically black color, but at closer attention, Merlin could see the black was iridescent — glowing green along the head and back, and blue beneath the massive wings and across the entire belly. The shiny, towering dragons viewed him with calm, piercing stares. He could not believe their size, but what was more terrifying to Merlin was their hideousness. With their horns, flanges, massive claws, and razor–sharp teeth they were unspeakably ugly. Merlin asked himself how Zaran could have conceived such horrors.

He, of course, had known exactly what to expect; particularly after the tour, the photos, and all of Zaran's detailed boasting. But only now, this moment, standing there in the midst of them, dwarfed by their awesome size, did Merlin fully comprehend their dreadful use. Suddenly he felt infinitesimally small; an insect among giants. His thoughts bombarded his mind like a laser shooting through a tube. His being was inundated with questions: Why? . . . Why build such things? . . . Is there really a need for such destructive creatures?

For the first time in his life, Merlin questioned the sanity of the State's "dynamic actions." This scene released in him a torrent of doubts that caused the well–built dam of propaganda to burst.

Quickly he pulled himself out of his thoughts. He instantly comprehended that his success with these creatures would depend totally on how much control he could maintain. He had to bury all his misgivings. He watched their creator. Yes, Zaran was in complete command. They seemed to know who was the master. Could Merlin achieve such superiority? He made up his mind that he would not be intimidated by their size, their purpose, or anything else about them.

At last Zaran introduced Merlin to the black beasts.

"This is Prince Merlin of whom you have heard so much. He will be working to enhance your life expectancy. You will cooperate fully with all his treatments and experimentations."

Spoken like a commander to his troops, thought Merlin. I must remember the tone of Zaran's voice.

But there was no instant response from the troops. Instead the dragons just stared at the intruder, and the long silence that followed was deafening. Merlin sensed some resentment toward him, which took him by surprise. Not that the creatures showed any emotion; they did not even move.

Zaran, Merlin, and the dragons waited.

After what seemed like an eternity of silence, the vast keep echoed with a loud, curiously mechanical voice. Rajak was at last acknowledging the command.

"Welcome—Prince—Merlin." There followed a long pause. "We—will—cooperate—fully."

"Thank you for your welcome," Merlin replied. "You will find that your cooperation will be beneficial."

There was nothing more to say, but Zaran attempted to fill the void with more conversation.

"I'll leave you now to your new patients while I take care of those matters necessary for your work."

But Merlin knew the audience was ended. "It's late, Zaran," he said. "I think it will be best to start tomorrow when we're all fresh." With confidence he turned, first toward Rajak, then back to Zaran. "Anyway, that will take the pressure off of you to ready all the details of my stay here tonight. Besides, before I begin I want to study some of the biological information you gave me today."

He turned and walked out with Zaran. Glancing back over his shoulder, his gaze was met by the glare of two ominous yellow–green eyes.

The two were met at the door by a laboratory assistant who was coming into the corridor. Zaran told him to take care of the lights and make sure the creatures were all right.

The exhausted Merlin was about to bid Zaran goodnight when his old friend sprang some new information on him; it set his adrenals going again.

"Well, my old friend, before you go, I want to tell you that we won't be working together after all." He beamed. Zaran had always loved taking people off guard, particularly his childhood friend. "I'll be gone by tomorrow."

"What? . . . When did this happen?" Merlin was confused. "I thought we were both to work on this project."

"That was what I thought, too, at least until this morning. It seems I have an opportunity to go on a very important assignment to work for the betterment of the State. Actually . . ." he laughed slightly, "it's a secret assignment." Merlin could see that he was thoroughly pleased with himself. "And anyway, I think you'll work better on your own."

At first Merlin argued in favor of Zaran staying, but at last he too was pleased by the news. He did not want to stand in the way of Zaran's future good, though in a sense he was relieved from the pressure of working alongside someone he thought was vastly superior. In certain ways, Zaran was much more gifted than he.

"I'm taking three dragons with me but not the six left in the lab," said Zaran, pointing toward the dragons' quarters. "I'm leaving them in your hands and you'd better take very good care of them or I promise they'll bite you." They both laughed, friends again, for the first time in a long while. They felt the tensions release themselves.

Then the two talked a bit longer, but this time it really was like old times. At first they recalled their recent exploits, then recollected childhood dreams. Afterward both agreed on MaReenie and laughed at how the beauty thought she was their boss. Finally the conversation reverted back to the work at hand. For the first time, Zaran showed real interest in Merlin's work. Now he asked many pertinent questions, particularly on Merlin's plans for the dragons. Up to that point, Zaran had been doing all the expounding about his work and allowing Merlin no opportunity to give any of his views. Merlin began explaining all of his recent experiments on longevity, and what methods he planned for use on Zaran's creatures. He continued with explanations of the work he had done on other animals tested. He even suggested possibilities for using the longevity serum on humans, though at this point in their history the Atlantians had achieved a very long life expectancy through selective breeding. Despite Zaran's occasional questioning, it became obvious to Merlin that somewhere in the middle of the discussion the other's mind had begun to drift away from the subject and on to his own assignment, its significance in his own plans, and its importance to the State. It was also plain that Zaran had become more and more uneasy about Merlin himself. For the discussion now in progress was revealing something that Zaran had never come to accept: Merlin was truly a genius. While pouring out a flood of information and ideas, Merlin was innocently showing his brilliance. Jealousy was cramping and squeezing Zaran's inner being. It was as if he were possessed by dissatisfaction — even while blessed with every possible talent — and could not bear the thought that his superiority might be slipping away.

And in fact, if Merlin's telepathic powers had not been temporarily forgotten, he would have perceived Zaran's concern easily: *What if he's more successful here while I'm off in that hellhole of Lemuria?* But Merlin could observe only that Zaran was becoming agitated. Wishing to offer reassurance, Merlin said, "I'll try to do you proud!"

"Oh–h–h . . . oh, yes — I have complete faith," Zaran stammered while being jarred back to reality. The two then said their farewells.

Zaran would be off to his secret assignment. Merlin would be left to work on the dragons.

9
Zaran's Mission

T he next morning when Merlin returned to the Research Center, he found that Zaran had indeed taken care of everything. The master of detail and efficiency made sure that Merlin would have the whole complex at his disposal, if he needed it. Therefore, he could concentrate totally on his work with the dragons. There was even a file on his desk containing more information about the creatures, together with a note of farewell and good luck in his new work. But Zaran had overanticipated his departure to Lemuria. Instead, at that very moment, he stood before Syus and the Council.

"Well, my dear Zaran, I'm glad you have decided to accept this assignment." Syus's voice echoed in the large, red room, resounding against the dark natural wood panels enclosing the massive council chairs. In this room, which adjoined Syus's private office, most of Atlantis's major military decisions were made. Occasionally, a military maneuver was decided by Syus himself, without the Council's advice; but that was rare.

Syus continued, "But then, you see, I knew you wouldn't refuse another chance to gain the honor of the State." He smiled wryly. "So — you are ready for immediate departure?"

"Yes, my dragons and I are at your command," Zaran announced proudly.

"Unfortunately for you," said Syus, "I now have changed my plans for an immediate military invasion of Lemuria. Something has come up which has altered everything." Syus sounded concerned. "But this mission will still give you a chance to prove what those expensive dragons can really . . ." The look on Zaran's face was changing.

"Now, now," Syus said appeasingly. "I realize that they have proven themselves in the control test. And certainly here in Atlantis they have shown that they are something to be reckoned with. This, however, is a different challenge. This assignment is more a reconnaissance mission rather than an offensive action. Naturally, if destruction is necessary to meet our aims, then destruction it shall be."

Zaran assured Syus and the Council that his dragons were capable of any assignment. He would stake his reputation on it and that was a lot to stake.

"Let us get down to it, shall we?" Syus addressed the Council and Zaran. He had some new information to give to them. "As you know, in the last month we have had two major power communications failures, along with some minor utilities interruptions. But what you don't know is that our investigations reveal that the source of these disruptions was on the continent of Lemuria."

Zaran broke in. "But, sir, my understanding was that the Lemurians were being monitored on a regular basis, and that they were basically a non-technological nation — a religious sect of some type, concerned only with stone monoliths and sacred burial mounds. When did they suddenly get military power capabilities?" Zaran was obviously confused, and the members of the Council shook their heads in agreement with him.

"Two days ago," replied Syus, "we sent a flight ship to gather intelligence concerning the tremendous power surge. It seemed routine; their communications were normal. When our ship hovered over the north–central section of the continent, they transmitted a picture. Then suddenly nothing. No communications whatsoever." Everyone in the room expressed surprise and concern. "The picture we received revealed nothing but a configuration of a stone circle with about twenty–five people standing around it. Nothing else."

"What do you mean, nothing else!" The Council was in an uproar.

"That is just what I mean — nothing else." Syus continued. "Not one ounce of evidence that there could have been anything unusual happening. Not one machine, not even so much as a piece of wire to indicate some primitive form of electricity. Nothing."

"Why were we not informed sooner?" one of the members demanded.

Syus ignored the question, and again turned his attention to Zaran. "I want you to start preparations for departure to Lemuria from the Cumbar base on a moment's notice. In turn, the Council and I will review all possible alternatives before you're off on your mission."

"My dragons and I are ready to serve Atlantis," Zaran said proudly. "I want to reassure you of their capabilities. They are the most powerful and modern piece of military equipment we have."

"Be ready — just in case," Syus answered. The conversation was over. Zaran bowed his head slightly, turned and departed. He would go to Cumbar, a station that had been carved from one of the mountains on Atlantis's west coast, and prepare himself and his beasts for future orders. Syus was left to hash out policy with the Council.

When Zaran arrived in the hills of Cumbar, his appearance surprised everyone at the installation. He had come unannounced to the massive facility that could house more than twenty-five dragons, plus men and armored fighting vehicles, flight craft, and other equipment. In ordinary circumstances, the personnel would have greeted Zaran with great ceremony, but his unexpected appearance gave them no warning. Hastily the director of the base put together a banquet in Zaran's honor. Zaran in turn informed the director that he had come only to check on some new procedures he was going to introduce into the dragons' training. The director, of course, agreed to comply in every way possible. No one but the ruler, Syus, and his military Council knew the real reason for Zaran's presence, and everyone obeyed all his instructions while suspecting nothing.

During his prolonged stay, time passed slowly for Zaran as he worked with the beasts. Syus apparently was taking his time to correlate the information Atlantian security had gathered to make the mission successful. He had promised to keep Zaran abreast if any new power surges had been reported, but there had been none. Not only that, but Zaran was informed of Syus's inability to obtain the approval of the Council for an all-out invasion of Lemuria. After hearing the peculiar data, they were afraid.

Although Zaran was becoming anxious to get on with his assignment, he used the time well. He readied the dragons for reconnaissance work. Of the two-hundred-odd that he had engineered over a three year period, the last twenty-three were the best. They had longer lifespans, greater intelligence, and much greater strength. They came in various sizes, shapes, and colors, each geared to a specialized training mission. Zaran knew them all personally, just as if they were his children. He was, after all, their creator.

Meanwhile, Merlin was working at Alta with six. One hundred seventy-five, the foundation of a military security network devised by Zaran and Syus, were on assignment all over Atlantis. The rest remained in Zaran's care at the baseport.

Why did Atlantis need these creatures of war? That was always the question posed by the Council. After all, Atlantis was the only nation on the earth with any technology. The rest of the world was struggling out of the Stone Age. Nonetheless, Zaran had convinced Syus of the necessity of the dragons and the Atlantians had funded the project. After all, though Atlantis possessed the top of the line in modern war machinery — flying crafts, guns, lasers, and missiles — only the dragons could function as a combination of all these weapon's capabilities. But with one important difference — the dragons were intelligent. Based on logic and orders, they could make decisions. The dragons would not only keep surveillance on the developing world but could destroy any growing threats without hesitation.

Syus and Zaran were both power mad, but Zaran had the upper edge — he was also brilliant. Even as a child he found that he had it in him to manipulate those who were his mental inferiors. He managed everyone but Kara, Merlin, MaReenie, and MaReenie's mother, Raena. She was the first to suspect that Zaran had inherited some of his mother's mental instability, and so became one of his first casualties. The boating "accident" got her out of the way. Kara was different. Even now he wouldn't tangle with her. But one day, things would be different — that was Zaran's constant thought.

In his determination to write himself even more prominently into Atlantian history, Zaran was resolved to make this assignment count. "I'm going to take Syus's place — and not too long from now," he would tell himself. "And when I do, the Council goes too!" These thoughts he quietly kept hidden in the dark recesses of his mind, where even Kara couldn't find them.

Meanwhile he remained at Cumbar and performed his assignment. The housing of the dragons at this installation was similar to that of Alta's complex; but here the dragons were the main reason for Cumbar's existence, whereas at Alta the scientific team and its equipment were of primary importance, the dragons only the basis for the scientist's experiments. The Cumbar facilities were much larger; there was even space for the magnificently horrible creatures to spread their wings. The men, on the other hand, looked like ants crawling around in the huge chambers.

After months of waiting, the orders finally came for Zaran's assignment. It was, of course, top secret. He had already picked out the six best dragons for the job, three of those housed at Cumbar and the deadly trio transfered from Alta. No one took much notice of his extra preparations, for he had established a routine of taking the dragons out for a day, even a week at a time. So when he requisitioned extra supplies and even a transport, the director took it in stride as more intense training, particularly since he himself had received orders from Syus personally to take care of any of Zaran's requests.

Finally, the time had come. The beasts knew that all the training had been for some purpose, but Zaran had not explained the reason for it until now. The six that he had chosen were being housed in a separate area, away from the rest of the facility, in a new area of the mountain. The seven of them — Zaran and his six dragons — had been out that day on maneuvers. When they returned to the base and were washed down and nourished, Zaran came in to talk to the beasts. The acoustics in the chamber were perfectly attuned; they had to be, or else the echo would be maddening.

"My pets," he said, almost lovingly. "We finally have our assignment. We are going to pay a little visit to our neighbors to the west." He grinned diabolically. "It seems they have been up to some mischief. It is up to us to ascertain just what it is and to correct them," he was sarcastic.

A large dragon asked, "Are — we — all — going?"

"Yes, all of us. We will fly to Port Quae in a transport, and from there you will fly me to a deserted area on the southern coastline of Lemuria."

"What — is — our — purpose — there?" inquired the smallest one, whose name was Xax.

"We must seek out the source of a large power surge that we picked up with our equipment. The location has been pinpointed." Zaran informed them. "The beam was so strong that it has at times disturbed and distorted our communications. Our great ruler, Syus, wants the plans for it, or if possible the device itself." Zaran sneered, "We could have gotten it long ago if you had been allowed to do the job for which you have been created."

"What — can — we — expect — to — encounter?" queried Xax. He was not only the smallest but had an experimental luminous, iridescent blue-green color.

"Up to now Lemuria has been an area populated by many diverse groups living a primitive existence. I know that a small Atlantian expedition was sent there about a hundred years ago — many of our people did not return. Those who did, brought back tales of barbarians with virtually no technology and hardly any government. These people supposedly performed tricks of magic, like a carnival, all day long. They called it mind power. But there was no real proof brought back to substantiate such claims. Personally, I'm intrigued." This was said to answer Xax's question.

Yes, he was a little more than intrigued. Mind power, that he understood. Limited manipulation of people he could handle. But what if he could really control people with his mind? Now that was real power! A power *he* could use!

The dragon sensed his thoughts. "We're — ready — to — serve — you."

how she is. She has to practically live with her subject. Remember when she painted yours. She was with you night and day." Zaran was reassuring the dragons and himself alike. While Merlin had been away all these years, Zaran had come to consider MaReenie his. He had no wish for Merlin to interfere now with his plans for the beautiful artist.

"I'm only taking four of you to the coast. The other two will remain at Port Quae. If I need you, I will send word," Zaran announced.

"A — question — Commander?" asked Xax. "What — about — leaving — the — Princess — with — Prince — Merlin — for — so — long — a — time?" The dragon hit the sore spot he aimed for.

"He'll be busy. I have seen to that!" Zaran announced confidently. "And so will she. I have had communication with the princess and she has promised to paint a portrait of my father. She will be staying out at the Old Miners Inn, where he vacations at this time of the year. You know

10
While Zaran is Away . . .

During the many months that Zaran was away from Alta, Merlin and MaReenie each worked on their separate State assignments. In all that time, Zaran made no effort to contact the scientist who was working on his dragons; he instead kept in touch with MaReenie — although, because his mission was so secret, he refrained from telling her where he was stationed. Nevertheless in his many calls to her, MaReenie acted as his newscaster. Naturally she always had news about Merlin, though she did not see much of him because of his work.

In contrast, the months after Zaran's departure passed swiftly for Merlin. He was totally engrossed in the work even when, at first, all his formulations were dismal failures. The specialist in longevity was being frustrated. Checking and rechecking, using every method of computation, Merlin as usual plodded on, toiling hard to find the answer. Then, after almost a half a year of constant false scents, the answer came. Not through careful experimentations or calculations but by accident, as is sometimes the true way of science. However, there was a twist; throughout the experiments, Merlin used sample tissues that had been prepared by Zaran. And Merlin always adhered to the specific instructions that Zaran presented as the only way the samples were to be utilized. Merlin, suspecting no intrigue, dutifully accepted the challenge, until, during a routine preparatory procedure, a laboratory assistant's accident destroyed all of Rajak's tissue samples. More had to be taken from the beast. In itself, this task was immense — the surgical procedure necessary to get the correct type of tissue was delicate in the extreme.

Before beginning the operation, Merlin searched the files to see which tissue Zaran had used. He studied all the papers in all the laboratories. He checked the computer banks. Nothing. Then, in desperation, he jimmied the lock on Zaran's desk and found, amid his personal notes, a scrap with what looked like a combination scribbled on it. Merlin felt like a thief in the night by going through Zaran's private papers, but he had to get to any information that would help him resolve his dilemma. Finally, after searching in the laboratory, Merlin decided to search the dragon's quarters. This could only be accomplished when they were all out of their keep simultaneously; otherwise the beasts would be suspicious of his action. He discovered a secretly hidden wall safe in one of the dragon's stalls. Naturally, in order to get to it, the beast had to be kept out, but without its suspecting anything. Otherwise it would have stood its ground. Merlin had already discovered that the dragons were not only intelligent but imbued with certain personality characteristics — most of them sinister. In addition, Zaran apparently had given them specific orders about their behavior towards Merlin. To say the least, they were unfriendly.

While the dragons were permitted an extra long exercise period Merlin opened the wall safe. There he found disks, which he then fed into the computer. All types of information spilled out. Not only were the tissue samples mutated in some way so that all the other experiments would not correlate and all of Merlin's work would be a failure; some basic data given to Merlin had also been falsified. Merlin watched the screen in disbelief. A half a year of his work was for nothing — nothing! Usually mild–mannered and easygoing, Merlin became enraged. At that moment it was Zaran's good fortune that his whereabouts were unknown to Merlin, who would have strangled him. But Merlin could only pull the disk out of the machine and close the laboratory.

All the way home in his hovercraft he continuously swore vengeance. "By all the gods that were ever thought of by all the peoples of the earth, Zaran, you bastard, if I ever see you again, I'm going to mutilate your body so that nothing remains but some ground up piece of meat!" But his words did little to improve his disposition. He landed the vehicle with a bump, banging the door closed behind him. Storming past Mupi into his apartment, he threw down his briefcase, then his clothes, and so on until finally, exhausted, he fell into bed. He snorted and fumed. Mupi cowered in the corner, his sanctuary from the flying objects. He knew — having read his master's mind — that Merlin wasn't mad at him. And naturally, Mupi believed all of Merlin's angry thoughts about Zaran, particularly after his brief experience with that madman. Finally, when Mupi felt that Merlin had calmed down a bit, he went over to the bed and snuggled up, to comfort his usually happy master.

"Oh Mupi!" Merlin took a deep breath and let it out slowly. "Why? . . . Why? He's played some pretty vicious pranks in his day, but this one is the most despicable."

Mupi pushed his nose up into Merlin's face and whined softly. Both knew the other's feelings. Merlin sat there, experiencing every conceivable negative emotion; depression, anger, hatred, betrayal, vengeance, and violence ran through his soul. Then finally the calm after the storm came over him; a calm that comes with decisiveness. Merlin knew exactly what he would do.

Now he stood up, jammed his fist in the air, and said with frigid certainty, "Zaran, when I finish my experiments with those damn beasts of yours, I'm going to make you look like the stinking heap of manure you really are!" He turned off the light that hung over his headboard and attempted to sleep. For Mupi, the night saw him sleeping on the floor in the corner of the room. Merlin's tossing and turning made rest at the foot of the bed an impossibility.

While Zaran was gone and Merlin was busy at the complex, MaReenie herself began working steadily on her numerous State commissions. She also had a few that Zaran assigned to her, particularly his request for a portrait of Arak, his father. She had never spent much time with the remote and distant man who kept to himself. He and Zaran had moved away from the other two families when Zaran was still a child. But even during the years that they lived nearby, the children were seldom invited to Arak's house. When Zaran was with Merlin and MaReenie, he seldom mentioned his father to either of his playmates, as if Arak didn't exist at all. So, naturally, when Zaran asked MaReenie to paint Arak's portrait, the request came as a surprise. Nevertheless, just as Zaran had predicted to the dragons, she went out to stay with him at the Old Miners Inn, trying to get to know her subject.

At first Arak was reticent, but MaReenie's way with people worked its magic and, before long, the old man opened up to her. She ate meals with him, they went on long walks, they even played cards and went dancing

to the old–time country music of the farm people. Yet, though Arak took care to show MaReenie a good time, she sensed a melancholy in him, as if he had a dark secret hidden away. And because she understood people, she knew that whatever it was she would never extract it from the white-haired old man.

It must be a great burden, she thought; he always looks as if he's hunched over with a heavy pack.

And indeed Arak looked much older than MaReenie's own father, Zirth, or Arthur, though he was many years younger. One day, after she had been at the inn about a week, he told her he had not had so much fun in all the years he had been going there. Then he said something very strange to the glowing MaReenie; it changed her mood entirely.

"You're not at all like Zaran. I almost feel I could trust you."

MaReenie's puzzlement was plain on her face. She didn't understand what was being said to her. Why wouldn't he trust Zaran?

He raised his eyebrows, sighed, then grinned and slapped his knees with his wrinkled hands. "Don't take it to heart, my dear," he said. "It was only the rambling of an old man — ready to die."

MaReenie spent more time with Arak than with any other person she had ever painted. Something about him fascinated her. Even after they left the inn, she continued to go back to Arak's apartment. She wanted to capture on canvas what she saw in him, but when the portrait was finished, she was still not satisfied. One day she mentioned this to Kara, but the smiling Lemurian only answered, "He's a very wonderful man who has had a great heartbreak to bear." Then Kara added, "My dear, I'm so glad you got to know him a little. I think one day it might make a difference for him as well as for you."

MaReenie never thought of Kara as secretive, but she felt that Kara knew all the details of this heartbreak. At any rate, MaReenie had to put it out of her mind. She was now very far behind with her work after taking so much time with Arak's portrait. The time was going by quickly and she had to buckle down to meet the deadlines of her other assignments. Catching up took many months — she saw Merlin infrequently and usu-ally only for dinner. And their meetings inevitably took place at Kara and Arthur's house thus limiting their time alone. Furthermore, every time MaReenie found herself in Kara's company, she was reminded of Arak's secret.

11
The Secret Cave

While the days passed into months and the months stretched into nearly a year, Kara watched for a sign — anything that would indicate the moment had come for her to reveal her story to Merlin. After Zaran's departure, Kara and Arthur had decided to wait, but it was finally Merlin himself, in his rage over Zaran's deceit, who cued the unfolding of Kara's drama. Yet even after she saw her son's fury, Kara waited many months, until the day of her wedding anniversary, to put her plan into action. This was to be a special anniversary — it marked the 125th year since she and Arthur had wed.

About a week before the date, Merlin naively asked Kara, "Let me know what you two would like for your anniversary. It's not every year my parents get to celebrate the big 125!" He kissed her on the cheek. "So your wish is my command, Mother." Then he went back to the laboratory to carry the day's work late into the night. Little did he know what that statement would have in store for him.

At long last the day dawned for which Kara had waited so long. If it could even be called dawn. The gloominess of the sky was enough to depress even the most buoyant heart. The clouds hung over Alta like a shroud, with the air so heavy that people felt as if they were being compressed in a bottle.

Kara — dressed in rugged traveling garb — turned away from the window and said to Arthur, "He's going to protest, you know, and especially now that the weather looks so awful." She again looked out at the grayness that laid claim to be the early morning light.

Arthur had been up earlier setting into motion the many details of the planned surprise. He told Kara, "I wager you he doesn't notice the weather at all. He'll be too busy worrying about the laboratory." By way of reply, Kara went over to Merlin's apartment and knocked at the door.

"Merlin, it's time to wake up, my dear," Kara spoke in a cheerful voice. There was no answer. She waited. Then again she knocked and repeated her message. Once more she waited — and finally heard a stumbling sound inside, followed by the click of a lock.

"What time is it anyway?" asked the squinting face at the crack of the opened door.

"Have you forgotten what day it is?" Kara's disappointed look was matched by the tone of her voice.

"Forgot what?"

"Today is our 125th anniversary. Remember, I told you I'd be ready to name my present," his mother answered.

"Oh yes, yes . . . Well, what can I give you?" Merlin asked, unaware that Kara had carefully laid a trap for him.

The trap thudded shut. "Today I would like the three of us to go on a short trip."

Though still half asleep, Merlin began the expected litany of protests about how much work he had and how important it was. To no avail. Kara was to have her way; this, she told him, would be a well–earned holiday; the people at the laboratory would take care of everything. His father was calling now, and yes, Merlin was to dress for a hike in the woods.

"What! Oh no!" The exasperated Merlin muttered to himself as he closed the door. "I *hate* walking in the woods! What a waste of time." His voice got louder but he was dressing anyway. "If this is *their* anniversary, why do I have to go and celebrate with them? I'm exhausted. I only had a few hours' sleep." Waving his hands in the air, he continued to protest until he found himself down in the atrium.

Arthur's voice answered his complaints from another room. "That is precisely why you're coming. You're completely overworked. Look at you. A day in the woods will do you a world of good."

Merlin took a deep breath. The long, impatient sigh did nothing to relieve his tensions, especially when he looked down and saw three huge backpacks lying on the polished floor. Arthur and Kara now entered the area, holding hands. Merlin immediately confronted them.

"What's this?" He pointed to the packs.

"We decided to camp out overnight. I thought it would be fun to show you what it was like on some of my campaigns," Arthur replied.

"What on earth! . . ." now Merlin became even more annoyed. "Oh father, we did this already, when I was little."

"That's right. But I'll wager you don't remember how to live off the land."

"Well, I don't have to. I'm not in that business," Merlin retorted, in a tone at once drowsy and arrogant.

"You will do it because we want you to." Arthur spoke with no–nonsense authority. "It's not up for discussion. Besides, it will make your mother happy. Isn't that right, my son?"

"All right," was Merlin's very reluctant reply. By this time, he ruefully remembered his grandiose "your wish is my command" promise to Kara. Apparently this was her wish. Even so, he felt that this shock tactic was not only unnecessary but totally out of character.

"I'm treated like a child." His angry thoughts were haughty. "I'm a grown man — a famous, important scientist. Why in the name of Raz am I putting up with this nonsense!" Again he looked down at the bags. "Aren't they at least bringing someone to help with the work?"

The answer to that question was no: the three loaded the bags into the hovercraft. Then they took off, heading northwest from Alta toward a vast wildlife preserve called Lawal: a tract of land that had been set aside during the old empire to protect the natural habitats of plants and animals. This area was only one of many such natural refuges the State maintained. Even within the most populated industrial cities, "natural spots" were scattered throughout the buzzing neighborhoods. Nothing was more jealously protected and guarded by the citizens than these small wilderness settings, and State policy was to help keep them free from human pollution.

But the Lawal Refuge was one of the largest of the game protectorates with the most breathtaking scenery in all of Atlantis. Although Alta had a tropical climate, just north, within fifty miles of the city, the landscape changed drastically. The country slowly began to turn hilly, then very mountainous. It was to the mountains of Lawal that the three celebrants headed, two of them cheerful and expectant, the third quite reluctant. From the hovercraft they watched the morning light burning away the mists of the night that hung in the valleys. At 100 miles per hour they were zooming toward their destination; the two and a half–hour flight offered a dazzling display of Lawal's spectacular sights. Great waterfalls, poised as if they were painted white against the mountains, rushed and splashed ever downward to create great whirling pools at their bases. The immense trees seemed to hug the sides of the cliffs; others jutted upward and outward as if trying to escape toward the higher elevations. The bubbling brooks spattered cheerfully toward the languid rivers that wound in and out at the foot of the green mountain range. Blossoms of every size and shape peered out — almost shyly — between the elephantine legs of the 200–foot trees, while others hung boldly from vines linking the uppermost limbs of the forest. Even in his state of mind, Merlin regarded the sight before him with wonder. Watching the deer scramble up the cliffsides, dancing toward the summit, he was beginning to mellow. The beauty of Lawal could not but leave him breathless.

They landed at the entrance to the preserve. Each reported in, showing

the official permission papers. This was merely a formality, but the guardians of Lawal had to keep track of anyone entering the protectorate in case of weather changes or accidents. Merlin left these details to Arthur while he and Kara started unloading the vehicle.

Now Merlin surprised Kara, saying, "It's too bad that we're only going to stay overnight. I'd forgotten how beautiful it was."

By now, Arthur was walking back to the craft and calling out exuberantly, "Well, let's get going. There's nothing like being out in nature to get the blood moving."

The three hikers marched along the main trail at a fast clip. Then, abruptly, Arthur turned off the path toward a stand of pines, lush with vegetation. It had been a particularly wet summer thus far, so the flowers were under and around the pines blooming profusely and the grasses turning a dewy, emerald green.

Arthur continued to lead the way, along a nearly hidden path. But presently, after an hour of tramping through the undergrowth, the beauty of the forest began to fade from Merlin's eyes. All he could think about was trying to keep up with the long strides of his parents ahead of him. Their spirits were high, and they sang as if exerting no energy. Finally, however, they rested briefly — all too briefly from Merlin's point of view — and ate. Then they resumed the hike, this time almost seeming to dance through and over the heavy vegetation. Merlin could not understand where they got all of their energy and stamina. He was supposed to be a young, strong, energetic male, but he could hardly claim a small fraction of their vitality. He had always loved nature, but at the moment he would have preferred a view from a plane — or better yet, a picture hanging on a wall somewhere in a more controlled environment.

And all the while, Arthur kept turning back and calling out, "Come along, Merlin, we don't want to lose you. Your mother wants to get to Red Crag before the sun goes down. It was one of the first places I brought her to when we first came to Alta. We don't want to miss the view at sunset. Come on . . ."

"Okay, but can't you slow down? After all, it is uphill." Having said this, Merlin became even more irritated at himself for being in such poor shape that two old people could outwalk him. He muttered something about not being part mountain goat as he continued trying to keep up.

Meanwhile, Kara commented constantly on the beauty of the butterflies, the birds, the flowers, and even the mushrooms on dead branches — or anything else she saw. The whole forest seemed to reach out and welcome the visitors happily. Even the pine needles seemed pleased to crunch under Merlin's feet. But to Merlin the excursion seemed more like a forced march ordered by some overzealous commander.

At last the troop reached its destination — just in time to watch what even Merlin was forced to agree was a spectacular sunset. He actually forgot his weariness watching the yellow ball of flame slowly turn magenta while the sky imperceptibly changed its striations to orange, pink, lavender, blue, and pale yellow. It was an all–too–short display of color, falling gradually into deep lavenders and purples, although the clouds continued to be streaked with the brilliant violets and reds of the setting sun. At last, in what seemed barely a moment, only the smallest hint of color remained at the horizon. Then the dark, gray–blue clouds — and gradually darkness — overtook the sky. As the last light faded, the three visitors stood silently, struck temporarily dumb by the performance nature had just given. And now, their energies at last began to flag; they felt limp and drained of color, like the night. The time had come to lie down on the ground and rest, surrounded by their own thoughts. When at last Kara broke the silence, she sounded almost like a thunderclap against the gentle stillness.

"You two have to get a fire going so I can get dinner ready."

Merlin surprised himself by agreeing wholeheartedly. With all the wonderment of the sunset he had temporarily forgotten he was starving. Now he remembered. He and Arthur hastened about, searching for enough dead wood to make a suitable fire. When at last it was blazing, Kara heated some soup; together with bread, cheese and fruit it made a fine repast. Merlin ate as if it were his last meal, while Kara and Arthur watched him and smiled at each other. When they finished, they lay back again, looking up at the few stars that blinked in an otherwise black sky.

"I think we might have some rain," Arthur said. "We'd better get the tent up for the night."

Merlin and Arthur erected the flimsy shelter. Though it offered little protection, it would at least keep off a drizzle. Because the temperature had started to cool, they crawled into their sleeping bags and Merlin now felt every bone and muscle in his body throbbing as he fell into the deep and trouble–free sleep that comes with total exhaustion. He had not been close to nature in years and his last thought before he dropped into oblivion was that he had had too much communing today.

Arthur was wrong about the rain. It did not fall that night, though next morning the tent was wet from the extraordinarily heavy dew that had accumulated all through the hours before dawn. But the sun had not even risen when Arthur nudged Merlin awake.

"Merlin," he spoke softly. "Get up. We are going farther into the park."

"Uh . . ." Merlin sat up with a bolt. "What time is it?" Then he looked around in the near–total blackness and said, "No. It's still dark. Good night!" Then he flung himself down and completely covered his head.

But finally Arthur's message came in clear.

"What!" He sat up again. "I thought this was an overnight trip. I can't stay. I have too much work to do." Not waiting for a reply, he said, "So if you two want to stay I'll send someone to pick you up in a day or so."

Merlin had not noticed that Kara was now awake, packing, or that she had heard her son's suggestion. But now she spoke — firmly. "Oh, no. YOU are the reason we're here. I don't wish to hear any more objections or excuses. Just get ready, Merlin. There's a reason for everything. Believe us, and please do as we ask."

Arthur added, more cheerfully, "Come on now, Merlin. This is a very special place. One that you'll remember all of your life."

By now Merlin's head was spinning — why were his parents being so domineering? Why so evasive? And *why* were they on this trip? Merlin submitted once more though now out of curiosity about his parents' baffling behavior. Apparently the only way to get satisfaction was to follow orders and go farther into the park.

Besides, just before dropping off to sleep, he had heard Arthur and Kara whisper softly to each other in a strange yet oddly familiar language. Though he could not understand any of the words, he remembered the peculiarities of that tongue. His scientist's mind would not rest until he knew the secret, surprise, or whatever.

Their new trek, deep into the park and up the mountain, was even more arduous than that of the day before. This time, though, the hiking was much easier for the reluctant Merlin. His attitude had changed, thus making the march an adventure instead of an ordeal, as on the previous day. Arthur was again in the lead, taking the three of them high into the park's least known areas. The march was grueling, even cruel, but at the end of the day they made camp again. And although exhausted, Merlin kept his ears sharp for any whispered conversation between his parents. But this time there was nothing to be heard. He drifted into a restless sleep on the cold ground.

Next morning the three continued their journey, only this time descending slightly and heading around the tree-crowned mountaintop. They continued down the slope for two more days until, at last, they looked out at a magnificent waterfall. It was not the largest but certainly the most beautiful in Atlantis and, because of its inaccessibility, the least frequented by visitors. The tremendous size — and force — of the plunging cascade offered its beholders an almost unparalleled experience of sight and sound. The waterfall's rhythms also seemed to welcome its three tired callers. Yet in spite of the scene's magnificence, Arthur informed Kara and Merlin that this was not their destination, but rather a cave behind the falls. Merlin found this odd; even his keen eyes could detect nothing behind the rushing flood — not even a path leading to the opening. But Arthur pointed to an all but invisible trail; it would take them to the hidden cave, he said. Merlin and Kara followed him closely and carefully, for the path was not only concealed but treacherously slippery. By now, Merlin had gotten into the full spirit of the adventure, wondering, as they passed behind the deafening thunder of the falls, how this place could be of any importance. Certainly the three were not going to be able to speak in the unending roar. But suddenly the mouth of the cave materialized — almost from nowhere — and when they entered, the noise all but stopped.

The cave's mouth had been narrow, but inside, the opening expanded into a cavernous hole; its ceiling rose to about sixty feet. Merlin surmised that the cave was deep. But how deep he did not realize until Arthur turned on their portable lights — which revealed the sparkle of many millions of crystals that lined the cave's walls and ceilings and threw back dancing reflections from the artificial illumination. Awed, the three visitors strolled through the great shimmering museum of light. Merlin made a point of examining the stones, which he said were a rare type of quartz.

"The interesting thing about this cave," said Arthur, "is that someone — or some people — have tunneled all the way out through to the other side of the mountain."

This fascinated Merlin with the possibilities of who, why, and what. He found no answers, but as he probed into the tunnel itself he saw that it was supported by massive beams of superbly worked craftsmanship. Later, Arthur told him and Kara a story about a strange race of squat little people — artisans of great renown — who lived in the mountains and mined jewels. Although Merlin thought the tale amusing — he remarked that it reminded him of the bedtime stories Kara told him when he was a child — he could not help but suspect there was more to this kernal of information.

By the time Arthur finished his narrative, Kara had readied a luscious stew made from roots they had found on the long walk, together with some dried ingredients brought from home. To weary hikers it was delectable and soothing. After eating they rested awhile, listening to the faint sound of the falls. And all along, Merlin's curiosity over the whole mystery of the journey grew — until it was no longer tolerable.

"Well, we are *here*," he said. "Now, are you going to tell me what this is all about or am I to die of curiosity? I can't believe that you brought me all the way here just to see this cave — a magnificent oddity though it may be."

Kara looked at him thoughtfully. Then she began what was to be a most fateful conversation for her son. "Tell me what you remember about the stories I used to tell you when you were little," she said.

Merlin's brows came together in concentration. "Oh, let me see . . . something about a faraway land and a strange but wonderful people who inhabited that place. . . . You know, I used to wish that I could go there, even if it *was* make–believe."

Kara watched him intently. "Do you remember the games I played with you?" she asked.

Merlin looked puzzled. Where was this leading? As if by rote, he rattled off a list of the usual games played by every Atlantian mother with her child, but suddenly he stopped short. There was another. But somehow, curiously, he could not say what it was . . . not aloud. Even there, in the hidden cave, he instinctively withheld his thoughts.

But then Kara broke through the barrier by saying, "And there was another one, a silent one . . ."

"Yes." Merlin hesitated. "A silent one." When he had said it he realized something important was happening. He was eager to learn what it was. He was also a little frightened.

"My son, we are all going to play that game now." Kara was speaking with quiet, earnest intensity. Arthur now shaded the portable lights and the three sat in the dimness.

"Close your eyes," Kara began, "and start to clear everything from your mind. As if you were trying to see nothingness."

At first, the years of neglected practice made the task impossible. How could one conceivably picture nothingness? Clearing his ever–active mind was much more difficult than filling it with thoughts. In their attempts to help him, Kara and Arthur offered many suggestions about techniques, but their efforts were fruitless.

It was not until the end of the second day that Merlin began to experience some success. The mental wall built over the years for his and his parents' protection finally began to crumble. And, as he took his first halting steps toward relearning the old knowledge, Merlin found himself much more relaxed and peaceful than ever before. Yet his mind was alert and quick.

In the five days that followed, he would learn a story much more fantastic than any Arthur could have told. Although hours passed without anyone speaking, images flowed into Merlin's mind fully formed, like a motion picture on a screen. The story unfolding in him was *his* story — and the tale of all of his loved ones. It was told wordlessly, first from Kara's point of view, then from Arthur's. Eventually, the entire one-hundred-sixty-five years of the story came alive before him. He relived the Lemurian lifestyle and history. He saw his mother, her family, and the meeting and eventual marriage that would bring Kara and Arthur to a new life in Atlantis. He saw the old empire and then the new state of Atlantis; both its good and its corruption. The State's headlong plunge into technology was seen for what it really was — the crushing desire to conquer not only this world but those of the universe.

Merlin learned of his ancestry, as well as Zaran's and MaReenie's, now comprehending the reason for the inseparable bond between them. He watched Raena's boating accident and observed the young Zaran's face. He learned that Zaran's mother had been mentally ill, eventually committing suicide in an institution for the insane where she had undergone brutal experiments at the hands of Atlantian scientist-doctors. He realized what Kara already knew — that Zaran had suffered greatly with that knowledge. And he was out to avenge her death, never believing or accepting her sickness. He had to prove his superiority. Kara revealed how she had attempted to help Zaran, only to have him rebel. Alone, his extraordinary cleverness and intelligence hid his secret from everyone else.

And at last, the incredible tale was told and updated to the moment of Zaran's secret assignment. Even Kara's suspicions of what role Zaran would play in the fate of her people was revealed to her son. Kara and Arthur even disclosed their desire to leave Atlantis and join the Lemurians in what could be their ultimate struggle for survival.

When all five days of the "game" were completed, Merlin's mind was filled to capacity and his body drained of every ounce of energy. Kara and Arthur were similarly affected. The trio lay in the cave, exhausted. Nothing was said. Nothing else needed to be said. Now it was time to rest, and so they slept, suspending all thoughts of their past for a full twenty-four hours. Then, refreshed, they started back to Alta. In reality, though, all three understood they had begun a much longer journey — to what end they did not know. But to that end they were now committed.

12

The Golden Stones

At exactly the same moment Merlin was complaining bitterly about his parents' unexpected trip to Lawal, MaReenie and her father were on their way to an island off the eastern coast of Atlantis.

Zirth, the old colonel, ex–officer under Arthur's command, had secretly planned a vacation to the island of Catiflus, where, as a child, MaReenie had stayed many times. In contrast to the reluctance of Merlin's departure, MaReenie went off on her vacation in high spirits. Excitedly, she boarded the boat that would take her to the small piece of rock she associated with a multitude of wonderful childhood memories. Though the place had once been the scene of happy times for Zirth, after his wife's death he had lost all interest in any of his old family activities — including trips to the island. Kara constantly encouraged him to continue with his life, even to marry again, but he refused, saying, "How could I find such perfection again?" Instead he found joy in watching his daughter grow to have many of her mother's qualities — rich in both physical and mental beauty. Now, many years later, she and her father were going to the place of her mother's death. Today, however, she was reminiscing about happier times and, naturally, she wondered why her father had had such a sudden change of heart about visiting Catiflus.

In their power boat, the two passengers sped toward the rocky shores. MaReenie watched the morning sunlight dance on the rough and choppy water while the boat bounced onward. Its white wake sprayed the passengers. MaReenie loved the salty taste on her lips, left by the damp breeze that messed and tangled her raven hair. The fishy smell opened her senses, conjuring up images of her childhood. Wrapped up in the excitement, she did not notice that her father was unusually quiet, particularly for a man who so enjoyed handling his boat — and talking about it. Zirth loved speed, whether on land, sea, or air. MaReenie had inherited some of the same wild spirit for she, too, enjoyed the feel of the boat battling its way against the heaving surface of the sea.

Not until the two had almost landed did MaReenie begin to realize that Zirth's penchant for speed was more than an enjoyable experience today — it was a means of escape from Alta. She now became aware that Zirth had continually been looking astern — as if expecting someone in pursuit. Perhaps, she thought, he's on the watch for intruders, seeking to share his isolated hideaway. But now, after they had landed, old Zirth hid the boat and hurried toward the partially boarded–up house. Instead of using one of the doors to enter, he went around to the side and behind some now completely overgrown hedges. With a whispered cry, he told MaReenie to follow him. Though puzzled by his actions, she instinctively obeyed.

Now, hidden behind some blossoming evergreens, Zirth opened a small doorway, which led into the first floor closet of the house. The musty smell of the place was literally enough to take the breath away. MaReenie could see that the sands were beginning to consume the abandoned building. However, at this moment her main concern was to follow the directions of her father, who was calling out for her to follow him down the basement stairs — and to close the door hard behind her. After being away from their cottage for so long, MaReenie wanted to have a look around, but Zirth was adamant; down the stairs she must go. He led her to another unused door which, when opened, revealed a passageway. Then, with an electric crystal torch in hand, the old colonel hurried along the dark, cobwebbed tunnel. MaReenie followed cautiously. At the end of the tunnel daylight could be seen. Warm rays streamed in through two small windows of an underground room.

MaReenie immediately noted that the room was surprisingly dry.

"Of course it is!" Zirth answered. "Your mother knew her business. This is on an earth line. Raena was always right about such things. That's why we all bought this piece of rock — Arthur, Arak, and I.

"Originally there were to be three houses here," he began to reminisce, "But first Zaran's mother got ill so Arak didn't have the spirit to continue the plan. Then, when Raena died, I just couldn't come here anymore." Then he straightened up and changed his tone. "Today is different, though, as you'll see in a little while. Don't ask about *it* yet, my daughter." He was emphatic, but MaReenie's curiosity was overflowing.

"But Papa, what's 'it'?" she wanted to know. Zirth answered by not answering. "Let's eat," he said "I packed this lunch myself. For the rest of our stay we'll be eating out of the foodstuffs stored here. As you can see, the one thing we won't do is die of starvation." He pointed to the north wall of cabinets. MaReenie went over and opened one of them. She found a storehouse of dried food.

The two sat under the small, oval windows at a drop–leaf table and ate their lunch. Zirth quietly reminded his daughter of the many good times they had had at the island; and more specifically, about Raena.

Because MaReenie's mother had been an exceptional artist, her works were still on display in many of the State's galleries. However, it was her metal sculptures, her personal favorites, of silver and gold that made her famous. Her pieces were so lifelike that everyone expected them to move at any moment. Husband and daughter both remembered her wonderful sense of humor and laughed at the many jokes she told. Somewhere in the middle of all their remembering, MaReenie suddenly jumped up and hugged her father. They had not talked like this in a long time.

"Maybe we should have come here sooner, Papa. It's as though Mama was here and we were all laughing together again."

Tears invaded Zirth's eyes and he attempted to hold them back.

"Let's finish, my dear. We have much more to do and the sooner we start, the better."

They finished the meal amid the laughter and tears of reminiscence, long overdue. When the two had cleared away the dishes, Zirth went to one of the packs they had brought with them. He pulled out a cloth bag and dumped its golden contents on the floor. They were the strange pieces given by Raena to MaReenie at each of her birthdays for twelve years. She had happily received these pieces; oddly shaped gold designs that looked like crude carved rocks. Raena had told her daughter that they were the pieces to a life puzzle and MaReenie was to play with them until one day she would find the right configuration for herself.

A few years after her mother's death, MaReenie found herself fingering the pieces when suddenly she received a strong current of energy, followed by a frightening mental image. After that, she wouldn't go near them. Even in her closeness to Kara, MaReenie never spoke to her about the experience with the golden stones. She sensed some danger connected with their use — and now her father had them.

"Do you remember these?" he asked.

"Yes, Mama gave them to me, but I had them put away. How did you find them?" MaReenie suddenly felt as if her privacy had been invaded. Zirth gave her a funny look.

"You'll soon find out, but first I must shut out the light from those windows." Zirth closed the open shutters.

"Papa, why are we hiding?" MaReenie asked. She was becoming afraid.

"My dear, you'll have all your answers in a while." Zirth could see that his daughter was trying to be patient. "I know," he said. "You've found the correct answer to the puzzle, haven't you?"

"What do you mean?" MaReenie replied.

"I felt the shock myself while I was meditating," Zirth answered. "Why didn't you keep on using them?"

"I was afraid, Papa." Now completely confused, MaReenie started to cry. "I sensed some danger or something terrifying about those things."

Zirth attempted to comfort her. "Well, my daughter, today you *must* begin to use them. Here there will be no danger, but through them you *will* find out some unpleasant things." Zirth was now holding MaReenie in his arms. "Your mother had planned to make a set of these for Merlin and one for Zaran, but she didn't have enough time to complete her work. I have a set for Merlin, but one stone is missing. Somehow, though, she never could start on Zaran's. It's too bad. He probably could have used them, but . . ." He hesitated, "Maybe it's better this way." By this time, Zirth was almost talking to himself.

Then he came back to the subject. "MaReenie, to begin properly I must first teach you some important techniques in the use of your stones. Will you trust me?" MaReenie nodded. Zirth then began to teach his daughter in the same way he was helped so many years before. "First, we must try to clear our minds of every thought . . ."

Zirth's task was much more difficult than that of Arthur and Kara. He alone had to prepare his daughter for the use of the stones and teach her to use her mind. Raena had not given MaReenie any of the help Kara had used with Merlin. In her eagerness to practice her art and her scientific knowledge, she had delayed working with MaReenie. As do most people, Raena felt she would have the time later and seemed to rely on the stones to do much to enhance MaReenie's receptiveness. But alas, Raena's time was cut short, and now it was Zirth who had to help his daughter use a power that he barely understood himself.

He knew Kara would be of some assistance later, but for the present he had to set their plan into motion by teaching MaReenie all she could learn through the use of her stones. It took her a week just to learn to control her mind and to find the right combination for *her* golden stones to aid her mental transmissions.

During that time, father and daughter rarely spoke aloud, as Zirth attempted, awkwardly, to communicate mentally. At first it was very frustrating to MaReenie, but once she mastered the technique, there was no stopping her. She had a thousand and one questions to be answered and Zirth tried to answer them all. Raena had been right. If her daughter was heir to any psychic ability, the stones would do their work.

With the twelve small stones in place, MaReenie placed her hands around them, felt the charge of power and began to watch the story of Lemuria unfold before her. Zirth had to keep his thoughts tightly controlled on the story, so as not to confuse and distract his daughter. But at that moment, in the light of the portable crystal light, MaReenie looked so much like Raena that he could hardly concentrate on anything but the story of their first meeting. He realized it was only a small part of the epic that had to be given to MaReenie, and struggled to widen his perceptions, but the sight of his now grown daughter released a flood of memories so long held back. He remembered the innocently spirited child who emerged to adulthood as a tease. To those who did now know her very well, she appeared somewhat superficial, but his daughter possessed a great sensitivity for others, which lay hidden behind her flashing eyes. She had always been aware of Merlin's great gifts and his lack of confidence. She recognized Zaran's dissatisfaction and his arrogance about his abilities; but to both she was always friend and mental equal.

Zirth had watched as his child's beauty blossomed and brought many suitors to her door, but they were all rejected. However, MaReenie did keep her admirers as friends, for, like her mother, she had the ability to gather people around her. Nonetheless, she was looking for something special in her life's partner, so MaReenie was continually drawn back to her two childhood friends.

Now, at the island, Zirth helped reveal, to her amazement, the reason for such a strong bond of love among the three companions. With mixed feelings, she used the stones to learn all about her heritage and that of her loved ones. The longer she worked with Zirth and held the stones, the more information she received. She learned that by changing the configurations slightly she could tap into vast stores of information — everything about the earth lines in Atlantis and their possible uses. At first, all this new knowledge was exciting, but later she was frightened at its implications of danger to everyone who might become involved in it. Even though she was using only a small fraction of her mental capabilities, MaReenie was still in complete awe of the fantastic revelations of the Lemurian's abilities. The pictures in her mind flowed swiftly, unfolding the complete story, and her feelings changed with each new scene. She was saddened by Zaran's tragic past — and terrified by his possible future. She shed tears of joy as she watched the love story of her father and mother and that of Kara and Arthur. She wept for Zaran's mother, her terrifying mental collapse, and its effect on her son. While she chastised herself mentally for her flippancy towards him and Merlin, MaReenie was also angry at her father and the others for secrets they kept, but understood their reasons.

When the two-week vacation was over and the visitors were packing to leave, MaReenie finally spoke out loud to Zirth. "How safe were we here, Papa?"

"Completely," he said confidently. "It's practically the only place that is. When we get back . . . well, I don't have to tell you the dangers of talking to anyone about this. By anyone I mean Zaran." Zirth's voice betrayed his suspicions. "Kara and Merlin will tell you more if they can, but be careful where you choose to communicate. We're all being watched — well, everyone in Atlantis is monitored in some way or another. You know that now."

"Oh Papa! What are we going to do?"

"Things will work out. They always do. As to the how or when — well, Arthur, Kara, and I are still working on that, but we wanted you and Merlin to be prepared to leave Atlantis when our plan is readied."

"And Zaran?" MaReenie asked anxiously.

"One does not sleep well with hungry tigers," was Zirth's reply. "MaReenie, he can't be trusted. He looks for power and has betrayed everyone in his way. You saw his face when the boat blew up and you've seen it again with the stones. You've watched him through the years. How do you think he's advanced so quickly in the political ranks — and why so many people have disappeared or have had to retire as mental cripples. There's an explosion of hatred brewing in that man and when it's detonated . . . I'm afraid the world as we know it will never be the same." Zirth was visibly shaken by his own words. "Come now. We've been away long enough."

They retraced their steps and returned home. Their trip back to Alta was made in silence; both were exhausted by their experience and drained by their fear of their future.

Lemuria was in danger because Atlantis was now on the move. Kara had sensed the power surge in Lemuria, and although she knew it would be used only for peaceful endeavors, Atlantis would view it as a threat. Syus was hungry for any power. He would want this power to add to his war–machine state and his move to world domination. Kara suspected Zaran of intrigue with Syus to overthrow Lemuria or destroy it utterly. Something must be done to prevent this destruction. But what could stop Atlantis?

13
Zaran Goes to Lemuria

The transport from Cumbar carrying its precious cargo of dragons, supplies, and Zaran landed outside the tropical city of Port Quae, located on the northwestern shores of the land now known as the South American continent. The dragons were unloaded along with Zaran's supplies and quartered in a very crude shelter built outside the city. Actually, the beasts needed no protection from the elements, but Zaran wanted to keep them hidden as much as possible. He planned to stay only a few days — just time enough to gather any local information about the Lemurians, and he would make any last-minute purchases or preparations here. Actually information about Lemuria was obtained with relative ease, for the continent's southern shore was situated only about 150 miles across the ocean, and free trade between the Port Quaens and the Lemurians was always open.

The information gathered by Zaran revealed practically nothing new. The Lemurians lived simply; they were friendly, trusting, and peaceful. But what did disturb Zaran was the complacent attitude of the people at Port Quae about the "so-called" power surge. Apparently over the years there had been many minor blackouts, but these were attributed to the unstable geological conditions of that part of the world with all of its volcanic and earthquake activities. Certainly not to the Lemurians; they were anything but technologically developed.

Or so the traders of Port Quae believed, for they had limited firsthand information about the Lemurians' interior countryside, except for the products made by the people.

After reviewing the aerial photos of the continent, Zaran decided to land at Lemuria's southwestern shores, but only after checking out the eastern half of the land; naturally, with what information he had gathered, the whole trip seemed to him like an easy assignment. Full of bravado for his impending victory over Lemuria's backward people, the overconfident invader readied his armored beasts. Yes, he thought; I will return triumphant and Merlin will have failed in his appointed task. I've seen to that.

The dawning of the second week at Port Quae saw four dark spots gliding across the clear morning sky. The dragons — with Zaran in a specially constructed cockpit device on Xax's back — were on their way to the peaceful and relatively uninhabited coastline of Lemuria.

During the near–one–hour ride, the flying was left to the beasts. Once arrived, they would circle around and seek a secluded landing area. At Port Quae they were told that Lemuria's east coast was dotted with caves that would be perfect for hiding four large beasts and a man.

As he sat on the small dragon's back, Zaran continued to muse about how easy it had been so far. "They're really stupid," he said to himself, "leaving their country wide open to attack like this."

What Zaran didn't realize and probably would never understand was that the Lemurians' thoughts did not include those of conquest or being conquered. They felt completely safe from attack; and because of their peaceful convictions they considered aggression only the acts of the insane.

When the "conquering forces" of Zaran's troop finally reached their target, the first order of business for the dragons was to scout the continent's eastern regions. Their findings would expand what information Zaran already possessed about the eastern terrain.

The continent of Lemuria was composed of three islands divided by a narrow channel of sea. If the water in the channel had been shallow, the Lemurians could have easily waded from any one island to any of the others. Instead, they were forced to use a system of deep–water buoys and lights to guide their rafts and other vessels. These navigational aids peppered the whole length of the channel. The two larger islands to the north and south were bordered on their eastern sides by great dry regions. Each of these areas, with its shriveled earth, was called Kaymaw. Here the onyx colored ground was streaked with the ochre of striated angular rock formations that dominated the landscape. In this vast, parched, seemingly deserted region were scattered scrawny plants, together with a hardy population of birds, reptiles, and insects that roamed freely yet hidden within the crevices of the alien scenery.

To the south, where Zaran's troop was to land, and to the west, the terrain was relatively flat, except for an occasional volcano that speared into the sky. The rich volcanic soil of this belt nurtured a lush diversity of plants and great rain forests. The contrast with Kaymaw was that of day with night. And, as the invaders prepared to land, Zaran stared in disbelief at the size of the plant life in this part of Lemuria. The fields of corn and wheat seemed to swallow and engulf the dragons. It was as if they had arrived at the home of giants fifty times their own size.

The beasts had chosen a place far inland on which to set down. After getting their bearings, they made their way through the fields, then out into the warm sunlight, moving quickly toward a densely wooded area. Once out of sight, the invaders reviewed their strategy — now taking into account their suddenly acquired knowledge of the giant vegetation. Zaran had also noted large monoliths, apparently placed at random all through the land. But through his power–sensing equipment, these large stones emitted nothing but silence.

The party's plan had not changed: they would head undetected toward the power source. At the moment, though, all of Zaran's equipment — and that of the dragons — was quiet.

"The Lemurians must be hiding their weapon," said Zaran. "They must have seen us." Silently he cursed his own carelessness. "Let's get to the caves. We'll wait there and see whether they plan to attack."

Luckily the five invaders found a suitable cave not too far from the place where they had landed. Now they settled down, all the while assuming that they might have been spotted on their arrival. For the rest of the day they waited. The next day, nothing having occurred, Zaran decided to venture out. With the clothes he brought with him, he disguised himself as a Lemurian, then left the cave to investigate the countryside.

But although he roamed until sunset, he encountered no one. Nor did he see any buildings — only miles of golden crops and an occasional monolith in the field. No two looked quite the same. Some were roundish, others appeared rectangular; some had been polished to a high gloss, and others were just large natural stones. More to the point, Zaran could get no power readings from any of these rocks — or from any direction in which he pointed his equipment.

"They must be decorations of some kind, or have some barbaric religious meaning," he said aloud as he continued to move through the gargantuan vegetation.

The sun was settling behind the western horizon when Zaran headed back to his dragons. It had been a waste of time and effort to land here, he decided. Somehow the information he had been given by his Atlantian co–scientists must be incorrect. Perhaps the power came from some other place.

But as he walked, he was surprised to find his frustration vanishing. Zaran was now experiencing a strange peace, actually thinking of how enjoyable the day had been. It had been a long time since he had had such feelings; not since before his mother had been taken away to the Institute For The Mentally Deficient. Yes, his attitude was definitely mellowing — his zeal and anger were not nearly as great as when he had left Cumbar. He felt as if a plug had been pulled, to let his hatred drain from his mind. Thus it was that when he got back to the cave, it was a different Zaran who greeted his beasts. At first they did not sense this change, and later said nothing while listening to their master tell of his day's lack of adventure. After eating, they took turns standing guard while Zaran slept.

The next morning again dawned in peace and so followed the whole day. Zaran started to think of how pleasant it would be to stay here and live a quiet life amid the towering plants. Not once did he bother to venture out into the fields, but stayed close to the cave and dreamed of the possibility of a peaceful life. He could not even muster up any envy or jealousy for Merlin as his thoughts wandered home. Naturally, his beasts were now confused and puzzled by his mood, but even they were beginning to sense the same feeling of peace — a totally alien sensation for these creatures of hate. They recovered by attempting their customary baiting and needling with Zaran, but this time he did not respond. At dusk, he turned on his portable lights, and warmed his supper. After finishing some Lemurian fruit, he was completely lulled by his sanguine thoughts.

And then he was abruptly jolted back to reality as his power meter began ticking.

"Damn! It was a trap!" Zaran shouted. "All this stupidity of peacefulness — just bait to prevent me from doing my job!" Now he whirled on the beasts and screamed, "Damn you! How could *you* have been taken in! I'll remember this!"

Instantly the four creatures were on their feet, ready for orders. Out of the cave they flew — now in the direction of the object for which they had come to Lemuria. Presently they saw an artificially constructed stone ridge below. As they circled it warily a flash of light suddenly turned the black sky into daylight. The four dragons plunged earthward to avoid detection, but after a few moments on the ground, Zaran's curiosity got the better of him as his power equipment went wild. He began to creep up the rocky obstruction. When he had reached the top, he cautiously peered over the ledge. What he saw left his eyes wide and his jaws open in disbelief. It simply was not logical. But it was happening.

The bare clearing held two concentric circles formed of immense, shiny black stones, each hewn into perfect right triangles. Inside the squat outer circle of stones was a smaller interior circle made up of seven tall triangles, all pointing toward a central structure carved from the same iridescent black rock. Fitted to its pinnacle were three inverted conical shapes of hammered gold, holding a crystal sphere. There were also twenty–one smaller triangles; at the base of every one sat a Lemurian, dressed in white with a red sash, reclining against an alcove that was hollowed into each of the stones and lined with hammered gold. With their eyes closed, the meditators sat cross–legged, the first three fingers of the right hand placed on the left knee. Radiating out from the crystal sphere were rings of lights.

Zaran stared in wonder as the sphere slowly rose out of its conical home and into the air, emitting brighter and brighter lights, its rays spreading into the darkness above and downward at the quiet Lemurians. As he

watched the great light surge through the black sky, Zaran abruptly felt drawn toward it. Without any warning, he found himself over the ridge, hurrying toward what he felt to be an aura of peace that welcomed him. But then, with the swiftness of a trap snapping shut, he stopped short. This wonderful, soothing tranquility suddenly became completely infuriating.

"What the hell is going on?" His mind screamed. "I'm suddenly being sucked out into the open!" He bolted back over the wall to hide again. Still, that feeling continued to haunt him. He turned and forced himself to leave. Then he saw the four dragons approaching.

"What the hell are you four doing!" he screamed at them. "Get back! I gave you no orders to move."

Xax answered, "There's — a — feeling."

Zaran's reply was an infuriated whisper. "What are you talking about? Are you creatures of destruction being invaded by a *feeling*! What have I created anyway?" He didn't wait for any answer. He left them, cursing softly but violently as he pushed his way through the heavy vegetation.

But even while rushing away he felt that "feeling" invade his mind. It was searching for something. Instantly Zaran understood that he must hide his mind as well as his body. It was not enough to look like a Lemurian — Zaran had to *be* a Lemurian, if he was to learn the secrets of this weird land. How could he keep this feeling–thing from penetrating his thoughts and yet try to find a means of capturing the sphere? He knew there was no way.

Zaran now made a decision. He spun around and headed back toward the stone circle. When he reached the ridge, he saw the dragons waiting. He ordered an attack. In a flash the beasts took to the air. Then, circling, they dove ruthlessly at the defenseless people sitting on the ground. Zaran remained on the ridge, his weapon in hand, firing carefully but rapidly. A number of Lemurians were killed. Yet the others did not run. "Are they crazy?" Zaran asked himself as he laid his weapon aside. But by the time he became aware of the surge it was too late.

It was a devastating counterattack. The overwhelming mind–forces of Lemuria were gathered in that circle, and the rings of light engulfing the entire clearing deflected the dragons' fire back at its point of origin. Almost immediately three of the monsters were reduced to ashes. Now terrified, Zaran could only call off Xax, by then the only remaining beast. The strafing dragon picked up Zaran in one claw and flew in retreat to the cave.

At this point, Zaran's frustration had overcome his panic and reached a point of hysteria. Once inside the cave, he signaled his remaining forces at Port Quae to meet him at specified coordinates. All he could do now was wait. He slowly let himself sink to the ground. Then he began to think aloud.

"There was nothing there but a circle of stones," he said, despair in his voice. "The power system must be built underground — and the stones have to act as transmitters." Then he hit the ground with his fists and shouted, "I have *got* to get back there!"

First, though, he must make further plans — and rest. Placing Xax as sentry, he gave orders to be awakened if anything unusual happened — or when the reinforcement beasts arrived.

Meanwhile, at the circle, there was chaos and grief. The suddenness of the attack had taken the Lemurians by surprise. These people had known of Zaran's presence, but they had hoped the peaceful messages they had sent mentally would win him over. They knew they had almost succeeded, but now they realized that some hate–filled force within the intruder was more powerful, and certainly more erratic, than their own. A mental call was sent to all nearby Lemurians to help with the dead — and to clean up the horrid debris left by the exploding dragons. Untiringly the work was done, though it took all night. The dead were buried within sight of the clearing, after which the beasts' almost unrecognizable carcasses were burned. When day dawned, the site was again clean. The only remaining sign of the previous night's tragedy were five fresh graves.

The Lemurians made no effort to pursue Zaran — that way led to certain death. They had not even meant to defend themselves. But the forces had been so strong that the peace–loving people could not stop the deflection of the dragon's fire. The Lemurians now knew Zaran's true heart. Certainly he would return for his revenge — and his booty. But there in the clearing that booty would remain, while the Lemurians would hide and wait, Zaran's presence always in their minds.

Zaran also waited and rested, but not peacefully. He remained alert, ready for an assault that never came. He could not understand why these people did not try to finish him off. That was what he would do to them . . . soon.

It had taken the dragons from Port Quae more than an hour to arrive at the cave. Zaran had briefed them on the events of the night before. By now, he had worked out a plan, but he told the new arrivals they would have to wait until morning for the details — it would be safer that way. Meanwhile, dragon sentries stood at their posts all night.

Early the next morning, Zaran awoke with a start, as if out of a nightmare. He had spent a fitful night dreaming continually of what had happened and what else could happen. While he ate, he sent Zork, one of the replacements, to survey the countryside. His orders were to maintain a high altitude, but to observe whatever activity was afoot. If he saw any

Lemurians, he was to capture them and bring them back. The beast returned — alone.

"No — one's — around — and — the — stone — circle — has — been — cleared — of — debris," Zork announced.

Zaran then sent out two more beasts to scout in a different direction, but they also returned with no news, saying there was absolutely no one anywhere. Zaran could not accept this, but he could wait. On the next two consecutive mornings, he again sent troops out in search of any signs of movement, with no success. On the fourth morning he decided to lead the dragons himself.

First, the evil squadron circled the grouping of black stones. Then Zaran ordered the dragons to land and remove one of the smaller stones which, he announced, would be taken back to Atlantis. To his astonishment, fury, and despair, none could be moved. Every possible force was exerted, but the stones were unyielding. Zaran even ordered the dragons to dig one out, believing that it was attached in some way to the great power station underground. The excavation only afforded the dragons some extra exercise. The stone could not be lifted and, unbelievably, Zaran found only more dirt under the digs.

Now in an almost unmanageable rage, Zaran even attempted to chip away some small piece of the black stone, but he could not; only a splinter of the hammered gold was finally hacked free. The invaders' attempts with the central column were equally futile — there was not so much as a hint of a sign of movement. Finally, at his wits' end, Zaran unthinkingly commanded two of the dragons to "blast the damned stones into oblivion." The mistake was irreparable — only the beasts went to oblivion, with the reflected rays of their blasts whirled back on themselves. Zaran could only scream his utter despair.

Now Zaran directed Xax to find any Lemurians, or else. The obedient beast flew off in search of inhabitants, but four days later he returned empty–clawed. Zaran cursed him. "How in hell's name can you tell me that you've found no one? They *can't* have disappeared! They're here! And I'm going to find one and wring out the information I want! And you're coming with me!"

Zaran was relentless. Day and night the two flew, even shooting animals and burning any unusual growth. Xax became exhausted — something that did not happen to dragons. And nothing was found. Zaran finally had to admit defeat. For all his efforts, he would return to Atlantis with only a piece of crudely hammered gold, one dragon, and nothing else. Apart from having to admit his failure to Syus, Zaran was a poor loser.

"Lemuria, you *will* pay for my humiliation!" he shouted, as he began the all–too–short journey back to his homeland.

14
Raena's Gift

The weeks that followed the unexpected vacations of Merlin and MaReenie were unusually busy with unfinished work, State activities and, of course, the planning of their families' departure from Atlantis. Merlin and MaReenie did not see each other during this period except at two State banquets, where they were summoned to perform their appointed duties. Not until the rumors of Zaran's return to Cumbar were everywhere in the city of Alta did Merlin attempt to contact MaReenie. The stories, which were rampant, depicted Zaran as anything but victorious, and Syus was apparently displeased with his prince, but so far no official announcement of Zaran's defeat had been issued. Merlin either ignored the questions put to him by his fellow scientists at the laboratory or defended Zaran as usual, simply to keep up pretenses.

No one at the laboratory understood what had happened during Merlin's initial experiments performed on the tissue samples which had been prepared for him by Zaran; all they knew was that Merlin was now proceeding with great success. However, in order to buy time to facilitate the escape plan, Merlin had delayed giving the dragons the full dosage of the serum, pretending that his current experiments would further perfect the formula.

"Don't want anything to happen to Zaran's babies. After all, he *is* my best friend and I did promise to take care of them," was Merlin's usual explanation.

Secretly, though, he could not bear to consider a future shared with everlasting beasts. He continually asked himself, "What will humanity think of us if we were to curse the future forever? And what will I think of myself?" But now his thoughts also turned to another matter: "I must get a message to MaReenie."

The midafternoon sun blazed down over the humid city as Mupi soared over Alta from the Old Laboratories across the canals toward what was called "New Town." Mupi watched the abrupt changes in the architecture of the city. Most of the older buildings had been replaced, but out in the residential area there were a few houses of the earlier style still standing. Of those, the most unusual ever built in all of Atlantis was the home of Zirth and his late wife Raena. Laughingly called the "horned house," it was basically of a small pyramidical style but had a large turned pinnacle

ending in a spiral. The horns that jutted out from its corners were in reality golden busts of people and animals.

Raena, once an artist/earth–line scientist in Lemuria, had designed the house as a power station of sorts. Built on an earth line, the structure collected power for psychic use. The "horns" were part of the collectors. Fellow residents considered the house an ugly oddity, but out of respect for one of its great artists, the government allowed it to stand. Now, when the happy Mupi landed, he perched himself on one of the "horns," and tapped at MaReenie's window with his beak.

As always, MaReenie was delighted to see Mupi. She thought the creature looked as if he belonged to her strange house. After opening the window and petting Mupi, MaReenie searched his collar. There it was.

"Oh you darling thing," she whispered to Mupi as she opened Merlin's letter. "Wait here until I see if your friend and master needs a reply."

My lovely MaReenie:

A few weeks ago, I spent some time at Lawal with my parents. It was their unusual way of celebrating a century and a quarter of marriage. As usual, it turned out to be an education. You know how Father loves to teach everyone about life in the wilds and tell old campaign stories. Well, I heard some beauts. If you are interested in hearing some tall tales, stop by and see me at the Hut.

Always,

M.

The "Hut" was the name Merlin gave to his parent's home. And the letter was friendly and absurd enough so that if it fell into the wrong hands, no one would be hurt.

MaReenie began her reply.

My Dearest M:

I was out in the wilds myself and it was great fun. I hadn't been camping in years. I heard plenty of old soldier campaign tales, too. Maybe we can compare notes and see just who was exaggerating about what detail. We'll have great laughs, dearest M. But why don't you come here instead? Father says you're becoming a stranger to the house. How about pleasing both of us? We'll expect you for tribute.
P.S. Please bring Mupi with you. I just *love* that funny creature!

Love,

MaR

Merlin, of course, would know that "tribute" was the evening meal, at which time Syus and his government were toasted with wine. The New Order had instituted the custom to insure loyalty from all.

After eating some fruit and a cracker that MaReenie gave him, Mupi flew back home, to find Merlin waiting for MaReenie's reply.

"So we're invited to tribute," Merlin announced.

Mupi rubbed against Merlin and made a throaty, purring sound, mixed with a whine.

"Well, I'm certainly glad she likes you, because I was planning to take you anyway. I haven't seen much of you lately. Come on, let's get ready."

Merlin had been extremely preoccupied since his return from Lawal. In fact the whole household had been busy. So Mupi's role as companion to the family, especially Merlin, had seemed somewhat usurped. Tonight, though, Merlin was attempting to make up for Mupi's lack of attention.

Dinner at Zirth's was always wonderful. Not only was the meal superb, but the company and the surroundings were, as ever, entertaining. Zirth and MaReenie told jokes and the three sang old songs. When Mupi whined in everyone laughed. Afterwards, Zirth brought out special pieces of Raena's work, some that only he and MaReenie had seen. Mupi sniffed each piece cautiously in an approving manner. Finally, Zirth presented Merlin with a wooden box containing some golden stones.

"I have kept these for perhaps too long," he said, "at any rate, there are only eleven pieces. The set was intended to have twelve."

Then he began to explain that it was a game invented by Raena. Merlin knew better. As Zirth talked, the curious Mupi put his head inside the box, sniffed around, and found something hidden along the inside of the lining. It was an old, unopened letter, addressed to Merlin. Mupi offered it to his master very reluctantly.

"I assume these are the rules," Merlin said, as he grabbed the envelope from Mupi's mouth.

"Yes," answered Zirth. "I have a set myself, and so does MaReenie. Raena died before she could make one for Zaran or anyone else."

"Well, I'll look over the rules when I get home. Too bad it's not complete," Merlin answered. Mupi whined in agreement, as if he knew what was being implied.

"In any event, it's really a child's game you might not have enjoyed playing anyway," said Zirth, "but you can still use the pieces as decorations. You know how valuable Raena's art is now. So that's quite a present.

"Well, children, I think it's my bedtime. Don't you two stay up too late either. Both of you are expected at the crystal pyramid bright and early tomorrow."

"Thank you for a wonderful evening," said Merlin. "I'm grateful for the beautiful gift."

"You're very welcome," replied Zirth. "The gift was really from Raena. I'm sorry it was so late in coming but since it was the last thing she worked on I just couldn't find it in my heart to give it up until now."

Merlin said, "I think I understand completely."

After Zirth had gone upstairs, Merlin and MaReenie realized that they could not talk about their experience — at least not aloud — and both were still too inexperienced with their new ability to keep a verbal conversation going while attempting to communicate mentally. Total silence for any long period would arouse the servants' suspicions. At any rate, they both knew what was happening. So after a few minutes of small talk, Merlin said goodnight.

Only when he was safe in his apartment did he open the envelope.

Then he said, aloud, "Come and sit over here, Mup. Let's see how this game is played."

Dear Merlin:

I have a feeling that you will not receive this present for many years after I have written this letter; certainly when you do get it, I will no longer be alive, but hopefully by that time someone will have told you about the past.

The stones in the box make up what I call a life game. Each person for whom I have made a set had their own peculiar configurations. In my home faraway, I have made these sets for many people; here in Alta only Zirth and MaReenie each have one, and now you. But Merlin, yours is different. I'm not sure why, but I could only make eleven pieces for you. I feel it is because you perhaps have a special destiny — not necessarily better or worse than the destinies of the rest of us, but certainly different. Now that you finally have the game in your possession, play with it every day as much as possible. It will brighten your mind and sharpen your inner vision. Somehow I know you will need it in the future.

Even now I can see that the man who will emerge out of the child will be great; certainly a hard worker. Merlin, try not to be totally obsessed by your work. Life to be lived must be filled with laughter, as well as sweat and tears. Lastly, I ask a favor. Please take care of MaReenie. She will need your steadiness. I only wish that I could have seen the outcome of all three of you children.

Love,

Raena

After he finished the letter, Merlin burned it, telling himself, "No one need know what she had written anyway after it lay hidden for so many years. Why cause any problems? And so what if she thought I'm to have a special destiny."

Merlin's thoughts betrayed him as Mupi read his friend's feelings. Merlin then said out loud to Mupi, "I will do the favor, though, of taking care of MaReenie. That is, if she'll let me. You know Mup, she's pretty independent."

Mupi whined in agreement.

Then Merlin began to finger the pieces and set them out in different patterns. After a while, he began to feel a strong sense of peacefulness. He attempted some of the techniques of meditation given to him at the cave, but Mupi would not cooperate. The lonely animal wanted attention. He licked at Merlin's face and rubbed his feathery body against Merlin's. He toppled the stones and flapped his wings. Mupi wanted to play and Merlin had to relent. He hid the stones and they went out for a romp. When they returned, Merlin was too exhausted to do anything but sleep.

Three days later Zaran returned, but he did not call any of his friends. Instead, Arthur and Kara were visited by Arak and were told of how his son had come back. And by his mood, said Arak, his mission had not been a success. Apparently more than one of his plans had gone awry and he was viciously furious about its failure. He was to have a meeting with Syus that afternoon. Arak was, from his manner, terribly afraid of what his son was about to do; and more so about his attitude toward Merlin and his success.

"Oh Arak, Zaran's just tired," said Kara. "After all, he's been working continuously for so long. Maybe what he needs is some time off to relax." She spoke as she felt someone might be listening. "Why don't we all go out to the garden and have some refreshment? Arak, I think you, too, have been overly concerned about Zaran. He'll be all right. After all, he is one of the great minds in Atlantis."

"Oh, I suppose you're right," Arak answered, gaining control of himself as they all rose to leave for the garden.

"Why, of course she is," Arthur agreed. "He's just overworked."

"Arak, you haven't seen my wildflower field!" Kara announced. "It's my favorite part of the whole property. I work out there at least a half–hour each day. It's my form of relaxation. I'm always eager to show it off, especially to those who enjoy nature the way you do."

Zaran's father got the message.

"I'll stay here," Arthur said. "I can see her working out there whenever I want. You go with Kara. You and she can name all the flowers to each other. I'm staying here with my cookies and fruit tea."

Out in the field, the two discussed the plan.

"Merlin is planning a trip next month to Kobbal," said Kara. "He'll be going to administer some 'special' serum to Zaran's dragons. He wants us to go the day before to Quae Qual, the resort town seventy miles up the coast. This will be a shopping trip for me and a reunion of some of Arthur's old command. We'll spend two nights there, and then Merlin will fly up to meet us — he'll have done his job by then. We've arranged to get a plane through an old friend of Arthur's to take us from Quae Qual to Port Quae — then on to Lemuria."

Having been given the basics, Arak then asked, "What about Zaran?"

"We'll have to play it by ear," Kara answered. "He can't get suspicious or he'll ruin everything. The main thing is that we don't want him to go with Merlin, but I'm afraid that's my son's problem." She hesitated, uncertain. "If it doesn't work out next month, then our only other chance will be the month following, when both Merlin and MaReenie are to go to Cumbar. But that plan has much more risk attached to it. The security at Cumbar is very tight and we would have to make plans more carefully with passage to Port Quae."

"MaReenie hasn't reconciled herself to leaving Zaran, has she?" Arak asked.

"She will, she will," Kara said confidently. "After she sees him this time, I think she'll see the truth that all of us have suspected all these years."

"I hope she's as strong as you think. Zaran might still get something out of her. I told you that his mind has gotten stronger since he was away. Even I found it almost impossible to keep my mind clear of all our plan. I despise myself for what I'm about to say. But he's evil, Kara. My son is riddled with hate."

15
Zaran Confronts his Ruler

rak left the home of his old commander and his wife reluctantly.
Though he envied Arthur and Kara's relationship, a way of life that
he and his own beautiful wife had not had the chance to experience, Arak
felt a peacefulness in his friend's house that he had experienced long ago
when he went with Arthur to Lemuria. Now, in his craft, he hovered
over Alta heading toward the large, sad, dwelling that he shared with his
overpowering son. The months of Zaran's assignment had been a great
relief for Arak; he had dreaded his son's return. In a way, he had always
felt uneasy with Zaran — a son who never called him "Father," but only
"Arak."

"Well at least he'll be gone when I get there," Arak said aloud, thank-
fully. He put the vehicle on autopilot and closed his eyes tightly, as if to
erase some unpleasant vision. "I just hope we can all get away from here,"
he continued, "and I pray that Merlin will be able to keep Zaran off the
scent."

At that point he began to worry. No one knew his son better than he did,
and until now no one else had seen the new, awful Zaran who had
returned to Atlantis. Perhaps all their plans would be dashed by the now
vengeful Zaran.

Arak landed, parked his vehicle, and proceeded toward the lift. Just
before entering the building he looked up and saw the lights that glowed
from the fifth–level apartment. "Oh no! He's still home!" he gasped. "By
the old gods, what's happened? I hope Syus hasn't refused to see him.
He'll be livid."

Arak was panicking. He did not feel as if he could stand to deal with Zaran any longer. "He should have gotten his own place years ago!" he admonished himself loudly as he entered the empty lift. But Arak knew he could not suggest a move to Zaran now. That subject had been broached many times before and Zaran had consistently refused to leave, furthermore, he had insinuated many threats. At the third floor, Arak abruptly stopped the lift.

"I don't have to go up there," he whispered to himself. "I'll just go back to Arthur's and stay the night." But then he realized that the confrontation must come sooner or later. It might as well be now. The lift took him to his floor, and the doors slid open to the foyer of his apartment. His home occupied one entire level of the small building, but still it was not large enough to escape the domineering presence of his son.

Reluctantly, he opened the door and tried to gather some courage.

"Oh, Zaran — you're still here," he said, as if pleasantly surprised. He hoped to keep things light.

"Yes," said Zaran. His tone was casual, almost friendly. "My meeting is postponed until late tonight. Apparently the secretary made a mistake with Syus's time, and he also had some other meetings that continued longer than expected. So the whole day was messed up. How was your visit with Arthur?"

"Very nice. I haven't been there in a while. Have you eaten supper yet?"

"No, actually," said Zaran. "Why don't we go down to that wonderful place across from the Rec Building that you like so much?"

"Well, I had a very late lunch and I'm not really very hungry, but why don't you go along without me?"

Apparent from the look on his son's face, that answer was incorrect. "Oh, I see. Are you by any chance trying to avoid me? Or is this your subtle way of humiliating me? No doubt you're ashamed — a glorified old campaigner like you saddled with the burden of a son who failed on Lemuria."

"Don't be silly. I'm happy to go with you, but I just won't eat. Maybe I'll have a drink, though." The thought of Zaran losing his temper was almost too much for the old man.

"Good!" Zaran's calm returned as suddenly as his other mood had overtaken him. "Anyway, Arak, I want to talk to you about something. Better yet, maybe we can go out later after my appointment. By then you'll be rested — and perhaps hungry." By now, Zaran was almost buoyant.

"All right," a relieved Arak agreed. "That will be better for me, if it's all right with you."

"Certainly. And I want to apologize for my behavior over the last few days. I was just overworked and under considerable stress. I've gotten control of myself now and I want you to know I plan for our lives to be completely different. I've turned over a new leaf, Arak. From now on I'm not going to allow any petty things to get to me."

Suddenly, Zaran seemed entirely sincere. "What's happened?" Arak asked himself. He knew something sinister was brewing in Zaran's brain, but he smiled and went over to his son, agreeing that everything would be fine. Then he excused himself and said if the two of them were going to be out on the town late at night, he had better rest. After all, he wasn't accustomed to such excitement. "By the way, Zaran," he added, "you should call and ask if the place stays open that late. If not, then make reservations somewhere else. I don't want our night on the town to be spoiled."

Now the old man retired to his room. But he did not sleep. He lay on his bed and listened until he heard Zaran leave a few hours later. Then he closed his eyes and slept soundly until Zaran came back.

Zaran left the apartment in a mood of grim determination. He had a plan, but for the moment he would have to check his temper, keep his ego under control, and confront Syus. His ride to the Crystal Pyramid seemed intolerably long. He knew this meeting would be humbling but he wanted to get it over and go on with what he considered his real business.

As usual, Zaran arrived on time and, considering the situation, in rather good spirits. The security guards checked him through the gates and he took the special automatic lift that carried one directly to Syus's suite as well as the council's offices. At its destination, the lift stopped with a slight jolt. Collecting himself, Zaran strode into the highly polished taupe-colored corridor with its black mirrored-looking floor. Since no one was about, he went over to Syus's office and knocked on the door. Almost immediately, a smiling Syus opened the door, and greeted Zaran cordially. He then took his place at the massive desk, while Zaran sat stiffly on the overstuffed couch that faced it. Unlike the formal red-and-dark-wood Council chamber, Syus's office was decorated in a very modern but casual style. The camel colors, mixed with rose and turquoise, gave the room a cheerful air, not at all what one might expect from the ruler of the most powerful nation on the face of the earth. Syus, however, understood his position and had learned to wield his power comfortably. He also found that the room made his visitors feel more at ease — giving him the political edge of a spider with a fly caught fast in its web.

But he showed nothing of the spider as he spoke to Zaran. "How was your trip from Cumbar to Atlantis?"

"Just fine," responded Zaran. "Xax and I flew back together. It was simpler than getting on a transport."

"Good!" answered the ruler abruptly. Then he changed the subject. "Have you seen what Merlin's doing with your other dragons? They tell me he had a very difficult time at first, something about their immensely complicated combination of biological structure and mechanics. But . . . he's on his way now. Studies on other creatures' tissues have proven unbelievably successful." To Zaran's great irritation, Syus seemed to be behaving like a proud father. "You should be delighted. Now your beasts will live forever!"

"Yes . . . Merlin's a good scientist," Zaran agreed. "I always knew he was a true genius!" Although saying this was like twisting a knife in his soul, Zaran reminded himself that he was not at Syus's office to make trouble. Not now.

The leader of all Atlantis casually rose and went to the wall of crystal windows looking out at his dominion. He paused for a moment, then turned to face Zaran.

"Well Zaran," he said, "you're not here for a chat. Shall we get down to business?" Syus's face took on a sterner cast as he walked back to his desk.

"Certainly," Zaran replied, trying to feign humility.

"I want to know exactly what happened!" For his part, Syus made no attempt to conceal a mounting anger. "Your reports from Port Quae and Cumbar don't satisfy me at all. By the Crystal, Zaran, you have failed utterly!"

Zaran's mind was clicking away. He had to keep control, but to be told he was an utter failure threatened his hold over himself. He took a deep breath. Then, very calmly and systematically, he began to recap what was already in his reports — although now he elaborated every minute detail. And, as he relived the events one by one, he made sure to cover himself in every way.

Syus was neither satisfied nor sympathetic. "But how could this be? You lost your dragons against an unseen force and unarmed people. By my weapon, this is incredible! I thought you told me that those beasts of yours were the ultimate in tactical weaponry — that they were invincible!" A tone of threatening sarcasm crept into his voice. "I'm beginning to think you're really not the genius you've made everyone believe you are. Perhaps I've made a mistake and should have named Merlin my successor instead of you. After all, he hasn't had two failures to his credit!"

Even more than the threats, the reference to Mupi came close to throwing Zaran completely out of control. He rose slowly from his chair, his eyes riveted on his ruler. With every last ounce of will, he composed himself, as now he focused only on his plan. Syus had left him no choice.

"I deeply regret that I am such a disappointment to you and our country," he told Syus, "but I beg to differ with you that the mission was a complete failure. We now know that Lemuria has a defensive weapon, but it seems to have little offensive capability, if any. That established, I believe that we could easily bring the Lemurians to their knees by using our remaining beasts, along with the newly–devised missiles." Zaran knew he was no longer in a weak position.

But Syus remained unimpressed. "Zaran, that weapon is still experimental. There is no verification of its real value."

Zaran shook his head. "I have been testing it at the Old Labs for a while — of course in minuscule form in comparison to what would have to be built for its use on the Lemurians. But we're being premature. Perhaps we won't have to use it at all. And at any rate, I should like to hear what the council has to say."

"What do you mean?" replied Syus, in surprise. "You have no meeting with the Council!"

Now Zaran smiled. "I know I don't, but I'm sending — or to put it more correctly — I have sent personal invitations to the top men to come to my home for a dinner party. Of course, I would be especially privileged by your presence as guest of honor . . . But I *will* have the dinner — without you if necessary."

It was Syus's turn to exercise self–control. "I'll think about it."

"Of course, I understand. After all, this is a last–minute development and your schedule is planned months in advance."

"When did you say it was?" asked Syus. His casual tone did not conceal his fury.

"I didn't say, but it's the day after tomorrow at seven o'clock. Formal, with entertainment and that special wine from Port Quae you like so much. As a matter of fact, I took the liberty of bringing back a case for you, along with some Kwee fruit. I planned to have it delivered tomorrow. At any rate, I do hope you come."

Later, when the two men said their farewells and Zaran went home to arrange for his dinner, Syus was left to wonder about the genius scientist, who undertook experiments without authorization. What motives could he possibly have . . . besides ambition?

16
A Dinner Politic—
The Taste of Power

Zaran and Arak's evening out after the former's meeting with Syus was a success, and although Zaran's mood was jubilant, he said nothing about his confrontation with Syus except to warn Arak that he had invited the ruler to a formal dinner at the house. He also asked Arak to help him plan a menu and arrange for some entertainment, explaining to his father that this dinner was in reality a meeting to help him, Zaran, get back into the good graces of the Council.

As a secretive person, Zaran normally never confided in Arak. That night, however, he did reveal his plan to exhibit to the Council and Syus a new campaign to conquer Lemuria. The stout-hearted Arak was horrified, but kept faith with his friends by pretending to be interested in the plan. Although he wanted to glean all possible information from his son, in no way did he attempt to search through Zaran's mind to find any further plans — not after Zaran's experiences in Lemuria. Arak sensed that his son had proven himself much too clever for that trick. Moreover, Zaran was not as open as he appeared, for the party was only the tip of the iceberg in a plot that was deep beneath the sea of his mind.

Arak naturally agreed to help with the dinner. He also told his son he understood perfectly why he would not be invited. After all, the old soldier knew well that State business had its levels of priority and this was Priority One. Besides which, he was completely happy to be left out of the situation; instead he would go over to Arthur and Kara's.

For the next day and a half, Zaran and Arak were immensely busy. Much had to be done in preparation for so important an event as the party; it had been years since the house had seen such bustle. The two men had the place cleaned to a sparkle; then some of Zaran's mother's beautiful linens were laid out, along with silver plates, crystal goblets, serving pieces, and all the cutlery appropriate to such an occasion. Servants were in and out, cleaning, fixing, arranging. Everything had to be perfect. In the middle of all the confusion, boxes and packages from Cumbar arrived with food, wines, and other delicacies for which Zaran had sent.

And all the while, Arak made many attempts to contact Arthur or Merlin, but either they were not at home, or Zaran or someone else was in the way. Finally, on the evening of the dinner, Arak reached Arthur and all but invited himself to his friend's house that night. To his disappointment he learned that Arthur and Kara, too, were on their way to a dinner. Nevertheless, Arthur told Arak he would be welcome to come afterwards — and the couple would be home early.

Then Arthur interrupted himself, remembering that he and Kara were going to Zirth's. It was MaReenie's birthday and Zirth was having a few people over. "So why don't you come with us, Arak? MaReenie will be surprised and thrilled to see you."

Arak agreed readily, adding, "In fact, I have just the gift for MaReenie."

By the time Arak had left, everything was ready for the party. The chef was completely in charge of the food and wines. All of the servers knew what to do and how their taskmaster expected it done. Zaran had only to wait for the entrance of his first guests. Nothing had been left to chance. Zaran had even written a speech and honed up on the rules of protocol. And when the first of the ministers arrived, the host was in perfect form. Now he had only to wait for Syus; and although the ruler had not notified him of his coming, Zaran had no doubt that this was one dinner Syus would not miss. As each guest entered, Zaran greeted him with equal aplomb. After all had gathered and were sampling wines from Port Quae and northern Atlantian provinces, the minister of internal affairs inquired about Syus's absence.

"I'm sure he'll be here," replied Zaran, easily. "No doubt he's had a long audience with some delegate from one of the provinces, but he'll come. We'll wait a little longer. It's bad form to start without him."

"Well, he'd better hurry! I'm famished!" complained the portly defense minister.

"You could do with a day or two of abstinence," said another of the guests, winking. They all laughed, including the minister.

Presently the talk started to stray from food and wine to the provinces, then gradually across the ocean, and finally to Port Quae. Zaran had been hoping to hold the conversation at bay and wait for Syus, but someone finally asked point–blank about Lemuria. There was no choice but to reply.

At that very moment the doorbell rang. Zaran rushed toward it like a camel in the desert races to a waterhole. When the door opened, it was the ruler. All rose. Zaran instantly became almost fawning in his obsequiousness. This could be seen to irritate Syus, who simply ignored Zaran as he moved about the room and greeted the other guests. He also joined in the wine tasting. Now slightly apart from the others, Zaran watched the festivities. If anyone at that moment had noticed him and the look on his face, he would have suspected what was to follow. But there were no suspicions as the host walked into the middle of the group and announced dinner was being served.

Every detail of the dinner was as flawless as Zaran could have hoped. The nine guests ate to their heart's content. Even Syus, a normally finicky eater, could not have been more pleased, not only with the food and wine but with the table itself and its appointments. After nine courses — including all manner of meat, fish, vegetables, and fruits — Zaran ordered the servers to present the pièce de résistance, a sugar fantasy of chocolate, cream, nuts, and strawberries, layered between thin sheets of feather–light sponge cake soaked in chocolate liqueur. And to accompany this flight of culinary madness was a rare sparkling wine from Port Quae, served in antique gold goblets. Zaran had purchased these some years previous on one of his many state trips. There were ten goblets in the rare set, along with matching dessert plates, and Zaran touched off an explosion of applause by announcing that each guest would be allowed to take his goblet home as a memento of the evening.

Zaran's generosity was almost too much for his guests. They could not believe that he would want to break up the set. He replied that he was in fact breaking nothing; were all present not friends and colleagues working for the good of Atlantis? So, in fact, he was only passing the goblets to family members who would always remain tied together. As he continued he found himself almost believing what he said. Then he concluded by telling the guests that after the meal, all would be taken down to the Old Laboratories and shown his plan for the conquest not only of Lemuria but possibly the entire galaxy. This was greeted with more applause; all the food and wine had made the ministers' brains a little fuzzy and they were ready to accept anything Zaran said as truth. Even Syus, normally clear–headed and immune to grandiose talk, had allowed the wine — and Zaran's words — to bend his thoughts.

At last Zaran told the guests that it was time to leave for the laboratories.

By this time Syus had become noticeably quiet. He was now carefully observing what he recognized as transparent political maneuvering on Zaran's part. Thus, while the rest of the party was preparing to leave on a shuttle arranged by Zaran to carry everyone over the laboratory, the ancient ruler remained seated. He informed Zaran that he had his own pilot and transportation; he would meet everyone at the laboratory. Zaran bowed his head in acquiescence.

Syus then stood up. "I want to see you the first thing in the morning!" he commanded. "I have some news that will greatly interest you."

Zaran turned to his guests as they boarded the shuttle. In minutes they were at the Old Laboratories. Here, Zaran surprised them. Instead of showing them his plan, he chose to continue the tale of Lemuria. This did not please his audience. They became restless, and ever more eager to see something or hear Zaran's plan. But Zaran paid them little attention and continued at his own pace, glancing frequently at Syus, who was seated at his far right. Then, suddenly, Syus collapsed.

Instantly Zaran raced to the fallen ruler's side, followed closely by the others. From all appearance Syus was having a heart attack or a stroke, — but he was also convulsing. A doctor was summoned immediately, and within minutes Syus was in an intensive care area with the best of Atlantis medical science trying to save his life. Every necessary instrument and method was brought to bear; even some experimental procedures and drugs were administered. But in the end Syus was dead.

Atlantis now plunged into mourning. The creator of a new age was dead. An elaborate funeral was held for the once master of the greatest nation on the face of the earth. And riding the immense waves of sorrow and shock was none else but the greatest prince of the grief–stricken nation, Zaran. His role as chief mourner at the funeral was undoubtedly his most impressive performance. Even he believed the act.

All prominent Atlantians attended the service. Naturally, Merlin, Arthur, Kara, MaReenie, Zirth, and Arak were among the most conspicuous, although their thoughts were more for whom Syus might have named as his successor than for his death. During the eulogies, the five sat, each concentrating on the turn of events; but away from their plan.

After the burial of Syus's ashes following his public cremation, an exclusive reception was held at the Crystal Pyramid. The elite were issued special invitations to attend this gathering, at which time there would be a private reading of the dead ruler's will. Then, according to procedure, a public reading would be broadcast throughout the country via the crystals. Among those given invitations — actually more in the nature of commands — were Merlin and his parents, MaReenie and her father, and Arak.

At the reading, all sat in their appointed seats. The will was very long. Syus was a generous man and he had many gifts for those who had served him well over his extremely long tenure in office. He also rewarded those who he called "my only real friends:" Arthur among them. To these compatriots, Syus granted complete immunity from governmental surveillance and freedom of travel. When the reader had finished with this extraordinary bequest, the five conspirators looked at each other. Escape for at least two of them was now assured. There were murmurs in the crowd and also expressions of surprise at such a gift.

But the reading continued. The tension mounted as everyone waited for the announcement of Syus's successor; however, the bequests went on endlessly. Then the reader began the sentence that everyone recognized as the start of the really important part of the document. In his own style, Syus had made them wait. He recounted the person's qualities, then qualifications and honors, and finally came the name. It threw the five would-be escapists into despair — Zaran was to follow Syus as ruler of all he surveyed. His name also struck a chord of surprised fear in many other Atlantians who were familiar with the successor's real character. Only Zaran was not surprised. He knew the contents of the will. In that room, though, sat two people who were also aware that had Zaran had his morning meeting with Syus, another name would have been read in Zaran's place. But they remained silent. That sort of knowledge was dangerous, and these two wished to remain alive. But for the five co-conspirators, Zaran's rise to the highest power changed everything.

17
Long Life and Happiness for the New Ruler

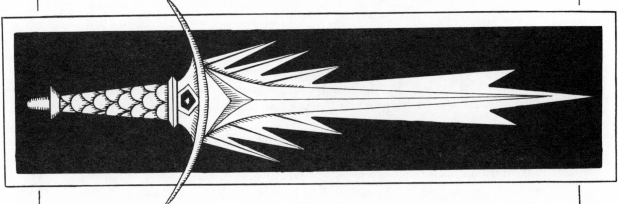

After both the private and public wills had been read, Zaran immediately took charge. Syus's belongings were moved out of the suite atop the pyramid and Zaran's appeared in their place. The new ruler requested that his father take over some rooms in the crystal building, but the old man pleaded that he be allowed to remain in his old home at least for now.

"After all, Zaran," he said, "you will have so many responsibilities — I don't want to be in the way. Besides, you might like to come and visit here for a change of pace when you get busy up at your new place. At any rate, it will take me time to get accustomed to the idea of moving. You know, my son, old people get very set in their ways and, Zaran, your father is old. Very old."

Zaran had been in better spirits over the last few days than Arak had seen him in many years, so the new ruler did not press his father to leave the old building. But he did insist on his coming to visit the pyramid at least once a week. To that Arak wholeheartedly agreed. Then Zaran suddenly hit upon the idea of a companion for Arak, someone to look after him. The old man grumpily answered that he did not want strangers living with him. After some discussion, Zaran grudgingly agreed to allow Arak to live alone. After all, he would have other ways of checking on the old man's well–being. Arak did not have to be told what "well–being" meant.

A day or two had passed when Zaran sent him a message that the two of them were to have a late supper at his new offices. Arak accepted the invitation — what other choice was there, really? Zaran sent an escort to bring him to the pyramid; that way he would not have to bother himself with transportation. Zaran was certainly and suddenly becoming considerate after his promotion — Arak wondered why. However, when he arrived at his son's quarters, Zaran's newly born thoughtfulness became all too clear to the old soldier.

As he entered the suite, he was greeted not only by his son but an entire staff. Zaran asked him if he would excuse him briefly; he had a few last-minute things to attend to before they could eat. Arak made himself comfortable on the sofa in an out-of-the-way corner of the room. From there, he observed his son. On the one hand, Zaran was completely in charge and seemed to be in his glory, but Arak also sensed stress and loneliness.

"So, he needs a friend," thought Arak, "and he has none. Not even Merlin and MaReenie. Well, well what could he want to say to me that he can't say to them?" But the more he observed Zaran the more a sense of danger permeated his mind; "Whatever it is, I know it will be immensely evil." Arak didn't want such knowledge — it could mean his death or death to the others. "Oh, my darling wife, if you can see me now, protect me from our son!" he prayed.

When he opened his eyes, everyone was gone and only Zaran was standing over him.

"Are you all right, Arak?" he inquired.

"Yes, yes. My old eyes were just tired."

"You must be famished."

"I *could* eat something," Arak answered politely, and then asked, "Do you keep this pace all day long?"

"Well yes, at least for now. You realize I'm trying to do a great deal in a short time and so it does seem to take more hours than the day has to offer to do the job. But honestly, I'm not tired. I seem to be thriving on all the pressure. This is just what I've always wanted. Let me tell you about some of my wonderful plans . . . Oh, but first let's get some food."

He pressed a button and a servant entered with some appetizers. He took Zaran's dinner orders and was gone. Zaran then offered Arak some wine and the two sat munching on vegetables and spreads, sipping wine while they waited for the meal. Zaran began to tell Arak of his development plans: in medical care, particularly in the mental health area; educational reforms, greater expenditures on research. To Arak these all sounded wonderful. Zaran sincerely wanted to provide up-to-date technology to the Atlantian outposts to improve life. As he talked, Zaran drank more than he ate. When at last the meal was served, he ordered more wine, which was quickly brought. Now Zaran's mood seemed to mellow.

"Have you seen MaReenie?" he asked.

"Yes, she always asks about you. I think she was disappointed that you didn't come to her birthday celebration, but she understood how important your dinner party was."

Zaran was startled. "What do you mean, she understood about my dinner party?"

Arak was puzzled by Zaran's reaction. "Well, you know you had to impress Syus and the Council with your abilities and your plan."

"Oh, yes. I had almost forgotten that." Zaran smiled warily.

"Forgotten? Zaran, how could you forget the night of Syus' death?"

"I meant the reason for the party. Actually I remember the dinner very well. It was a culinary triumph and a political masterpiece." Zaran laughed, unpleasantly, as if he possessed some hidden knowledge.

"What do you mean?"

Zaran poured some more wine for Arak and himself. "Brace yourself, my father! You know that is the first time I've called you 'father'?" He did not wait for an answer — his indifference to what Arak thought about that statement was obvious.

"Your son is now the most powerful person in the land, all because of that dinner you helped me plan." No less obviously, Zaran was becoming drunk and cocky. "And this room is the only place in all of Atlantis that I could now say out loud what I'm about to tell you . . . And oddly enough, you're the only person in all of Atlantis to whom I could tell it."

Zaran swaggered to the middle of the room. "I am ruler of all the world, thanks to the stroke of a brush on the plate from which Syus ate." At first, Arak was uncertain just what his son was telling him. But Zaran unleashed the full impact of his statement. "I discovered a wonderful substance which, when taken internally, waits patiently for hours, then strikes its victims by mocking heart attack, stroke, or a strain of epilepsy for which there is no cure." By now Zaran was laughing loudly and slurring his words. "And furthermore," he continued, "the greater the effort made to cure the patient by drugs, the more violently it works until its victim is dead. And the substance is impossible to trace. Isn't that marvelous?" The laughter suddenly stopped. Then Zaran was silent for a time.

Arak stared in horror at the evil standing before him. He could not believe what he was hearing. The blood ran from his face. He truly feared his own son, his diabolical flesh and blood. He shrank away from him. Destruction was closing in. Yes, Zaran's terrible truth was indeed too awful to bear alone.

Now Zaran's mood saddened as he drank more wine. "I really didn't want to kill Syus. You must believe me. But he left me no choice." He was slurring the words more now and sobbing. "He was going to name Merlin heir to take my place. I just could *not* let him do that. You understand, don't you, Arak? Not after all my work and loyalty. And just because of that Lemurian incident and that idiotic creature. I planned to do too much good to have him deprive me of my place."

Arak could not stand to look at his son. But when he forced himself to look, it was with disgust, hatred, pity, and — most of all — fear. Fear of the stranger who sat before him. The drunken Zaran had fork in hand and was pushing his food around. Then he looked up at his father.

"I promise to make up for Syus's death, Father. He was old anyway. I will make Atlantis good for all its people, not just those of us here on the mainland, but everywhere. You'll see — the world will live in unity and technology when I'm finished." Apparently Zaran needed his father's approval. Arak tried to pull himself together. He did not even want to look at Zaran, much less talk to him, but he felt he must.

"But my son, if you plan all this good, why have you started by enforcing so much military security? Why have you taken away the people's freedom of movement?" Arak knew full well that tomorrow the drunken murderer now before him would probably not remember any of this night's conversation.

"These are only temporary measures until I can establish order," Zaran answered quickly.

Shaking his head, Arak then replied, "I didn't realize there was any chaos when you took power."

"Oh yes. And there were many dissidents who wouldn't cooperate, but that's all being taken care of." Then Zaran asked, "You do understand, don't you, why I had to do what I did?"

Arak answered with absolute certainty. "I understand completely, my son. Don't worry. I do understand." By now, Arak was weak with exhaustion and asked Zaran if he could leave. He could not stand to be in the same room with this drunken evil that sat before him.

"Yes, of course. You're not accustomed to the wee hours of the morning. Enjoy the dawn on your way home. It's almost time for daybreak."

As Arak left and was taken home, the dawn of a new day was indeed breaking through the darkness of the warm night. But Arak missed the pink view, for his thoughts were fixed on how to get a message to Arthur or Merlin without suspicion. And his thoughts depressed him.

"By the old gods, what have I spawned into this world? He will destroy us utterly!"

18
Merlin Readies Himself for His Destiny

Almost within moments of being named Syus's heir, Zaran began to exert his power onto what he would refer to as "The Mother of the World." He began by tightening all security at the borders. Two days later, all official leaves were cancelled; schedules were rearranged, and the people soon realized that this was no transitional government carrying on where Syus had left off, but a new power being exerted on them. With the new government, there also came a new wave of fanaticism from a small group of extremists. If during Syus's tenure the Atlantians were living under what in later centuries would be known as "Big Brother," this latest oppression would have to be called "Wicked Stepfather"; even the most loyal of its citizens felt the pressure. Alta became an armed camp. The military received top priority, and every high-ranking retiree was called back into service. Even Arthur and Arak were drafted back to their old regiment — and gone were all of Arthur's immunities. Zaran reneged on everything.

As for Merlin, the security around him tightened like a hangman's noose, encircling and pressuring him into action. The final squeeze at last came in the form of a "requested audience" from Zaran. Merlin kept hoping against hope that somehow all the atrocities foisted on Atlantis at Zaran's hand would simply disappear, or at least that they would not touch *his* life, but he knew that was impossible. Eventually he would have to deal with Zaran. Perhaps this was what Raena had foreseen as his peculiar destiny, he thought. But at the moment he was frantically preparing the files for Zaran's inspection; no time to wonder about his destiny now. If Zaran discovered his intrigue, he would have no destiny about which to worry.

Because none of his assistants had the slightest knowledge of his deception, Merlin had to prepare the major presentations himself. All verifications were justified with experimental data. Merlin had now been working on these records for some time, but he had not expected to put the files to such immediate use — many of them still had to be organized for Zaran's keen perusal.

When the day of his audience with the new master of Atlantis finally arrived, Merlin realized that he had been so preoccupied with his tasks that he had forgotten to purchase a new uniform of Zaran's design, which was now mandatory for all appearances before the ruler. Even if that person had no military standing, he would still have to appear in this special uniform. "Remember, we are all soldiers of our 'Mother,' Atlantis," Zaran would say in his speeches. Kara and Arthur, however, had not forgotten, and early that morning they appeared at Merlin's door with the new outfit. "After all, there's no use in antagonizing the 'ruler,' especially over something so trivial," said Kara.

Once in uniform, Merlin looked at himself in the mirror. A worn, overworked, tired, pale stranger looked back at him.

Merlin shrugged and turned to Mupi. "Well, Mup. I don't think this outfit does anything to help my appearance."

Mupi whined in agreement. Unlike the formal red–and–silver dress suit of Syus's office, this drab, greenish brown jumpsuit was very dull indeed.

After stopping by to say goodbye to his parents, he was off to see Zaran. There were more hovercraft in the air these days, but nearly all bore military insignia.

"Where is he getting all these people from?" Merlin asked himself, noticing the extra–large throngs below in Alta. Since Zaran's climb to power,

Merlin had tried to erase everything from his mind — Zaran's tyranny, the dragons, and even Lemuria. But he now at last realized that his world would never again be the same. He could never, as he once did, work in his laboratory with the complete absorption of a scientist free from politics, intrigue, and plots. Merlin was now living in reality, but oh how he longed for the innocence that he would never recapture.

His craft arrived at the Crystal Palace all too soon. He was there at the parking bay with more than sufficient time to undergo all the new, more elaborate security checks that would grant him access to his destination at the building's pinnacle. At last, in the lift, he found himself alone again. Suddenly, he broke out in a cold sweat, and trembled with fear. Until now, he had been so preoccupied with all the preparations for this meeting that he had overlooked a most important fact — his childhood rival, Zaran, held the ultimate power of life and death over him. And now, a prince of Atlantis, with falsified documents in hand, was on his way up to see this ruler. Furthermore, it was no ordinary dictator he was seeing, but a fellow scientist and creator of the very creature on which Merlin was presently experimenting.

"By the power, what have I done!" he said to himself. "Zaran will know immediately that I have been playing games with those creatures!" He had to pull himself together and carefully play his hand. There were lives at stake — the lives of people he loved and those with whom he worked. Zaran would never believe their innocence in the matter. The lift stopped with a jolt. Merlin straightened himself out, took a deep breath, held his head high and stepped out to meet his destiny.

At the desk in the hall outside Zaran's office was yet another security check. The guard told Merlin to wait, and he sat in one of the chairs provided. Looking about him, he saw that the decor of the taupe–colored hallway, corridors, and reception area had not changed, but that the atmosphere certainly had. More personnel milled around, bustling in and out of the Council chambers and the ministers' offices, which were also located on this floor. Everyone, male and female alike, wore that dull brown uniform designed by Zaran. Merlin continued to wait and watch. An hour passed, then two. Finally Merlin approached the guard to ask about his appointment.

"You will have to wait. There is a major council meeting this morning and that takes priority."

Merlin returned to his chair. His alternating fear and resolve to be strong were blending into impatience. However, after four hours, he simply fell asleep — only to jump to attention as he heard his name called. Then, hastily rubbing the sleep from his eyes, arranging his clothes and hair, he picked up his file and went in to see his ruler.

Zaran was seated at a great dark, wooden desk in front of a row of the sheer–draped windows. The afternoon sun was streaming in and onto desk, and from Merlin's vantage point, Zaran looked like a brown, jump-suited god bathed in a halo of light. The ruler stood up and went to greet Merlin in a friendly manner.

"Well, Merlin, it was good of you to come," Zaran said as he held out his hand.

Merlin knew his protocol. He stood at attention and bowed his head. "Greetings from one in your service," was his answer.

"Oh come on now," Zaran said. "We grew up together. We're friends. There's no ceremony between us."

"Hello Zaran," Merlin smiled in relief. "Mother and Father send their love — and MaReenie sends hers, too. We all wish you long life and a happy rule."

Zaran beamed. "Please thank everyone for their good wishes. I'm plan-ning a dinner so we can all get together again. There's nothing like old friends and family to bring pleasure into one's life. . . . But now, Merlin, let me see what's been happening with my dragons under your care."

Merlin handed him the two thick files, explaining that much more data was being compiled daily. Zaran opened the cover, strolled over to his desk, and began to read the material. Offhandedly, he offered Merlin lunch, to which Merlin agreed. Then almost as if entering another dimen-sion, Zaran became completely absorbed in what he was reading. Merlin took a seat on the couch located along the right wall of the office and waited. This seemed to be a day of waiting. But this time Merlin, filled with apprehension, did not fall asleep. It was late at night when Zaran completed the two files.

"You've done a good job," he told Merlin. "But now I want to take a more personal role in the dragon project. So from this moment on, you'll report to me directly. Also be prepared for me to visit the laboratories occasion-ally. I mean to keep in touch with my creations. I want them to know that I'm still their master." His voice became a bolt of steel. "Do you under-stand?"

"Yes, of course," answered Merlin, feeling slightly relieved that his report had passed Zaran's scrutiny. "I was only acting as Syus directed. Actually, if you have someone else in mind to relieve me, I'd be happy to relinquish the project altogether."

"You may not." Zaran flashed his eyes. "For now, I want you to continue your work. Anyway, what could be more important or fascinating to you than this project?"

"Nothing, absolutely nothing," Merlin replied quickly. "I only want to do whatever you think will be best. As a scientist you know that we all work for the good of the State at whatever task we are assigned. I just wanted you to know that I'm willing to do your exact bidding."

"Good. Then you'll stay on the project. Very well, that's all, Merlin. There are people still waiting to see me."

Merlin looked at him in disbelief. "There are people still waiting?"

"Yes," Zaran answered matter–of–factly, as if that were the norm. "After all, I have a whole country to get into shape."

"Yes, of course! I didn't realize," Merlin stammered. "Take care of yourself, Zaran."

Despite what Zaran had just told him, Merlin was still surprised, on reentering the reception area, to find the room filled with tired people, all anxiously looking at him. He left the building by the route he took on arriving, being halted once more at all the same security checkpoints. As he finally headed his craft homeward, he almost pitied Zaran.

"Could he really want power so much that he would endure such a life?" he asked himself. "What kind of existance could that be, anyway? If he makes us prisoners in this country, he's only imprisoning himself, too, and in a smaller cell — the Crystal Pyramid."

19
A Queen for Atlantis

Working feverishly on her "dream paintings," as she called the new series of works based on Lemuria, MaReenie had been up long before the glow of dawn touched the dark sky. Alone in the house, she sat at her boards, oblivious to the commotion outside. Today was market day, and Zirth, along with the servants, was away visiting with the local farmers and crafts people. Many of the city dwellers flocked to the countryside vendors as a form of entertainment. Though the government had attempted to curtail such activities — labeling the system inefficient and reporting that the quality of the goods was inferior to those products produced and purchased in the State control stores — the Atlantians gathered around the markets anyway. Normally MaReenie too would have been out that morning, enjoying the fresh air and the multitudes of people, smells, and colorful products, but she was so engrossed in her work of late that she felt no need for such an outing. So, when a voice at the inter-communication system called our her name, the sound startled her. She answered in a slightly annoyed tone, hoping that whoever was at the door would go away. But the voice that came back was clearly familiar.

"On my stars! Zaran, it's you!" was her answer.

"Come on and let me in!" It sounded more like a plea. "You can't be that angry with me! I've come to beg forgiveness for neglecting you."

"Just a moment," said MaReenie, hastily shoving the new paintings into a closet and bringing out her more conventional work, just in case Zaran asked to see her studio. Then she rushed to the door. As she passed a mirror, it reflected an image of a disheveled woman. MaReenie stopped short in exasperation, attempting to fix her trailing curls and straighten her paint–blotted tunic. Even as she reached the door, she was still trying to get her face in shape in order to greet the master of Atlantis. Then with her hand on the doorknob, she pressed out a long breath, then breathed in deeply, all the while thinking of how awful she must look.

In the doorway, dressed in the formal red and silver uniform of the ruler with all the trappings including his Excalibur, stood the smiling Zaran, surrounded by an entourage of guards and onlookers.

"Hello! Hello!" he cried. "You look as *beautiful* as ever!"

"Oh, Zaran, you look wonderful in your uniform! But — you caught me working. Come on in . . ." she spoke casually, but then remembered to whom she was speaking. Now she greeted her ruler formally. "The great ruler of our Mother country is always welcome in our home."

She bowed her head and with a sweeping hand movement stood to the side to allow him to enter.

Zaran shook his head and smiled. "Don't do that! We're friends." Then he turned to his escorts and told them to wait outside.

As he walked in, Zaran closed the door and asked, "Now is that the way to greet your most ardent admirer?"

MaReenie looked up, smiled and said, "No, of course not," as she gave him a big hug.

The two then talked in the large foyer, basking in the reflection of the colorful skylight now set aglow by the rising sun. Zaran looked around, but MaReenie quickly led him toward the back of the horned house. Here, in a solarium–type room with windows on three sides and a profusion of blooming plants shedding a rich perfume in the air, MaReenie entertained her guest.

"Can I get you something to drink or eat?" she offered.

"No, thank you," Zaran answered. "I came to see *you*, not for anything else." He sat down and patted the ornately carved settee. "Come sit by me."

MaReenie complied, saying, "Oh Zaran, it's been such a long time since we've seen each other or talked. How have you been?"

"I'm fine and I have a lot to tell you." He began to relate much of what had happened to him since Syus's death, then continued for almost an hour and a half. Actually, she learned little more than what she had already heard in the public news. Zaran told her about his work, but he never mentioned Lemuria, and, of course, said nothing about his role as Syus's poisoner. He did, however, describe the dinner party, and explained how it was such a political success for him. As he talked about his ascent to power, his eyes danced with excitement. Then, for no apparent reason, he abruptly changed the subject. "What are you working on these days? Is your painting going well?"

"I couldn't be happier with my work," she said, as she stood up and walked over to one of the plants and smelled the blossoms. "I've so many commissions now that I'll be busy for the next five years."

Zaran followed her, coming, finally, to the point. "But how about the rest of your life? Are you content just to live here with your father?" His hands rested briefly on her shoulders, then stroked her hair.

MaReenie hesitated, then said, "Well, for right now I suppose I am." Now she turned and asked, "What is this all about, Zaran?" She walked to the far wall, pausing to pick some dead leaves from a topiary. Realizing that his approach was not accomplishing the results he wanted, Zaran altered his tactic.

"Oh, I almost forgot!" he said as he turned toward the door. "I have something for you. A belated birthday present. I hope you like it. Wait just a moment." He ran out of the room to the guard at the front door and gave an order. Then, in barely two minutes, he returned with the guard behind him, carrying several large boxes and two smaller ones. After setting the packages down on the table in the garden room, the guard was immediately dismissed.

"Are these all for me?" asked MaReenie, in almost childlike delight.

"Yes. I'm sorry they're late, but I didn't forget your birthday. I was just very busy. Forgive me?" Zaran handed her the largest box.

"Oh yes, of course." MaReenie was alreadying opening the large one at Zaran's direction. The first box contained a traditional folk dress of the people who lived in the mountain regions outside of Port Quae. Every part of the costume, from hat to shoes — and an elaborate coat — was there.

"They're wonderful!" she cried, taking special note of the workmanship and design as each box was opened. Finally, she flung her arms around Zaran and hugged and kissed him. "Oh Zaran, everything is just beautiful!"

"Not as beautiful as the person who'll wear it," Zaran replied.

"Oh, you're a darling! You always know just what to say."

"Well, actually, right now, I'm having a lot of trouble saying what I want to . . ." Zaran looked at the floor, feigning shyness. "Could we go over here and sit down?" He pointed to a bench in the corner of the room. She obliged. As he looked deep into her eyes, he took her hand in his.

"MaReenie, darling," he started "You must know how I feel about you, and how I've felt about you since we were children. I know I've been very neglectful lately, but with my work and all the pressure of what has happened recently, well . . . I've been so preoccupied. But now, my MaReenie, well now that I have things under control . . ." She felt his grip tighten on her hand, and became aware that he was looking straight into her eyes. "I have come to ask you to be my wife and share my life as ruler of Atlantis."

MaReenie lowered her gaze. She had waited a long time for this moment, but now with Zaran holding tight to her and offering his life and a country all in one proposal, she felt a chill running through her body. Something about it did not ring true for her.

"Oh Zaran," she said as she hesitated for a second, "I'm honored."

Squeezing her hand slightly, he said, as if relieved, "Then it's settled. I'll talk to your father today. He can't possibly have any objections. After all, I'm the ruler and what more could any father want for his daughter?"

"Zaran . . ." she attempted to interrupt, but he was already walking out as if he had settled some minor problem and was off to more important matters.

"Zaran," she called insistently. "I did *not* say yes."

He stopped short, then slowly turned and deliberately walked back towards her.

"I have to think about it," she said solemnly as she looked at his face and eyes. "This is a major decision in my life and I have to consider not only my feelings for you, but also . . . well, my father."

"Your father?" Zaran closed his eyes ever so slightly. Then he said, "Your father will be well cared for. He can move in with us at the Pyramid if you wish."

"That's extremely generous of you," she gratefully acknowledged. "Most bridegrooms wouldn't want their father–in–law moving in with them."

"Well, actually he'd be good company for you. At present, my schedule is very full and at times you might get lonely. So he could fill in the gaps until you have our children. You do want children?" Zaran inquired of her.

"Of course, I want children," answered MaReenie, "But, . . ."

"So you are agreed." Zaran smiled confidently.

"I still want time to think it over," MaReenie insisted.

Zaran clenched his teeth. "How much time do you want?" His voice had become less gentle.

"I don't know. Until I have the answer. Zaran, what's the rush? You've waited this long to ask me. Certainly I can take a few days to give you the answer."

He walked close to her, then embraced her and kissed her firmly, strongly and passionately. At first she melted into his arms, but his burst of true affection was short lived. It was as if Zaran's passion was being measured out in just the right amounts, the way one might apply just the right amount of pressure to open a tightly closed jar. MaReenie began to feel suffocated and struggled to loosen his grip. That was a mistake. It offended Zaran. The more she struggled to get loose, the tighter he held her until he began hurting her.

Finally, with one last desperate attempt, she broke away and ran to the other side of the room near the door. She was confused — and fearful. Never before had she been afraid of Zaran. In the past, she had handled him easily, but now the beauty watched the prince become a beast. He stood there, breathing heavily — almost snorting. His left eye began to twitch, at first just slightly, but the longer he looked at her the stronger the twitch became. He glared at his would–be–queen, frustrated at his loss of control, trying desperately to regain his composure.

"Zaran, what's happened to you." MaReenie's voice was slightly higher pitched.

"You pulled away," Zaran stared and said as if it were impossible for her to reject him.

"I told you I need some time to think it over," she said. "I don't like to feel pressured."

"MaReenie, you must understand something now. There can only be one answer. You are mine; you have always been mine; and no one else is going to have you!" He drew himself out to his full height and now spoke in the tone of a master commanding his slave. "Is that clear?"

"What kind of statement is that?" she demanded.

"I mean that you will say yes. And not only say yes, but come to me willingly and wholeheartedly." He smiled in deadly seriousness. "I am now ruler of this country; furthermore, I need an intelligent helpmate, one with beauty and charisma. One that I can use to unite the people. You have all those qualities. You are also sensible and, therefore, you will be happy to oblige me completely. Believe me, all those people whom you love so dearly will be kept under my generous protection. I am certain you understand exactly what I mean." He was smiling now and bowing his head towards her as if in supplication. Then he added, "Don't take too long to say yes. I'm not a patient man. And remember that when you come, you must do so freely and passionately." His look was intense, deadly. He turned and walked out the door, leaving MaReenie shaking in the corner of the room. She covered her face, slowly dropped to the floor, and began sobbing uncontrollably.

20
The Engagement

When the urgent message from Arak was received by Arthur and Zirth, they feared that escape might be futile. Arak's message included the statement, "I have a gift for each of you from my son," their code indicating that something terrible had transpired concerning Zaran, and he requested that the three meet at the wine vendor's stall on the next market day.

Anxiously, the two appeared at the appointed time, and by the look on Arak's face as he approached the stall, his friends knew instantly that he did indeed bear grim news. Rather than incurring any bystanders suspicions, Arthur took up a ploy to relieve tensions. He turned to his companion and said in a loud voice, "Well, Zirth, I can see by the look on Arak's face that he's reluctant to give us the gifts. They must be expensive — so he's trying to keep them for himself."

Arak took the cue. "Well, it's just that I doubt if either of you has a palate sophisticated enough to appreciate this wine, and I don't want to waste such a great gift on you." He held up his prizes in the air.

"Now we know where we stand, Arthur," said Zirth. "After all the years of wine tasting we've endured with this amateur and after all the experience we've given him, he now decides he's an expert."

Then laughing, the two embraced their gift bearer, and the three turned to greet the wine merchant who was just opening his stall. The merchant gave each a sample of a new vintage from the north, which the three colleagues deemed "lethal." After more talk and wine tasting they finally made their purchases, then set off to browse through the crowded market. Arthur, with a shopping list from Kara, enlisted the aid of the other two to help fill the order. When they were finished, they carried the bundles to their crafts. Then they walked cautiously into the adjoining cornfield — where Arak at last gave them his news. Arthur could see that the old man could no longer contain himself.

When Arak had finished, Arthur said, "These are grim tidings that you bear. He's much more dangerous than we had suspected."

"He's kept his secrets well," added Zirth. "What are we to do now?"

"Now," Arak answered, "we must plan more carefully than ever."

"We'll certainly be next if we don't cooperate with him," Arthur concluded. Then, looking around, he said quietly, "Let's get back; there are some men watching us."

As they approached their crafts, Arthur began to converse jovially with his companions. He said, "Why don't you two come over to my house and we can have a picnic out in the field in back of the house. Kara is sort of expecting you. I know she's going over to pick up MaReenie." He noted the time. "It's later than I thought — she's probably left already. We could cook out. The fish is fresh and we can flame it over an open fire. What do you say? It also gives us the perfect excuse to try our new wines."

"You say Kara's picking up MaReenie?" Zirth queried. "Well, I hope she has better luck getting her out of the house than I've had."

"Well Zirth," Arthur replied, "all I can say to that is that my wife seems to have a way with her. Don't you agree?"

Both Zirth and Arak nodded. Arthur said, "Good! Then it's all settled. Besides, all this fresh air is making me hungry. We'll meet at the house." He went over to his hovercraft.

"I'll race you two home," Zirth called out. Zirth was always ready for sport; he had never grown up when it came to speeding. But today Arak was so impatient to get away from the crowds at the market that he ended up winning the race. This took Arthur and Zirth by complete surprise, since they always considered their friend rather stodgy.

Arthur had been correct about Kara having gone to MaReenie's. But when Kara arrived, she was amazed to find a crowd of onlookers just dispersing as Zaran's official craft took off. Seeing the front door open, she didn't bother to announce herself on the intercommunication device. However, when she stepped over the threshold, she was seized by a frightening premonition. Fearfully, Kara called out, "MaReenie, darling! Are you there?"

The sounds of sobbing were clear, though the voice that answered was muffled by tears.

"Mama K! I'm over here!" MaReenie sounded frantic as Kara ran through the doorway — to find that MaReenie, fortunately, was not injured.

"What happened?" Kara cried out. "MaReenie, did someone attack you?"

At first MaReenie could hardly speak coherently but after a few moments in Kara's arms, she became calmer. Then she began to blurt out everything, but Kara quieted her, deciding it would wiser if she did not speak aloud. So instead, MaReenie mentally communicated everything to her "Mama K." Although horrified by MaReenie's story, Kara continued to comfort her fearful charge. At last MaReenie was ready to listen as Kara spoke to her in soothing tones.

"Darling," she said, "he just wants you for his wife. Zaran has gotten accustomed to power — he doesn't want to be told no. My dear, I know Zaran does love you; it's just that he doesn't know just to convince you of his love. This was his clumsy way of doing it."

Kara then placed her left hand over her own forehead, closed her eyes and began rubbing her brow and side of her face. She knew it would be hard to handle this turn of events. Again she took the now calmer MaReenie into a loving embrace, and mentally sent the young woman a message.

"This makes our plan more difficult." Kara held MaReenie's face in her hand and continued speaking silently: "You have to be brave, my child. I know you can! And you must promise not to question what we tell you to do. We are all going to be safe."

As MaReenie's mood lightened, Kara began to speak audibly again. "Now, then. I came over to invite you for lunch. Arthur is bringing your father and Arak over to the house after the market and Merlin will be there, too. You will come, won't you?" Kara was smiling now.

"Oh yes!" replied MaReenie. "Just let me change my clothes and I'll be right with you."

When Kara and MaReenie arrived at the "hut," Merlin was the only one there to greet them. Instantly MaReenie flew into his arms and began crying quietly. Kara motioned Merlin to take the tearful woman out to the garden, but Merlin refused. He sent her his thoughts, explaining that he had just discovered two new surveillance devices, one in the bird feeder, the other in the roof of her new gazebo. In a flash, Kara returned the thought, commanding that he and MaReenie were only to communicate mentally. Both agreed, but even so, Merlin got most of his information from Kara because MaReenie remained distraught.

When the racers arrived, however, Kara had things somewhat under control. She immediately made what had transpired known to Arthur — conveying the news while the two greeted each other aloud as though the race was the most important happening of the day. After congratulating Arak on winning, Kara went out to finish preparations for lunch. Arthur in turn took Zirth and Arak out to the field to set up the fire, and to relay the details of Zaran's unorthodox proposal. The picnickers ate quietly — no one even remembered the wine; they were too immersed in troubled thoughts.

After they had eaten, Arak, Zirth, and Arthur agreed the best thing for MaReenie to do was to wait a few days and then, of course, to accept Zaran's proposal. At first MaReenie was horrified. How could they ask her to marry that monster? Merlin also would not agree, but in the end the two relented, reassured by Arthur and the others that MaReenie would not really have to marry Zaran, but just agree to his proposal. With luck, the betrothal would buy enough time for them to put their plan into action. By the time the date of the wedding had arrived, they would all be far away.

So MaReenie agreed to do their bidding. She would shortly invite Zaran to lunch, and then give him the answer he had demanded.

The intervening days gave Arthur, Zirth, Arak, and Merlin a little time to work out the details of an escape plan. Much of their plan relied on the amount of influence each man could use to secure border clearances, travel permits, and other official documents. But on the eve of the luncheon date, many of the particulars had yet to be resolved, and the four men were growing desperate when — in a moment of inspiration — MaReenie saw a way to use the lunch itself as a means to buy the group far more time than they could ever have hoped.

Zaran arrived early — and was surprised not only by Zirth's presence but also Arak's. He had not expected a public acknowledgment from MaReenie. But she was all smiles as she took him into the dining area. By now, he too was smiling when the two men stood up to greet him. After everyone was seated, Zirth stood up and proposed a toast to the happy couple. He wished them long life and happiness together. Then he added how he would have wished that Raena could have been able to see their beautiful daughter. Arak made a similar toast, adding how lucky Zaran was to have such a wonderful woman as MaReenie be his helpmate through life. MaReenie and Zaran each acknowledged their good wishes. Zaran then rose from his chair and began his own speech.

"Zirth, I had planned to come to you privately and ask for MaReenie's hand, but since she herself has chosen a more public way of acknowledging my proposal I hereby enter my public plea for your daughter's hand." He held his wine glass in Zirth's direction.

Zirth replied. "By tradition a ruler of the realm need not personally enter a plea for his intended, but rather, he must send a commissioner to do so. Zaran, MaReenie acted as your commissioner — and she was the loveliest commissioner you could have sent." His own glass was now held out toward Zaran. "It will be an honor for our families to be joined together officially."

Then MaReenie spoke to Zaran. "It had always been my wish to have a large wedding with all the ceremonial trappings that could be afforded by my father. But now your father has added to my joy by offering to help finance a more elaborate ceremony. I hope that this will be acceptable to you."

"Certainly I think a public display will be most suitable," Zaran agreed, again toasting the two men.

"Actually, Zaran," Arak inquired, "might not an elaborate official State wedding be more appropriate, and do much for the morale of the people?"

"What do you mean?" Zaran asked coolly.

"Well, there has not been a State wedding of a ruler since long before Syus's time. You know that he chose to remain unmarried, and that his predecessor was already married when he took office. So the last time all of Atlantis has participated in a happy and sentimental occasion such as a State marriage was during the old Empire. I know of no better way to get the attention of all well–wishers than to hold a public wedding. And you could capitalize on the fact that MaReenie is the most decorated woman in the State, not to mention her popularity with the common folk and the intense interest her work always generates. In keeping your marriage a private affair, my son, I think you might be missing a great political opportunity."

Everyone held their breath as Zaran gazed at each one with a surprised look on his face. He sat staring at the three of them while he clenched his jaws rhythmically. Then he stood up — almost jumped — and said "Arak, that's the most brilliant piece of political strategy I've ever heard described. Why didn't I think of that myself? Pure genius, pure genius." Zaran went to his father and shook his hand. The three co–conspirators flashed glances at each other.

"It worked," Zirth told himself, mentally congratulating his daughter for the plan she had devised.

"What's more," declared Zaran, "there's no need for either of you to make any preparations. I'm arranging for the wedding myself." Then he turned to MaReenie and said, "My darling, you can have the biggest damn wedding that your heart desires. Do whatever you want so long as it will include all of Atlantis."

"Oh! Thank you! Zaran, thank you!" There were tears in her eyes as she jumped up and rushed over to embrace Zaran. She was playing her part exceedingly well: ever since the earlier meeting, just the thought of Zaran touching her made MaReenie feel as if she were covered with filth.

Later, after the luncheon, Zaran took MaReenie by the hand and strolled into the sunroom where he had acted so brutally. He placed his arms around her and whispered, "Forgive me, my darling."

The thought stabbed her, but she smiled at him and said, "Oh Zaran, I realized that you just didn't know how to convince me of your love. But now, with these wedding plans, you've made it all wonderfully clear."

Presently Zaran bid his luncheon partners farewell: State duties could not wait. "Let me know what you need," he told MaReenie, kissing her goodbye. "And give me an itinerary as you plan it. I want to know all the details."

When the ruler departed, Zirth and Arak congratulated each other on their brilliant performance, while MaReenie sat alone — wondering what kind of life, if any, she would have if their escape plan failed.

21
MaReenie Dies

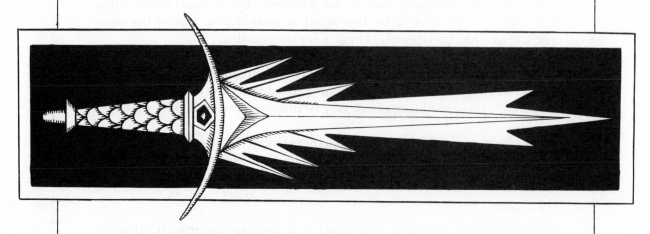

The weeks following the engagement luncheon were passing quickly for the escape planners. Even though travel permits were now much easier to obtain since Zaran had given orders for MaReenie and her party to be accommodated whenever possible in their efforts to arrange the wedding spectacle, there still was much to do. Because the grand scale of MaReenie's wedding itinerary often brought her to the provinces on shopping expeditions, she also had the opportunity to arrange visits with provincial governors. Whenever possible she and her companions — sometimes Arak, occasionally Zirth and Arthur, but always Kara — would seek out escape information. Of course, wherever she went, the ruler's intended made the best impression imaginable. The reports sent to Zaran by his informants only solidified his belief that not only had he chosen well, but also that the State wedding would do much to aid him in getting the good will of all Atlantians. Both plans appeared to be working.

The next phase of the escape operation began when Merlin requested an audience with Zaran, during which the dragon's caretaker outlined his plan to commence the mass injection of the beasts with his newly improved serum. He informed the ruler of his desire to personally supervise the whole operation in order to prevent any mishaps. The trip would take him all over the continent, since the dragons were scattered everywhere; Merlin estimated three to four months of solid work.

Zaran was impressed. "You seem to have thought of everything. But I would prefer it if you could remain in Alta, in the lab, and allow your assistants to do this work. After all, I wouldn't want you to miss the wedding," he said.

Respectfully, Merlin demurred. "In effect, Zaran, I'll be working on my Alta–based project because I plan to take the material with me. That way all the new data gathered on my trip can be put to immediate use. I can make on–the–spot improvements if necessary. As for the wedding, I wouldn't miss it for the world. By the way, I want to congratulate you again. MaReenie's a wonderful girl!"

"Thank you," replied Zaran matter–of–factly. "After all, as my main witness it wouldn't do for you to be away. But back to the dragon project for a minute. How many people are you taking with you?"

"Only one assistant. The rest of my party will consist of lab people, mainly to help with the loading and unloading of equipment."

"Humh . . . I could alleviate some security difficulties for you, if you allow me to arrange for you and your assistant to be met at each of your destinations by competent lab people who could do your bidding."

"Well, that would be just fine. Candidly, I'd prefer not to have to deal with all the security problems of transporting any extra people," Merlin answered.

Zaran smiled. "Merlin, Merlin, will you ever change? You still want only to hide away somewhere with your work and not be bothered by the realities of life, don't you?"

"I guess so," answered Merlin with a sigh. "You'll probably never really know just how much I wish I could forget about the world outside of my family and my work."

"Well, just leave it to me! I understand you very well. Don't worry, I'll take care of the whole move for you." He pushed a button and a secretary appeared to take down his detailed orders for Merlin's trip. Then Zaran turned back to Merlin and said, "Just follow him and tell him what you want done. He'll make all the arrangements. And if you're not satisfied, let me know."

Thus far, the powerful ruler was accommodating the group perfectly. Now with Zaran's approval, Merlin had enough help to move equipment and data without question from the security people. "Sometimes it's better to let Zaran's ego do the work for you," he said to himself as he left the ruler's office. "And what an ego!" He could not help smiling through each of the security checks.

Feverishly, Merlin spent the next week packing. By keeping late–night hours he was also able to work undisturbed. Since he could not leave the laboratory totally empty, he spent the time erasing programs from the master controls, carefully replacing them with false data. In most cases, what he was packing would eventually be destroyed, but for now he had to make it look as if he was planning to work on this trip. He had already perfected the longevity serum and now, together with a new precious fluid that he would administer directly to the dragons, he would complete his part in the conspiracy.

Meanwhile, now that the entire group had been granted the freedom to travel within the country, Arthur and Arak had to find some means of getting off the continent and to their ultimate destination. Every attempt to secure any type of seagoing vessel proved unsuccessful, since all shipping lines had been commandeered for military use. Even fishing boats or commercial shippers were now under military authority. Unfortunately, because their own hovercrafts simply did not have the flight range, the only remaining alternative was to find a transport craft. Arthur and Arak proceeded to inquire discreetly about the availability of such a machine. Perhaps one that needed repairs. With their engineering and mechanical expertise they could renovate a damaged craft.

Though Zaran had relaxed security in the interest of getting the wedding off the ground, he was a naturally suspicious and jealous man who needed constant reassurances about his loved one's loyalty. Consequently, he decided that it would be prudent to enlist two of MaReenie's former suitors and one of Arthur's friends to obtain information about MaReenie's activities when she was not acting in an official capacity. Daily, sometimes even hourly, the ruler's agents reported any unusual activity of the group, and Zaran began to get a vaguely interesting picture of his friends' private lives.

One day, while continuing to seek transportation, Arthur, Zirth, and Arak received some intelligence of their own: an underground network of citizens was working to help people escape from Atlantis. Thus far most of their attempts had failed because security was so intense. Moreover, the group had schemed only among themselves, thereby implicating no one else in case of discovery. Therefore, Arthur and Arak were astonished on being approached by a man who not only guessed their undertaking but also insisted on helping them. Of course their new friend had an ulterior motive: up until now no one of any rank had attempted to escape, and if this plan proved viable, it would give others hope.

It was from this man that Arthur, Zirth, and Arak finally acquired an old, dilapidated transport. It required extensive repairs, but the price was right and the two men began immediately to rebuild the craft. Almost at once, Zaran learned about their purchase, but at first he disregarded the news as one of Arthur's eccentricities. Arthur had always been an avid collector of antiques; even his present hovercraft, which was in daily use, was one of the first models built by the old Empire. Eventually, the entire family had been bitten by the same bug. Zaran told one of his informants, "Even Merlin collects old toys. Why a scientist would want to keep children's playthings I don't know, but he does. Even Arak goes over and helps with Arthur's renovations of old machinery." He announced in disgust, "I guess when people get that old they begin to hoard the things of the past . . . Anyway, I want something more concrete than my father and Arthur spending good money on an old piece of junk. What about MaReenie? What has she been up to?"

"As far as we can see, nothing but wedding activities," the informant answered.

"When you come back, you'd better have something a little more substantial than that! The woman *does* have a life, after all. Do you understand?"

Yet the information regarding the transport did not sit well with Zaran. He could understand Zirth buying such a relic, since speed and racing was a hobby the old man relished. But Arthur, Arak, and Zirth — together? Zaran wrung his hands in frustration. It was all too obvious that if anything was to be carried out to perfection, that thing must be done by him personally. And with that, he set out immediately to find the man who sold the aircraft.

The unfortunate seller, Ival, was a weak-willed man, and a coward to boot — easy prey for Zaran. An old crony of Arak's, he had served with him on the Lemurian campaign. He told Zaran more than enough about Kara, spilling out bits of the conversations that had taken place between Arthur and Arak. It seemed clear that a trip was in the offing, which in Zaran's mind proved without a shadow of a doubt the group's intentions.

But when he left the man, commending him for his service to the State, Zaran lost control of his passions as a terrible suspicion assailed him. MaReenie — had she really used the wedding as a ploy? After all, the entire debacle was her idea, not Zaran's. The old informer was a man Zaran intended to see again. He would force the shattered man to help him destroy the conspirators, then one by one he would eliminate any person who could know of this plot. Thus when these heroes and heroines of Atlantis met their fate, Zaran would be pitied for the loss of his family and friends.

On the day of the planned departure to the Quae Qual reunion, spirits were high at the Yonaja house. However, when Arthur received a communication from Arak, his heart fell.

"Arthur, he wants to come!" the voice said.

"Who wants to come?" asked Arthur.

"Zaran!" the voice answered.

Arthur's reply finally came. "Oh how nice!" Arak understood Arthur's answer. "Oh well, I guess you'll have better transportation than any of us.

But we will all get together once we arrive," Arthur reassured him. "Are you still staying with us at the new Excalibur Inn?"

"Oh you don't understand. He's coming with us." Arak spoke rather dejectedly at the thought of having to spend the trip with his son.

As Arthur closed the communicator, he felt the blood drain from his face. Just then Kara came into the room. When she looked at her husband, a wave of alarm swept through her.

"Are you all right?" she demanded.

"Zaran is coming with us to the reunion."

"Oh my crystals!" Kara exclaimed — then, remembering, she replied in their mental way, "What are we going to do?"

"Nothing. Everything's been planned. Only now we must be ten times more careful."

"What about Merlin?" asked Kara, continuing the mental conversation.

"Our son can take care of the remainder of the plan with Arak," Arthur said confidently. "It will be easier for Merlin and Arak to escape alone than it would if all six of us tried it together."

"I still want to discuss it with the rest of the group," she said.

"Very well. But I don't know how you can discuss it with Merlin. Especially when he's away," Arthur flashed back.

"I have my ways." Kara winked. Then she began speaking aloud. "I need to get my best dress packed. We might be invited to dine with the ruler and his father. That will be an honor."

"Yes," said Arthur aloud. "I'd better get my new uniform out, though they say he still wears the red and silver for more formal occasions."

"Isn't that nice!" Kara replied.

Zaran arrived at the terminal in particularly good humor. His usual entourage of guards and aides was noticeably absent. He had sent them ahead to the Quae Qual. After cordial greetings, he told Arthur and the others that he was especially pleased that they had allowed him to go with them. He felt he was losing touch with his old friends, and now they could have a reunion of their own.

"It's too bad that Merlin isn't here with us," Zaran remarked. "But I do get to see him quite often." Smiling, he then sat with MaReenie. His behavior to her was conspicuously affectionate.

"Zaran, dear," said MaReenie, "I'm so excited to see you! But why this sudden change in your schedule?"

"I wanted to be with you, darling," he smiled. "You know, I've been a thoughtless lover. You've been away doing such a marvelous job making friends for me all over this continent and I haven't seen much of you." His smile broadened. "So I decided that before the wedding took place, I'd like us to have some special time together."

"How very thoughtful, dear," answered MaReenie. "But you know we *are* going to be together for the rest of our lives."

"That's true." Zaran smiled warmly. "But it won't be quite the same, will it? Anyway I wanted to see this wonderful machine that Arak and Arthur have been renovating." The party was now boarding the craft.

"Of course we're not finished with the renovation," said Arthur. "In fact, we've only begun. These things take a lot of hard work. I hope you won't be disappointed when you see the inside. You would have been much more comfortable in your own vessel."

"Yes, that's true, but I'll be happier here with all of you," Zaran told him.

Though the vehicle was rather plain, Zaran still wanted the grand tour and insisted on being shown everything. And they did show it all to him. Arak pointed out the new equipment he had installed in order to make the awkward antique easier to fly. These modernizations were concealed so that the craft's original design was not outwardly disturbed.

"You know," said Arak, "they wasted a lot of space back then with bulky instruments. Arthur and I have kept the old panels. We just gutted the workings and hooked up all the new data banks in the back. Makes the whole thing handle like a new craft. Of course we can't go as fast as the new ones, but we're not in a hurry."

"I see you've also started working on the inside," Zaran commented.

"Yes," Arthur answered. "Kara and MaReenie insisted that we do something about that. You know how women are. They like their comfort."

The conversation continued in this vein. And indeed, the entire trip was spent talking alternately about the craft, trips with MaReenie, childhood days, Zaran's plans for the future of the country, and his work as a ruler. The atmosphere was like that of a family get–together. Zaran seemed his old self, and the conspirators forgot their worries about being discovered. After all, they had not concealed anything about their ship. Arthur actually said he hoped that he and Kara could do some more traveling after the wedding. They had received invitations for return visits from many of the governors and their wives. Zaran said he didn't see why not. Perhaps Arthur could act more in his old diplomatic capacity. That was, of course, if he was up to it.

That evening, when the party arrived at the Quae Qual air terminal, they were greeted by a State envoy, carrying an official invitation to dine with the ruler. Outwardly, they of course pretended to be honored, but secretly they feared the possibilities of sharing Syus's fate.

However, Zaran's dinner turned out to be thoroughly enjoyable. He had invited the entire regiment. Old warriors greeted each other joyously. Some would again be serving in Zaran's new military regime, others would not, but all were savoring each other's company. Only a few who had made the trip to Lemuria were still alive; but of those there that night, no one spoke of their assignment. So it was that except for the five who anticipated meeting the same fate as the unfortunate Syus, all reveled in the light–hearted spirit of the party, not to mention the excellent food and wines. After the dinner, when a few hours had passed, even the five settled into the pleasure of seeing old friends; now realizing that for them, there would be a tomorrow after all.

The next day was filled with prearranged activities and meetings; those in charge of the get–together had planned more of a convention rather than just a reunion, but everyone concentrated on the business of having a good time. All had decided that they might as well enjoy what might be their last celebration together in Atlantis, after all, the members of the regiment were getting very old. The five conspirators, too, enjoyed the reunion. Even though the escape had been planned well ahead of time, any possible last–minute changes were to be resolved in advance by Arthur and Arak in between the many parties they attended.

Zaran insisted on spending almost every waking moment with MaReenie, a most trying experience for her. At wit's end after the first few hours, she kept imagining how it would be to live an entire lifetime with this man — it was a concept just too unbearable to comprehend. Zaran, meanwhile, was totally accommodating. He took MaReenie shopping and sightseeing — often including Kara in their plans — though none of Quae Qual's beauty could divert his gaze from MaReenie. At each of their stops, people offered their best wishes, commenting on what a beautiful couple they made together — so good–looking, charming, and socially attuned. Zaran, in fact, was having the best time in his life.

On the last day of the reunion, a grand breakfast was conceived, with Zaran as the guest of honor at this last meeting. There were parting speeches and tears. The gathering had been so successful that the group resolved to meet again in five years. Elections were held to appoint a committee to begin working on the project and Zirth, Arthur, and Arak were chosen to serve as entertainment chairmen.

The afternoon of the departure was so hectic that Zaran told MaReenie he would not see her until they met at the air terminal. He was very pressed for time to complete his audience at Quae Qual. MaReenie was relieved.

For even though Zaran had been more than pleasant, her nerves were strung out to the breaking point. Besides which, each of the conspirators had duties to tend.

When they arrived at their craft, Zaran was waiting there. His vehicle was also being readied on the same docking bay.

"I understand Arak will be going back to Alta with you," Arthur said. Although well aware of the vehicle's destination, Zaran asked what it was nevertheless.

"We're taking some supplies to Merlin," said Arthur. "But first we'll be dropping Zirth and MaReenie at Tamplokee. They're attending the wedding of Neera Sabame, one of MaReenie's old school friends. MaReenie is one of the witnesses. After we visit with Merlin for a few days, Kara and I will return to pick up MaReenie and Zirth and head home to Alta. We still have to make the final preparations" — he smiled — "for the wedding of the millenium."

"Well, MaReenie will certainly keep you busy," Zaran said absentmindedly as he looked around the docking bay. "Excuse me. I want to say goodbye to her." He shook Arthur's hand. "Have a good trip. I'll see you soon." The ruler walked over to MaReenie. "I'm going to miss you, my darling MaReenie," he said as he took her in his arms and kissed her. Then he held her for a long time, finally breaking his embrace and gazing deeply into her face, as if he were memorizing her every feature. "I can't tell you how much these last few days have meant to me. You are really a wonderful person to be with. I'm going to miss you terribly." He embraced her again.

"Zaran darling," said MaReenie, "I'll see you in about a week."

The ruler of Atlantis then watched MaReenie board the aircraft. After a few moments, all access and service vehicles pulled away. The craft took off. Zaran continued to watch intently as the ancient transport pulled up and out over the bay. Then as the craft began to ascend and make its turn to come back over land, there was a crack of thunder and a flash of light, followed by billows of orange and black clouds of smoke and fire. The transport fell into a million shattered pieces, littering the water. Zaran stood riveted to the ground as he watched every instant of the terrible sight. Tears streamed from his eyes.

"MaReenie darling, there was no other way."

22
A Murderer Reigns

While Arthur, Kara, Zirth, and MaReenie packed to leave for the air terminal, Arak remained busy — seemingly with the last details of the newly formed committee, actually with preparations for the final phase of the escape. Leaving the conference room on the second floor of the Excalibur Inn, he headed toward the site of his planned rendezvous with his Quae Qual contact. Then he noticed a disturbance in the room across the way. Pushing through the crowd, he found himself kneeling at the side of a cold, still body. It was Ival, the man who had sold him and Arthur the antique transport. Shaken, he looked around at the other shocked people, asking what had happened. The onlookers shook their heads, not knowing what to say. The one volunteered an answer.

"He's been despondent about something. I don't know what it was, but all this week he was in very low spirits."

"Yes, that's right," chimed in another. "Something about having to do something he didn't want to do. But what it was, he wouldn't say."

A medical team arrived to remove the body. Arak couldn't believe the man had committed suicide. He went up to his thirtieth–floor room. Under the door was a letter. He picked it up and as he walked over to a chair by the window, began reading it.

"Oh no! No!" he cried out. Instantly he called Arthur's room — no one answered. He tried Zirth, but he was also gone; then MaReenie. She too had left.

He dashed to the lift. Of course it did not respond to his frantic pushing on the call lights. "Damn everyone's leaving at the same time!" Then he remembered the public communicator in the hall. From there he called down to the desk, all the while watching the lift. He was told that Arthur, Kara, Zirth, and MaReenie had already left the inn. Then he directed the communicator to send an emergency long distance message.

"Merlin, I am delayed by . . ." At that moment the lift arrived. "Just sign it 'Arak' — just send it as it is."

The lift was unbearably slow, stopping at almost every floor. When it finally reached ground level, Arak pushed his way out and ran to the first available transit tube out to the air terminal. The ride would only take a few minutes from the inn. The nervous Arak sat looking out at the scene rushing by him. The picture blurred before his eyes as he thought of the letter in his pocket. He took it out and read it again.

Dear Arak,

I will be dead when you receive this letter, but I do not want to go without telling you what I have done to you and Arthur. Though he was my friend, I have betrayed him — as well as the princess. Arak, your son has his ways to force a weak man to do his bidding.
When I realized that he planned to kill the princess, I knew I didn't want to live anymore. How could I when she, her father, Arthur, and Kara would also be dead because of my treachery? Rotar and Sim have also done his bidding and there are others. He means to have Merlin too. I am glad not to be living in a world such as the one that Zaran will make for all Atlantians. You *must* warn them! Try to save yourself — and to forgive me.

Ival

Arak got out at the terminal stop and ran panting towards Docking Bay 12. He stopped short next to Zaran and watched the sky as the blue transport rose in the air and over the bay. He was too late.

He stood looking at the horror of the falling debris and fiery clouds. He covered his face. Zaran stood there crying. Arak looked up at his son's face. Could it be that he had not meant to harm them?

But then Zaran said, "MaReenie, there was no other way."

Arak glared at the creature before him. Then he turned and ran away. Zaran ran after the old man.

"Arak, don't be a fool!" he called out. "You can't get far. Besides, Father, you must go home to Alta with me." He caught up to him and placed his hand on his shoulder. "There will be a State funeral equal to the one for Syus. Only this time Atlantis will truly be in mourning" — his voice had a tone of sarcasm — "we have all lost our loved ones . . . And now I must meet with the news media."

The security around Zaran and Arak tightened almost instantaneously. They were rushed out of the terminal and into Zaran's waiting aircraft. Before Arak realized what had happened, they were on their way to Alta and the Crystal Pyramid.

When the two arrived at the top of the pyramid's docking port, accompanied by a platoon of security officers, Zaran gave his first news broadcast to the shocked people of Atlantis. Infiltrators from the strange continent of Lemuria, he said, had, earlier today, killed Princess MaReenie in cold blood. Most Atlantians had, up until now, only some vague notions about Lemuria, but when Zaran completed his speech the country's temperament was ready — actually eager — for war. Appalled, Arak listened to his son's lies with mounting revulsion at what he as a father had produced. Zaran must be destroyed.

But how?

After the news conference, the two men confronted each other in Zaran's office.

"I was too clever for all of you, wasn't I?" Zaran seemed actually to revel.

"Yes, I guess you were." Arak's voice was toneless, empty of expression.

"Well, don't take it too badly. I know you will miss your friends, but after all, *you* are still alive. If it's any consolation, I'll tell you this much: I didn't *want* to eliminate MaReenie, but I had to. I had no other choice. She really wasn't going to marry me — I knew that all along — and she would have made me look like some stupid schoolboy left waiting at the doorstep. I *couldn't* have that! Everyone would have laughed at me! At *me*! But not now. Now, my countrymen are *with me*! Grieving *my* loss as well as their own." It was almost a shout of triumph.

"I would like to leave," said Arak. "I don't feel well. I'm too tired."

"You're staying here tonight," Zaran ordered, "where you'll be safe."

Arak did not refuse. He allowed himself to be shown to a room where he fell into utter oblivion.

But only three hours later, he was dragged back into consciousness by two servants who helped him dress for dinner. It was now very late and he had not eaten since breakfast. But he was still bone weary and tried to remain in his room. Zaran would not have it: father and son would eat together. As the old man entered the dining room, Zaran motioned him to a chair, saying "This won't take too long." He smiled that Zaran smile.

Arak dutifully trudged over to the chair. The servants poured wine and began serving the meal. It was a light dinner. Zaran said he should not tax his system this late at night, especially after such a trying day. Arak could have cared less what Zaran said or thought. The two ate quietly. Arak said nothing and Zaran did not berate him. After the meal was over, Arak attempted to leave but Zaran said he wanted to talk. As they walked into the next room, Zaran said he had some news that might interest Arak. Again he bade his father sit. Arak chose a large brown couch while Zaran sat in a cream colored chair facing him. Swirling the wine in his glass, the ruler smiled as he stared at Arak.

"You have been a bad boy, Arak." He continued to smile as he stood up and slowly walked around the room.

"Really," Arak remarked. "What am I supposed to have done now?"

"You sent a message to my old friend, Merlin." Zaran's smile broadened.

"What makes you think I did that?" Arak asked.

Zaran's smile dropped. "Because I have a copy of that message." He threw the copy of the message at Arak. It said, "Merlin, I am delayed . . . Bye, Arak."

"Well, for your information, I didn't say 'Bye, Arak.' I was going to tell him that I was delayed by the events that had taken place such as my coming back to Alta with you. But the lift came just at the time I was dictating the message. Moreover, I was late getting out to say goodbye to my friends at the air terminal."

"I don't believe you. This message was a code to Merlin," Zaran argued. "I think it told him to leave, because now he's missing." Zaran looked very intently at his father's face.

"Missing? Perhaps he's just gone to Quae Qual to the site of the accident."

"No, he's missing. He's not at Quae Qual or anywhere else, I tell you. But I think I know where he has gone."

"Where?"

"To Lemuria — where all of you were going," Zaran replied.

"Lemuria? Why would he go there?"

Zaran then proceeded to tell his father all he had learned about Kara, Arthur, Zirth, Raena, and MaReenie.

"Well . . . well," Arak remarked. "So, do you also know about your mother and me?"

"Yes."

"So, now what are you going to do?"

"I'm going to get Merlin." Zaran smiled and sat down beside Arak.

"Why . . . ?" Arak began. "Zaran, there is no one in Atlantis to challenge you. You have ultimate power. Merlin just wants to be left alone. He has no ambitions. Let him go. You'll never see him again. Those people only want to live in peace. They'll never seek conquest."

"Ah, but you don't understand." Zaran's eyes were bright. "*I* seek conquest. I want that power the Lemurians have."

"What power?" Then Arak smiled. "Oh, you mean the use of the mind? Well I can show you that if that's all you want."

At that moment, Zaran's face changed. Something was wrong. Arak looked at his son's face — the ruler looked scared. Arak laughed and shook his head.

"You fool! You arrogant killer!" he said. "So you poisoned me, too? Well, good! I deserve it for having given life to such as you. So you won't get it after all." His laughter became louder.

"I will — I *will* get it!" Zaran shouted. "Or Lemuria won't be left on the face of the earth!"

Resolute, Arak rose. "I think I will go to bed to die, my son." He began walking toward the door. Then he paused, turned, and said, "Leave those people alone, Zaran. This power you want will destroy you. For once be satisfied with having the rest of the world."

Zaran was screaming, "I'll get it! And I'll get Merlin, too! He has it, doesn't he?! Answer me!"

"Leave it alone," Arak said.

"I will *have* it! I don't care what it takes! Just like MaReenie — *I* wanted her and *no one else* was going to have her!"

Just then Arak fell against the doorway.

His face an explosion of rage and guilt, Zaran ran over to his father. "You're just like her!" he whispered hoarsely, tears streaming down his face. "Why did you leave me no alternative?"

"Zaran — shut up." Arak's voice could scarcely be heard. "You're a mad man."

"I'll get Merlin for this!" roared Zaran.

"You never get anyone but yourself," Arak answered with his dying breath.

Zaran frantically screamed for help. The guards rushed in to find their ruler sobbing deeply as he cradled his dead father's body in his arms.

23
The Great Escape

While MaReenie and Kara immersed themselves in wedding preparations, traveling, and entertaining State officials, the reclusive
Merlin — accompanied by his assistant, Detrie — was quietly executing his
part of the master plan. His father, Zirth, and Arak continued to plan their
escape while Merlin systematically visited all the dragon installations. At
each he was warmly welcomed, not so much for his now–famous work on
the beasts, but rather as a popular celebrity. His reputation as a quiet,
easygoing person preceded him, and although the base directors had
strictest orders that his work was to be given highest priority, they were
always pleasantly surpised on meeting the informal, affable prince who
had charge of the project. And, of course, everyone was delighted with
the curious, friendly little Mupi. They were indeed a remarkable pair of
supervisors.

After months of work, only the dragons at Alta remained uninjected.
Merlin was saving old Rajak and the other five for last. And by this time
the serum that he was injecting into the beasts was completely perfected
and totally reliable.

As for Zaran, his occasional dispatches to Merlin expressed elation at the
consistent reports of the dragons' increased activity and newfound
strength. Every reflex had been sharpened; even their evil brains oper-
ated as cleanly as a razor's edge — and every bit as menacingly. Merlin
shuddered whenever he thought of those monsters loosed upon the skies
of the world. Mupi also cringed at the possibilities.

"But not for long," Merlin smiled as he read his friend's mind. "Not for
long."

He had yet to hear from Arak and Arthur about his own escape plan. They were still setting up all the details at Alta. And now during the reunion at Quae Qual, Arak would finalize all the details with those who were helping get MaReenie, Zirth, Kara, and Arthur out of Atlantis. Arak would then get in touch with Merlin in Alta when the reunions ended and then, soon after, they would leave. The plan, so far, was working like a clock; meanwhile Merlin kept working as usual.

Even with all of Zaran's cooperation and assistance, the job was grinding. At each station, equipment and supplies had to be unpacked and then, when the work was completed, repacked and forwarded to the next installation. At each stop, Merlin discarded one, two, or three pieces of equipment, sometimes requesting that they be stored at the installation and at other times sending it back to Alta. He also was slowly discarding all tapes, disks, or papers that contained any "real" data.

At first Detrie suspected nothing, but as time passed and the team arrived at each new place with fewer and fewer supplies, he began to question Merlin directly, asking, "I can't understand why we're leaving so much equipment behind. Aren't we going to continue to work on the serum?"

"Yes, of course." said Merlin. "I give you work to do every day. However, when I left Alta, I wanted every piece of equipment necessary to cope with any conceivable difficulty. Now I see that we don't need half of what we brought. Besides, some of it's malfunctioning, so I'm sending it back for repairs. You should be grateful, Detrie — it's a lot less equipment for us to be packing up at each installation. If we don't need it, we shouldn't drag it around."

Detrie was not wholly satisfied with his superior's explanation. Nor was he happy with certain new experiments he was being asked to perform. To some degree they were not related to life extension, although Merlin had explained the reasons for them. At any rate, Detrie felt it necessary to contact Alta's head of security. A very tough woman. They arranged between them when and how Detrie would report on Merlin's activities. She, in turn, would forward the information directly to Zaran.

Although Detrie was an intelligent, cunning, ambitious man, he proved to be no match for his superior — or even Mupi, for that matter. Merlin, accustomed to the ways and means of the new regime, was well aware that every disgruntled employee of Atlantis could easily find a willing ear. Because of this state of affairs, he found himself being forced into what Zaran called "the realities of life." Now certain he was under scrutiny, Merlin had Mupi tune into people's thoughts, listen to conversations, and generally act as his counterintelligence agent. Since no one remotely suspected that Mupi had any more intelligence than a dog or even a bird, particularly now when the creature was acting even more clumsy and erratic with the stress of constant moving, Mupi roamed freely throughout the bases. Wherever he went he begged treats and attention, all the while tapping into people's thoughts and sorting conversations; even looking at secret data screens.

But it was not until one of his nightly prowlings that Mupi finally heard Detrie talking on a long–distance communicator — thus accidentally discovering the assistant's secret. Not wanting to arouse Detrie's suspicions, he bounded into the office panting and begging in his customary way. Startled, the traitor at first tried to push him out; however, when the pet settled casually under the desk, Detrie continued his conversation. By listening carefully at first, Mupi gathered that this was a routine weekly report. But when he decided to listen into Detrie's thoughts, he became thoroughly frightened: the ruler, having learned of the escape plan and MaReenie's deceit, was planning to kill his betrothed. It was of utmost importance that Merlin be detained at the installation, but Detrie had not yet been given the date.

Mupi wanted to rush out to tell Merlin, but any abrupt movement would cause a disturbance. So he waited patiently under the desk for Detrie to end his report, determined to behave normally. That meant he must start begging for food. The ruse worked. After petting him and speaking a few words of baby–talk, Detrie finally tossed Mupi half a banana. Mupi wolfed it down, tripped over a stool, became entangled with himself, and bounded out at last — to the sounds of Detrie's laughter — making his way like a ricocheting bullet to Merlin's office.

When he arrived at the door, Merlin absent–mindedly greeted him with his familiar "Hi, Mup." Then he began to reproach the creature for staying out so late. "Where have you been? Eating, no doubt. You're getting much too fat with all the food everyone's giving you."

Mupi paid no attention. As soon as Merlin had finished scolding him, he got his thoughts together and flashed the awful news to his master. Merlin was dumbstruck — but careful not to react outwardly. Casually, he petted Mupi's head and proceeded to leave.

"Come on Mup. It's later than you think," he said aloud. Mupi just whined.

Out of the office and past the security checks they hurried, then on to the overhead tube system that would take them one block from their apartment complex. Throughout the entire trip, Merlin conversed telepathically with his friend.

"You know tomorrow — or should I say this morning — is the last day of the reunion. I wonder if Zaran is planning something for tomorrow?" Receiving Merlin's thought-question, Mupi whined in doubt.

"I must get a message to Mother and let her know. What time is it over there?" Merlin looked at the time calculator on his wrist. "Let's see, it's about three hours difference to Quae Qual from here, so it must be half past seven by now. They'll be starting that breakfast by now. They're all early birds. By the time I get home and I set up, it will be eight o'clock. I just wish this thing would move faster!"

When finally the tubes reached their destination, the two were at their home in a flash. Merlin, fearing some type of visual surveillance, quickly dressed for bed as usual and turned out the lights. Once in the dark, he pulled out the stones that Raena had made for him and began to send warning to his mother. Because he was so distracted with worry, it took a long time before he could properly respond to the power within him. Ultimately contact was made, but the message had come too late, Kara said. Nothing could be changed; they were already boarding the aircraft. It seemed to Merlin that Kara was experiencing some difficulty — her message was distant, odd. Suddenly Merlin's mind was alerted to an order from his mother.

"Merlin, get out of there this instant! Do you understand? Get out! You know our destination. Go there!"

Kara's son shot back his urgent question, "What about Arak? I can't just leave him!"

The answer came. It was unthinkable! "If Zaran knows our plan, then Arak is a dead man. He understood the danger but he is an honorable friend. He will never betray us. Escape! Do you understand? Save *your-self!* Make his sacrifice mean something!"

With that his mind was stunned. Mupi, who had been mentally eaves-dropping, acted more excited and fearful. He was anxious to leave. Merlin had to think now. How could he save himself and Mupi, too? How? An idea struck him, and he was on the communicator instantly, calling an old friend of Arthur — No time to worry about listening devices. While he waited for an answer, he started regretting having left the dragons at Alta for last. Just then a sleepy voice at the other end made a gruff "Hello! Who's calling at this uncivilized hour?"

"Is that you, District man Kobar?" Merlin asked.

"Yes. Who is this maniac calling?" the angry voice replied.

"It's Merlin, sir." His voice was respectful. "I'm sorry to wake you at this early hour but I need a favor and quick." He took a swallow and started. "I completely forgot about the reunion of my father's old regiment at Quae Qual this week, and I had planned to surprise them with a visit, but you know the work I've been doing has kept me so busy it totally slipped my mind."

"Yes. Yes." The other had become less angry. "You haven't changed a bit, my boy."

Merlin continued. "Well I was wondering if I could borrow your old racer, sir. I'll take good care of it. I'd be back tomorrow. I'm leaving for Alta tomorrow. Father will be away on some State assignment, and I won't get to see him. How about it, sir? I'll bring you back some brandy and some of those wonderful Quae Qual sausages."

"Brandy and sausages?" the voice laughed. "Make the sausages garlic and it's a deal. And you can tell your father his son's a charmer."

"Thank, you sir! I'll be there in a few minutes." Merlin closed the mechanism and turned to Mupi. "Now we have a way! Let's get out of here! I just wish I could have finished off those big ones in Alta. I have a feeling I'll live to regret it."

He packed only necessities, which included stones, scientific data, serum, and his Excalibur weapon. Extra precautions were taken against being followed. After all, he didn't want to cause his father's old friend any extra problems. When they arrived at Kobar's house, the racer had been primed for Merlin.

Designed to hold two flyers for a type of long distance racing that had been the "in" sport during the days of the old Empire, the midnight blue racer had been a champion in its day. But such craft had become obsolete with the development of newer, faster Atlantian machines. And the sport itself had long ago been abolished as a wasteful use of time. However, Kobar maintained his ship as a hobby and flew it around the countryside.

With assurances of safe flying and a cargo of brandy and sausage on his return, Merlin was off. Hoping that he would not be missed at once, he headed over the water to avoid being spotted against the dark sky. For, should Zaran suspect anything, he would certainly send the beasts in his pursuit. In any case, the five–hour trip was especially grueling. Merlin was unaccustomed to maneuvering an antique at such high speed, and it was an effort to push the old bucket as fast as she would go. As for the co-pilot, Mupi, he vacillated between sleep and continual nervous whining. At last the exhausted pilot and his passenger arrived, but not at Quae Qual. Instead, Merlin hovered over an abandoned racing field in a valley hidden among the mountains outside Cumbar. Out of practice, Merlin made a landing as "smooth" as the condition of the broken landing field. Man and beast got out. Adjacent to the area were two buildings — one a clubhouse, the other a tower. Both were in need of repair and appeared empty.

"I'm afraid they've either left or perhaps . . . ." Merlin could hardly say it. "Perhaps something's happened to them." Leading Mupi toward the buildings, Merlin started thinking about Kara's message, and the thought knocked hard in his brain. He peered in to the window of the stone building and saw nothing but his reflection.

"We've got to get out of here," said Merlin. "But where can we go without being spotted?" And indeed, at that very moment the pair heard a large transport closing in fast. Mupi flew to the racer, but Merlin could not make it. He was halfway there when jumpsuit–uniformed members of Zaran's guard poured from the machine. Their weapons were drawn and leveled at Merlin. Instinctively Merlin whirled to face the enemy, reaching for his super–powerful excalibur. Its scabbard was empty; Merlin had left the weapon aboard the racer. There was nothing to do but hold up his hands.

"You've got us!" he called out to the guards. "Don't shoot! I'm not armed."

"You're a damned fool!" the guards' commander shouted at him. "When you're escaping, you'd better be prepared to kill or be killed!" The man broke into a smile.

"What?" the bewildered Merlin shouted back. "Who the hell are you?"

"Friends, my careless fellow. Otherwise you and that strange creature would be smoldering ashes by now!" He took Merlin by the arm and motioned for the men to remove the baggage from the craft. Merlin was then hurried to the waiting transport. Six people were inside — four of them the most important people in the young man's life. Arthur, Kara, Zirth, and MaReenie all rushed at him. Merlin was all but thrown to the ground by their embraces.

"What happened?" . . . "How did you get away?" . . . "We're all back together again!" Merlin was crying tears of relief and joy. Mupi worked his way into the middle of the group, and trying to nuzzle and nip everyone at once. The leader questioned Merlin about the racer. Merlin asked if brandy and sausages could be procured for the district man. He was assured that all would be arranged: someone would pick up the brandy and sausages and fly the ancient craft back to its ancient owner.

"One day I'll have to tell him what a *real* friend he is," said Arthur.

As the transport and its crew, cargo, and passengers were lifting off, Arthur began to answer Merlin's questions about the escape.

24
No Need to Return to Atlantis

Together and safe at last, the group listened while Arthur commenced the story of how Zaran had been foiled.

"Unfortunately, Merlin, we were already boarding the craft when your mother got your thought message," he began. "There we were, saying goodbye to Zaran, trying desperately to pretend we'd all meet again at Alta. We couldn't change our plan at that point. Anyway, I think MaReenie had the most difficult job. For the whole week of the reunion she had to be in Zaran's company."

MaReenie broke in, "The entire time he acted exceptionally tender and attentive towards all of us. It's hard to imagine that all the time he was planning our deaths. How could he be so cold and cruel?"

Merlin looked at MaReenie, sharing her bewilderment. "Let me take over," Zirth said. "We had planned to enter the old transport in the usual manner, but then with the help of these underground people" — he pointed to the crew on board — "we exited through the service doors and into the attached ground vehicles that were supposedly bringing on food and baggage. That part went all right. Your father and Arak worked out the brilliant details of rigging the old transport for an explosion. You know, Merlin, Arak's a genius with electronics. He wired that ship and hid all he'd done. No one suspected. Not even Zaran. We showed him everything on board during our flight to Quae Qual."

"How can you be sure of that when he found out about the escape?" Merlin asked.

"Because," Arthur interrupted, "After we got your message and got into the transport, Zirth opened the panel to plug in the explosion device. He found the bomb planted by Zaran's people. All those so-called experts that he has working for him — they didn't even hide that thing." Arthur explained, "Their device was set to explode three minutes after takeoff, which would put us out in the bay. That suited us perfectly, but just to make sure that they wouldn't bungle anything, Zirth timed ours to go off simultaneously."

Kara added, "It *was* a tremendous explosion." They all laughed.

Merlin sighed in relief, then shouted "You're free, really free! And I want you to stay that way! Father, please drop me off at Port Quae. I must go back and finish my job."

"What!" MaReenie and Kara cried out almost at the same moment. MaReenie added, "You *can't* go back. He'll kill you. The man is completely mad, Merlin. He'll stop at nothing."

"Exactly!" agreed Arthur.

Merlin nodded, smiling. "You're right," he said. "He'll stop at nothing as long as I'm alive. Don't you see? All of you are free. He thinks you're dead. But he knows by now that I've escaped. And he also knows that we were headed for Lemuria. So as long as I'm free, he'll go to Lemuria and only the heavens know what evil plan he has in store for any who aids me. To keep him from Lemuria, I must go back. Besides, those creatures in Alta haven't been injected."

"Oh no, my son!" Kara cried. But Arthur knew that Merlin was right. Zaran had to die, else they would never be truly safe. Even the Lemurians would not be able to withstand an all-out military assault from Atlantis. Merlin tried to assure his mother that he would return safely, but to no avail; but at the moment the thought of his remaining was too horrible for her to bear.

MaReenie was no less distraught. Just when she thought she could finally have the love she so desperately wanted, he would place himself in new peril. Merlin embraced her, but she could only weep. All the joy of the escape had suddenly been washed away.

Now the underground leader came back, to tell them of a communication that was being intercepted. Arthur and Merlin went forward to listen; they were followed by the others.

"Attention! All pilots, DRAGON priority! Look out for antique midnight blue racer, cover number 8-7-2-9-0. Belongs to district man Kobar of

Duryd. Pilot of vehicle is wanted in connection with Quae Qual explosion. If spotted, report coordinates immediately. Capture alive if possible, but do not hesitate to destroy vehicle if pilot attempts evasion. Acknowledge."

Merlin ordered the leader to warn the pilot of the racer at once.

"He's already heard the news. Your on–board equipment is up to date. We checked it out before he left. He'll know what to do if he's spotted."

"*What* will he do?" asked Arthur.

"Take evasive action."

"No!" Merlin shouted. "You must tell him to set down. I won't have him do anything to get himself killed!"

"Prince Merlin, sir." The leader replied. "He has two choices. One is to set down and be tortured for information, undoubtedly being killed even if he confesses all he knows. The other is to make a run for it and be killed instantly. Which would you choose?"

Merlin shut his eyes and cradled his face in his open hands. "My miserable life isn't worth his sacrifice."

"Well," said the leader, "the pilot thought you were worth it — he volunteered. And I have a feeling you're going to make his sacrifice worthwhile."

"He should be getting to Quae Qual soon," said the pilot of the transport. Then voices were heard on the transport speaker. Merlin didn't want to listen but he had no choice. First there was the usual back–and–forth banter of pilots in the area — interrupted suddenly by a strange, mechanical-sounding voice.

"He — is — spotted. Coordinates — are — sectors — fifteen — by — sectors — one — eight — five — outside — Quae — Qual. — He — is — *mine!* — Rajak — reporting."

Now the pilot was ordered to land. No reply. Rajak repeated his command. After a few seconds' interval, the explosion was heard. Finally, the awful voice drummed out the news. "Rajak — reporting. — Racer — terminated — in — chase. — Prince — Merlin — is — dead."

On the transport, the silent, grieving people heard the shouts of victory being screamed into the communication network. Only the escapees mourned the dead man — a man they never knew. They shut off the system.

"Consider yourself free," said the leader to Merlin. "There is no need for you ever to return to Atlantis."

Merlin was stunned by the man's words. Yes, to Zaran and the rest of his countrymen, he was dead. Rajak had personally terminated him. Somehow though, he still questioned his right to escape, leaving the world in Zaran's hands. And what about those creatures? How long would they last? Would Zaran not use them anyway? His questions received a bombardment of answers by family and transport crew alike. Arthur did not refute his son's feelings, but instead offered an alternative.

"Merlin, come to Lemuria with us. Rest your body as well as your mind. Learn what you can from these ancestors of yours. After all, if you are destined to confront Zaran, it would be best to do so with preparation. Time is the great healer, my son. And you must be strong if and when you meet such an adversary. Besides, there are those of us here who need you in order to help start new lives."

Merlin studied the faces of the people on board the craft as he listened to Arthur. His father was wise. Now was not the time to go back. Yes, he had much to learn and he needed rest. Rest — he had almost forgotten what that was like. He would take this opportunity — both the good and the bad — but he would begin by taking advantage of the sleeping area at the back of the transport. He was in a deep slumber even as the craft took off.

Ironically, the group landed at almost the exact spot where Zaran had touched down so many months before. Instead of the isolation that had greeted Zaran, throngs were there to celebrate properly the homecoming of a great Lemurian lady, her family, and friends.

As soon as the ship touched down, Merlin was prodded by MaReenie.

"We're here, Merlin dear," she announced. "We're here in Lemuria. Get up! There are people who want to meet you."

The groggy Merlin opened his eyes, his mind still fogged. "Where are we?"

Joyously MaReenie told him, "Merlin, we're finally home."

25
The Dragons Are Dying

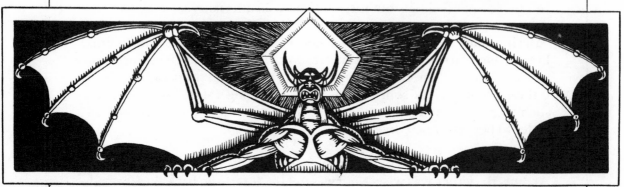

*I*n the sixteen months following the conspirators' deaths, Zaran found himself in a turmoil of activity. Following his inauguration, he had abolished the Council and consolidated his forces within the government. For the first time within even the Atlantians' long memory, one leader now held absolute control over the State. However, not all of Zaran's decisions were unilateral, for he relied on agents and spies to help formulate his policies.

But despite his successful maneuverings, despite his becoming the total governing force of Atlantis, Zaran's life reeked with dissatisfaction. As each day passed, he came increasingly to comprehend the awful truth of his actions. *He* had killed all the people who had filled his life with meaning. Consequently the passing of each new month found him spending more time in the dragons' quarters, talking to the beasts who had become his only friends. He continued drinking heavily to block out his fear and isolation.

Still, he did not feel guilty. After all, whose fault was it that he had been forced into his extreme actions? Drunk, he would sit in the lounge chair he had dragged into a dragon stall, Xax lying close by, resting his massive head next to his human master. The ruler raved on about how his friends had left him no choice, all the while stroking the head of the bored beast. Zaran carried his burden alone for the dragons offered no sympathy. Indeed, as was their nature, the evil creatures sometimes toyed with the inebriated ruler, tormenting him to the point of rage. To add to his misery, Zaran's position as ruler left him surrounded by opportunist jackals, fawning followers, or complete incompetents whom he, himself, had appointed. Nowhere could he find a mental equal, even someone he could trust.

This day it was still to early to drink. Having spent the morning dealing with the many problems of state business, the weary ruler sat in his spartan office at the Crystal Pyramid. Even after all his detailed instructions on proper protocol, he was startled when his door abruptly burst open.

"Something's wrong with the newly arrived dragon from Cumbar," a messenger frantically blurted out. "He's down! And we can't get him up!"

"Imbecile! Why wasn't I informed sooner!" raged Zaran.

"Sire, it just happened!" Terrified, the messenger continued. "At this very moment the team is working on all the data but their leader thought it would be better to inform you personally."

Zaran flew out of his office and over to the Old Labs. And, at the very moment he stamped into the facility, the team met him with their analysis of their situation and proceeded to show him all the test results.

"There's been a trauma in the dragon's biological systems," the team's leader began. "Prior to this, all previous tests indicated regeneration taking place at an accelerated rate — it's been documented that the beasts were actually growing younger and stronger. But the tests performed today on the Cumbar arrival reveal just the opposite, and we haven't yet determined the cause. For some reason, the systems are reversing and the dragon is aging — at an incredible rate."

The dragon specialist took a breath. "Moreover, I have just received word that this rapid aging process has been reported at the *Cumbar* installation as well, affecting all the remaining dragons housed there. It could be a virus. It could be a genetic defect."

That analysis was received by Zaran with fury. He lashed out at the team, accusing them of sabotage, incompetence, stupidity, and anything else that occurred to him. He demanded an immediate reversal of the dragons' aging process, and promised severe penalties for failure. The team of scientists could only stand dumbfounded and helpless — until a voice on the speaker was heard to say, "The Cumbar dragon is dead." Zaran's eyes almost flashed fire with hate and disbelief. Then the director at Cumbar came onto the speaker, announcing, "All of the beasts at this installation are down. What are your wishes, sir?" Instantaneously Zaran shot back the order for an autopsy of the dead beasts. At the same time, he demanded an immediate and thorough examination of the remaining dragons in all the installations. He would have answers and a cure, he shouted; nothing less would be acceptable.

One month later every dragon in Atlantis, except for those in the Alta laboratory, were dead. With each day, another of the ruler's creations had passed quietly from a condition of extreme weakness into total systemic arrest — and even more unbearable for Zaran, none of Atlantis's teams of scientists could find the reason for the beasts' death. Frustrated by their incompetence, Zaran decided to take personal control of the testing.

Incredibly, this work was added to his already debilitating schedule — but Zaran had suspicions. And, after many endless nights in the laboratory, those suspicions finally bore fruit — he discovered the ingeniously hidden fallacies in the data bank along with the discovery that much of the bank's equipment had been sabotaged to give faulty readings. Afterwards — even in sleep — Zaran could be heard cursing the dead Merlin. And, though he worked feverishly to reverse the aging process, the dragons continued to die. Zaran could only grieve that he had been unable to torture Merlin personally.

One afternoon a recently returned envoy from Lemuria stepped into this poisoned atmosphere, and Zaran — although exhausted and on the brink of collapse — took time out to meet the diplomat whose assignment it was to encourage trade between the Lemurians and Atlantis. Recently, in a rare display of good will, Zaran had sought intelligence on Lemuria by cultivating peaceful relations — even though, because his missions had proved unsuccessful, his patience with the Lemurians was wearing thin. Now, when Gruger, the envoy, was announced, Zaran decided he would glean whatever information he could, and then order punishment for his failures.

"Send in Gruger. I'm ready to see him," he directed his nervous secretary. At first Zaran was uncharacteristically affable toward the visitor, throwing him off guard with quiet, intelligent questions, though the scant information set his teeth on edge. The Lemurians had ignored all recent efforts made by Atlantis to acquire trade agreements for the stones and their use. Zaran became angered when they offered only to trade crafts and crops for any unusual plants and animals found in Atlantis — and to welcome a very limited number of visitors.

"Actually, sir," said the envoy, "these people feel that we have very little to offer them. They also can't or won't grasp your interest in their stones when Atlantis has so much technology."

"So they can't or won't?" Zaran snapped impatiently. "Well, if they insist I'll have to convince them of my sincere interest won't I?" He closed his eyes as if dreaming and smiled with evil joy — then came back to reality and fixed the envoy with a glare of steel.

"I'm disappointed in you Gruger! You've failed in your assignment. And you know the penalty for — " His eyes popped wide in near shock as the envoy interrupted him.

"Forgive me, sir! I beg you to forgive me for intruding. But I have not completed my report."

Zaran leaned forward eagerly. "You mean you *got* them to trade?"

"No, sir, I regret to inform you that I haven't. However —" he paused. "I *do* have evidence that certain people who all Atlantis believed were dead might still be alive and well in Lemuria, mainly in the province of Elyria."

Zaran's jaw tightened and his eyes grew very small. As if in slow motion he rose from his desk and gradually approached the envoy, who at this moment was beginning to fear for his life.

"What are you saying?" Zaran's voice was almost a hiss.

The envoy swabbed his brow with a handkerchief, gulped, and began his account.

"Quite by chance, on the day before I was to return home, I decided to visit the far northwestern province of Elyria. It's a mountainous region and sparsely populated, but the main village is quite large. Happily I arrived on market day."

"Get to the point!"

"Yes, sir, of course. While I was going through the makeshift stalls I spotted a strange creature with a baby harnessed to its back. The beast was unmistakably dead prince Merlin's pet, Mupi. I followed far behind until I could clearly see the face of the woman who held the creature's harness. It was Princess MaReenie — or it had to be a twin sister."

Zaran seized the envoy by the neck. "Is it true?! You had better not be playing some joke on me!"

"No! No!" Gasping for breath, the envoy struggled to talk. "I swear it's true! I saw them — and there's more!" Zaran released the half–choked man and threw him to the floor, where he cringed. Then Zaran got a grip on his temper.

"Forget I did that," he said. "I was simply overcome with relief." But relief, he knew, was not the word for what he felt. "Let's hear the rest of it."

"Of course sir," said the envoy. "But may I be permitted first to say how happy I am to have been able to bring you good news — and to voice my hope that this news will counterbalance your disappointment for the delay in getting the Lemurians to trade."

Zaran nodded impatiently and the envoy continued. "I learned not to seek information from any Lemurian adults, so I pumped the facts from some children. Yes, it was indeed MaReenie that I saw. She is now married to" the diplomat hesitated "to Merlin and the child is their baby."

Zaran's face was now drained white. The envoy continued. "They live high in the mountains outside the village, along with Merlin's parents. Zirth maintains a home alone in the village. Kara has apparently become one of the leaders of Lemuria and Arthur serves as her advisor. The family is considered one of the happiest." His voice dropped off.

Up to this moment the envoy had been fairly safe. But now he told Zaran what he heard of escape from Atlantis. Zaran screamed. Guards rushed into his office and saw the envoy cowering in a corner. Zaran spun, faced the officer of the guards, and pointed at the envoy.

"Take him away and don't let him talk to anyone," he ordered. "He's gone mad, totally lost his mind! The Lemurians have poisoned his mind!" Instantly the guards dragged away the only person, other than Zaran, who knew about the successful escape.

When he was at last alone again Zaran sat quietly at his desk for a long while, the image of regal composure, while his mind rapidly wove a plan of death for those who had deceived him. Then, abruptly, he jumped up, left the office, and rushed to the old Labs. His need to talk was like a raging thirst — but he could entrust the escape story only to Rajak and Xax. The two dragons listened impassively to the long, complex narrative.

When he finished, Zaran said, almost happily, "Well, things are looking up! Life won't be so dull after all. But I'll have to keep my wits about me — no more drinking for the time being. At last I have a worthy adversary. I know now just how clever he is — yes, much more clever than I could have imagined."

26
Farewell to Lemuria

The next day, Zaran announced his plans for a major news conference, to be aired, live, at three p.m., and every citizen of Atlantis was advised to tune it in. It was not boring. Zaran opened with a threatening speech concerning the infiltration of Lemurian dissidents into the State. He spoke of them as savages who wished to reduce Atlantis to barbarism. All progressive Atlantian innovations would be eliminated, and all their high–tech creature comforts destroyed. Zaran fabricated revolutionary plots, which he said the State had squelched, and linked the Lemurian mental power to brainwashing. Blaming the death of the beloved Prince Merlin and the others on the Lemurians, Zaran also hinted at the use of drugs and poisons in food and water supplies. The speech was a tour de force of demagoguery.

It was also a complete success. The continent was in an uproar. Calls and messages were 100 percent in favor of ridding the country of the subversive infiltrators — by any means necessary. This was just what Zaran wanted to hear. Two days later he was back on the air to reassure his distraught people and announcing that although his plans could only be successful if kept totally secret, Atlantis would soon have the situation totally under control. The details would be released only when it was perfectly safe to do so.

Zaran had already summoned his chief military advisors and ordered an immediate, all–out attack on the northwestern province of Lemuria. He wanted the region leveled; no survivors. There was much discussion about the fallout from Zaran's proposed mass launching of high–power missiles and the drifting wind currents in that area. But Zaran did not care about these particulars. He wanted Elyria completely destroyed, and soon.

"This will teach them a lesson," he told his officers. "We won't be affected by any drifting fallout — and as for the target region, Atlantis has no need to colonize that part of the world anyway."

A general asked, "But what about our colonies at Port Quae and other coastal places near the continent? They're in the path of the prevailing wind currents."

"All who can be evacuated in the next twenty–four hours will survive,"

Zaran replied coldly. "Now on to more important business. Unfortunately, only five of the special missiles have been armed with the new war heads. Nonetheless, these will still contain sufficient force to do the job. All five will be aimed at the target areas indicated on the map and duplicated in the orders before you. I alone will give the order for their launching. Understood? . . . Any questions? . . . Very well. Before any of you leave, you must swear to complete secrecy about the plan of attack. I must warn you that if for any reason it fails in its objective, all of you will pay for the indiscretion with your lives. Is *that* understood? . . . Good. Raise your right hands . . ."

Meanwhile, in Lemuria, life went on at its unhurried pace. With the help of their new Lemurian friends, Merlin and his family found immense happiness in the mountains of Elyria. The world seemed so much simpler; their Atlantian past behind them, all dedicated themselves to learning about the magnitude of the power within them. All their activities in and around their new living houses brought them closer to true peace, and as they worked in the fields and meditated with the help of the stone circles, they found harmony with nature and all its creatures. Their minds and bodies were being healed — the trauma of their experiences in Atlantis, a rapidly fading scar.

However, even with this new sense of peace and happiness, the new arrivals, Merlin and MaReenie in particular, remembered the importance of always keeping a low public profile. They even changed their outward appearance, Merlin by letting his hair and beard grow, MaReenie by wearing her hair in bangs and braids, and both adopting the Lemurian dress. The others likewise attempted to alter their looks. They were naturally — and painfully — aware of Zaran's diplomatic endeavors, and realized the peril for their friends if they were discovered. This danger, however, did not in any way prevent them from aiding the recently expanded underground movement in Atlantis. All actively helped with the settling in of the few who escaped the mother dictatorship.

Therefore, it was natural that they were stunned when Zirth arrived at the house with news of their having been discovered.

"I have just now learned that a stranger was asking a few of the children some questions about you," he told MaReenie and Merlin. "This person also wanted information about Arthur, Kara, and me too! There have been so many strangers in the village lately with all the new immigrants that the children were taken unaware."

"I know it wasn't their fault," said Merlin. "I shouldn't have taken Mupi to the market. But he's been so anxious to see the village and the children that I gave in. Besides, he hates being away from the baby."

"We'll have to leave the area," said MaReenie.

"Do you think that's necessary?" asked Zirth.

"Father, Zaran is an evil man. He'll do *anything* to *anyone* to achieve his end."

"Before we jump to conclusions," Merlin proposed, "let's talk it over with my parents."

MaReenie and Zirth nodded. When they were approached with the news, Kara and Arthur agreed with MaReenie.

"These people are in imminent danger," Arthur pointed out. "As a matter of fact, that probably applies to all of Lemuria. We'll have to get word to the leaders."

Merlin clenched his fists. "I'm so sorry. All of this is my fault."

"My son," said Kara, "we can all be lulled into mistakes. And you were acting out of friendship for Mupi, not out of thoughtlessness for the Lemurians. They understood the dangers involved when they accepted us into their land, but they too acted with love and compassion. The fact is, Merlin, Zaran would have attacked this beautiful land regardless of whether or not you and MaReenie had been discovered here. The Lemurians have seen that madman's true face — and he has, through them, experienced true power, however briefly. The Lemurians were frightened by the encounter, of course. But Zaran — Zaran was terrified. And what terrifies Zaran, he will destroy.''

Thought messages were transmitted to every corner of Lemuria. In many cases, people chose to remain in their homes, but an equal number opted to leave. Preparations were begun for a mass evacuation of the continent. As anticipated, those who had decided on staying aided the people who were leaving by building the boats, rafts, and balloons that would carry their friends to safety. There were very few flying craft in Lemuria — only those that had landed with the recent migration. Even so, all preparations were completed swiftly.

Then every Lemurian was stopped short — they knew. Missiles had been launched.

While many sought refuge to the north, east and south of Lemuria, Merlin and his family, although among the last to leave, traveled to the central valley of Laz, an area located beyond the ocean, in the interior of the continent now known as China.

After openly announcing his intentions to attack, Zaran anticipated some type of evacuation, though certainly not a migration of this size. Nevertheless he sent his small squadron of healthy dragons to annihilate all those leaving Lemuria. Only the shortage of beasts kept the invaders from annihilating every last Lemurian man, woman, and child.

On reaching their destination, Merlin, MaReenie, and Mupi helped the 150 passengers from their transport to disembark, unload the cargo, and find shelter. Soon Kara and Arthur landed their small craft, carefully hiding it in the foliage before unloading. There were six additional people aboard.

MaReenie and Merlin were herding the last of Kara and Arthur's passengers into a heavily wooded area when they caught sight of Zirth's craft in the distance.

Zirth, who carried a group of children and older people to the valley refuge, began readying the transport to set down in a clearing. MaReenie watched her father's descent from the forest's edge. But he was not alone in the sky — was it an unexpected arrival of fleeing Lemurians? MaReenie narrowed her eyes, focusing on the spot looming ever larger against the face of the sun. Then she gasped in horror. The dragon Rajak was circling the area at the precise moment of Zirth's landing. Sickeningly, the fiery breath of the beast blasted the craft as it hit the ground. Hiding in the eastern hills that surrounded the valley, the refugees stared dumbly at the carnage as the craft exploded in a gray cloud pierced by orange and white flames. Pieces of metal shattered into a million fragments. Then the dragon shot off another charge, and the craft — with its human cargo — completly disappeared in the inferno. The anguished onlookers could take no comfort in the knowledge that being safely hidden they were spared from the telescopic eyesight of the murderous beast. At last, when the thing had flown away, MaReenie turned, flung herself sobbing into Merlin's arms. First she cried for her father and then for his helpless passengers. But presently she found herself weeping with rage — at the beast's creator. "Merlin, something has to be done about Zaran. He's out to destroy the world."

MaReenie cried herself to sleep while the remaining survivors settled in for the night. At last it came — the thunderous clap of the blast; the mountains to the west glowed as if ten thousand suns were rising. For some it was too much to bear and they cried out, feeling the deaths of their fellow men deep within their sensitive souls. The hideous glow seemed to last an eternity, but presently it began to fade, and then vanished altogether, leaving a handful of living dead on the broken land. As the sky blackened, each was left alone in his own sorrow.

Only Merlin could not grieve. His mind overflowed with thoughts of revenge.

Then, suddenly, a voice cut sharply but gently into his consciousness. He looked up. Kara was staring down at him. "Merlin, your mind screams loudly with dreadful thoughts. My son, you cannot change what has already happened."

Merlin stood up and took his mother's arm, leading her away from the sleeping throng. But she continued to talk to him. "Listen to me. Evil men like Zaran always end up destroying themselves, along with everything that they have created. His own people will punish him, not you, Merlin."

But her frustrated son would not agree. "Mother, MaReenie is right! Something has to be done about Zaran! What's the matter with you? Don't you care about the destruction of your own people?"

"Merlin, my own people will find a way to defend themselves. It will not be in a battle. But they *will* fight — by surviving and building anew elsewhere. But you . . . you are in danger! You must *not* carry this hate in your heart. It may not destroy you immediately. Indeed, it may for the moment appear to make you stronger. But if you play Zaran's game, this revenge may very well cost you all that is dear to you."

Kara dropped her gaze. The terrible truth pierced her heart. Her son's mind was set. He would kill Zaran.

27
They Find a River Valley

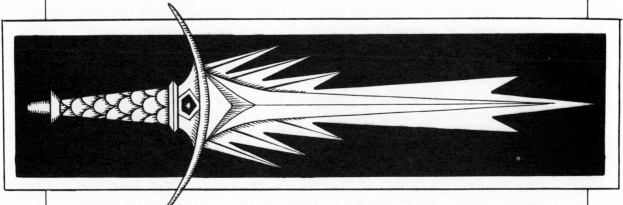

The dragons unquestionably understood Zaran's simple orders — all escaping Lemurians were to be destroyed. So the tireless killers menaced the sky, their eyes and sensors probing for any sign of movement. Even at this incredible range the dragons were deadly accurate, clearly deserving of their reputation as the ultimate in war machinery. The highly intelligent mass murderers worked independently, without constant instructions. A single order set into motion an endless chain of logical action, in this case, true atrocities, halted only when the initial order had been fulfilled. Had Merlin not been one of the hunted, he would have better appreciated the genius of Zaran's work; but at the moment he could concentrate only on trying to save 156 Lemurians from being slaughtered by the beasts. The Lemurians had no weapons and although Merlin was armed with his Excalibur blaster, it was totally useless at long range and equally ineffective — on full power, even at close range — against a dragon in his prime. Consequently, in order to survive, Merlin had to recall every tactical trick he had ever learned — and then invent new ones. The masses of people moved only at night, and then only when assured that the dragons were patrolling elsewhere above Lemuria. Even these nocturnal travels became increasingly difficult, since the beasts, for some reason, were converging more and more in and around the valley.

The hills were honeycombed with caves, so hiding was not difficult. But Merlin did not want to stay in the caves forever, and trapped by the constant dragon surveillance. No fires could be lit, no food could be gathered, and certainly no escape was possible. But even with the dragons' never-ending proximity, the Lemurians patiently and quietly obeyed Kara's and Arthur's orders. They would have to wait it out. And wait they did,

while the fire–blasting creatures roamed the skies freely and even targeted the caves. Rocks melted. Sand took fire. Cave walls burst. But the
Lemurians remained hidden.

Then one day the dragons abruptly stopped the destruction and flew off.
Dehydrated and weak, the half–roasted refugees still waited until Kara
finally gave the order that released them into the open air. But the land
they found was a smoking, horizonless boneyard. The beasts had done
their work well: not one survivor could be found. Between molten rocks
and bursts of fire, the people from the caves huddled together, but they
would not yet feel grateful for their survival — they could only mourn the
deaths of their friends and loved ones. When at last Merlin, Kara, and
Arthur counted the toll only fifty–seven plus Mupi were still alive. The
small craft had been destroyed, but miraculously the hidden transport
had survived the attack. Uncertain as to how long the dragons would be
gone, Merlin constantly watched the skies. And, since the group had no
idea whether the sudden withdrawal was permanent or not, Kara and
Arthur hastily ushered them into the transport and departed at once,
even farther into the interior of present–day China. The flight seemed
almost endless as the craft winged westward even beyond China, finally
putting down in a region once known as Sumeria.

Debarking, the passengers found themselves in a lush river valley. Here,
to their astonishment, they were met by people who at once began literally to worship them — having thought of their descent from the heavens
as miraculous. Being treated as gods did not please the Lemurians, who
knew themselves to be all too mortal. But no matter how much they
resisted the idea, their primeval hosts continued to worship them. However, after a week of this behavior, Kara, determined to end the idolatry,
finally insisted that unless they were treated as human beings she and the
others would leave. At this, the inhabitants relented somewhat, but they
never fully abandoned the idea that gods had come to live in their midst.

The Lemurians had already endured much and they knew they could not
go back to their dead continent. They agreed that this fertile land was the
perfect place for them to settle. Weary of being pursued, and ready to
start anew, Kara, Arthur, and the others came to call the valley home. In
time the indigenous peoples would need a gentle push toward civilization, and with what little possessions they had stacked in the transport,
the Lemurians could bring a touch of modernity to their kind if unedu-
cated hosts.

The weeks passed into months as the group threw themselves into the
arduous work of rebuilding their damaged lives. Though Merlin helped
with the building of new housing for the group and teaching the inhabitants agricultural techniques, his mind remained riveted far across the
world in Alta. The hard work of erecting a new home left everyone

exhausted, but still the brooding prince could see that his wife, his parents, and the others were happy — secure in the knowledge that they were safe at last from the dragons.

After most of the harder work was completed and the Lemurians were beginning to settle down, MaReenie went for her daily visit to Kara's hut. Mupi and Merlin were out tending the newly-planted fields.

"Mama K! Mama K!" MaReenie called out as she carried her little boy over the threshold of his grandmother's house. Apparently MaReenie had arrived early — no one seemed to be at home.

"I'm over here, my dear," Kara called out, "out in the back."

MaReenie hurried to the rear of the red-brown painted hut and out to the small garden plot in which Kara was kneeling. "Mama K," she asked, "are you very busy?"

"No, why?" Kara replied as she got up to greet her daughter-in-law. Tenderly she kissed little Arak, then started to walk back to her house. MaReenie followed.

"I'd like to talk to you about . . ." She hesitated.

"Merlin." Kara finished.

"Yes. How did you know?" asked MaReenie, momentarily forgetting her mother-in-law's powers. Then, remembering: "Oh, of course." She smiled. "You heard my thoughts." But now the serious look on her face returned. "Oh Mama K, I'm so worried about him. He's determined to go to Alta and confront Zaran. I have tried talking to him but nothing I say will alter his thoughts. What can I do?"

Lovingly Kara took her grandson into her arms and smiled at him. Then she answered, "MaReenie, I have already spoken to him about his wish for revenge. And at that time he was resolute." Unhappily she gazed in her daughter-in-law's eyes. "I feel this passion can only bring sorrow." Kara placed Arak on the mat, then stared out of the opening in the wall. "Once we began to settle down here I thought he would forget Zaran in his happiness. Unfortunately I was wrong."

MaReenie's eyes welled up with tears. "I just can't stay here while he goes off to be killed by that madman."

"My dear, you have a child to raise. What else can you do?"

"Well, if he goes — I mean, when he goes — I'm going with him!"

"What about little Arak?"

"I'll take him with me, and Mupi too!"

"I think you're foolish!" Kara spoke sharply. "Don't you realize a woman with a child in tow will be more of a liability than an asset? If you feel you must go then leave the child with us. He'll be much safer here . . . Until you come back."

"I don't know how I can leave him." MaReenie clutched at little Arak as if he were already being left with Kara.

"Have you talked about your feelings to Merlin?" asked Kara.

"Oh no!" MaReenie said dejectedly. "He's so preoccupied with his own thoughts."

"My dear, you must. And I urge you to meditate, my child. Then you will find what is right for you. I don't want either of you to leave. You shouldn't spend your youth like this. Both of you are missing so much. I wanted you to experience years of happiness together in peace. Instead, you both have begun your life together with danger lurking every-where."

MaReenie was resolute. "No matter what, I can't let him leave without me. Not now! Besides, life without him would be worthless. Mama K, it's taken me so long to realize that I was always in love with him. I was just too stupid to know it. So now that I have him I won't lose him again. Better to enjoy a short time with him than spend a lifetime alone."

"What are you saying, MaReenie?" responded Kara. "Don't talk like that. You both will be all right. Merlin will take care of the two of you!"

Afterwards the two women drank hot herbal tea while little Arak played on the mat covering the dirt floor. They continued to talk for a long time. By late afternoon MaReenie returned to her house and her waiting hus-band. Pensively Kara stood in her own doorway, watching the young mother and child walk toward their new home. The rays of the setting sun stained the landscape red when Kara turned to answer the call of her husband coming home from the fields.

28
Homeward Bound

*I*n the course of Zaran's attack on Lemuria, the ruler of Atlantis kept a keen eye on dragon activities. Also, to ensure his success, he employed a vast fleet of military aircraft to help cover the areas not tended by his beasts. The five super–missiles had been fatal to the peaceful continent. While each had been precisely targeted to ensure maximum results, it was the delicately balanced natural formation of that part of the world that affected the greatest destruction. Touched off by the explosives, the land became a rumbling mass of volcanic and seismic devastation, which was compounded by fallout and incredible winds. Thanks to Zaran's inhumanity the pitiful survivors were offered no assistance. Indeed, Zaran took pleasure in waiting for them to perish cruelly in the aftermath of the destruction. A unique people were destroyed and their peaceful way of life wiped from the face of the earth. Those who found safety in other parts of the world would start again, but they never would regain the paradise that was once Lemuria.

In contrast, on Atlantis, the master of violence grew stronger than ever before. Zaran rejoiced at his victory. He supposed he had eradicated Merlin and the rest of his enclave, and his military advisors — not wishing to incur his wrath — encouraged his fantasy of complete victory. Quickly these same advisors began bringing into Alta a stream of representatives from the remaining cultures and inferior races from all over the globe; and soon the mad ruler was being hailed as a god.

For Merlin, time ticked by slowly as he prepared to return to his native land with the stubborn MaReenie in tow, though they decided to take Kara's advice — and leave little Arak with his grandparents. Likewise, Mupi also would remain behind. The loyal creature was torn between his love for Merlin and his newfound bond with little Arak. Moreover, like Kara and Arthur, Mupi had had enough of violence. Luckily, the decision to stay was not his to make; Merlin ordered the creature to protect his son and his son's grandparents.

The first hurdle to overcome in his attempt to journey to Alta was the matter of the trip itself. The faithful transport was by now running low on power. However, with Arthur's help Merlin redirected the energy generated by the ship's console power pack. It would now run the craft itself instead of the massive electronic equipment on board. Flying manually would be necessary but the trip would not be a long one — the transport, now stripped to the bare hulk, would fly very fast.

Beyond making rudimentary travel arrangements, Merlin left the rest of the details open. He hoped to contact the underground, if one remained, at Kobbal. On the other hand, if the underground had been disbanded and no help could be found, then he and MaReenie, disguised as envoys from Sumeria, would present themselves personally to Zaran. Both Kara and Arthur felt the whole venture was too chancy, but by now they knew that Merlin would no longer heed their counsel — not while a single dragon remained alive.

Finally the day of departure arrived. And, as the craft ascended into the sky, MaReenie watched the figures of Arthur, Kara, little Arak, and Mupi shrink into dots on the ground below. Friends had also come to wish them a safe journey and victory; but tearfully MaReenie could only gaze at her tiny family that she was leaving behind.

"Why the tears, darling?" Merlin teased. "We won't be gone that long. And besides, between Mother and Mupi, our son will be completely spoiled."

"Oh I know he'll be well cared for. It's just that I've never left him before and, well, I'm afraid I'll miss something new that he'll do!"

"Well, I promise you when this is over, we'll never have to leave home again," Merlin said. "Besides, you didn't have to come. I'm perfectly willing to set the ship down if you'd rather stay."

"No, of course not. I made up my mind. I don't want you to leave me behind either. So I'm in a pickle."

MaReenie laughed and so did Merlin. But there was much to do now that flying the transport was to be done manually, so the two busily exchanged instructions, all the while keeping their eyes peeled for dragons. Once airborne and on course, Merlin found himself staring at the beauty beside him. Her alabaster skin was now tanned from working in the hot sun, and her once delicately manicured hands had become rough and calloused from handling a hoe and washing clothes in the river. Gone were the raven curls — instead, she wore her hair tightly braided into a coronet at the top of her head; and no longer did she wear elegant clothes. In fact, MaReenie was dressed like a savage peasant, but to Merlin she had never been more beautiful. He broke the silence.

"MaReenie, do you have any regrets?"

MaReenie turned to her husband and shot him a curious look. "What are you thinking about? I have no regrets — except one."

"What's that?"

"That I didn't marry you sooner."

Merlin leaned over to kiss her. After their lips parted, he grinned broadly and reflected, "But my darling, I didn't ask you sooner."

She answered, "I know, but I should have asked you."

For the remainder of the flight, the two reminisced about their life in Atlantis. For a split second, Merlin wished he could turn back the clock and do a few things differently, but he instantly realized that he would probably have done everything the same way.

MaReenie seemed to second him. "Merlin dear, we could never go back, even when Zaran and his beasts are gone. You and I are so different today. We want something else out of life. With our parents' help we've found the true importance of life. Atlantis is too steeped in materialism, too ready for violence. We might have been able to teach them a different way of life when Lemuria was still strong. But not now — I'm afraid to say that for the most part the Atlantians are lost to their philosophy of conquest and superiority."

"I hope you're wrong about the Atlantians being lost to their philosophy. After all, it's for their future — and our son's — that I'm returning."

"Merlin, I'm afraid that you'll have to leave Atlantis to her own future. But have you really thought about Arak's?"

"All right," he said, "let's hear your plans." And with that, MaReenie described her blueprint for a school to teach Arak and the other children the Lemurian way, yet integrating the best of the Sumerian beliefs and Atlantian knowledge. She touched on every aspect of their lives, including their future children.

"*Future* children?" Merlin almost lost control of the craft. "MaReenie, our *present* child gives us plenty to worry about."

"You mean our present *children*."

"What? . . . Why didn't you tell me before we left?"

"Merlin, darling, would it have made a difference? Would you have given up your plan to return to meet Zaran?" She challenged him.

"I might have postponed it!" He answered. "One thing for sure, you *wouldn't* be in this plane right now."

"No, my love, we'll do this thing together. It's for our children and their children. Besides, as you said before, this won't take that long and I'm perfectly healthy. So lead on, Prince Merlin! You and your princess will conquer the future."

Merlin now initiated his descent, and approximately twenty–five feet from the ground, the craft gave a violent jolt — followed immediately by the deafening crack of an explosion. After that Merlin remembered nothing.

He had no idea of how much time had passed, or where he was, when the tearing pain in his head brought him back to consciousness. But he seemed to be in something like a hospital bed, and he could make out someone in a doctor's gown through the fog of pain.

"Where —" He tried to sit up, but the doctor held him back gently.

"You're with friends, so just rest for a bit."

"And my wife?" The pain made talking almost impossible.

"She's here too! Don't concern yourself. You're both safe," he reassured him.

"What . . . happened?"

"You were spotted by Rajak," said the doctor. "Zaran had all the call letters and markings changed on all craft, along with the channel frequencies. So the dragon knew the instant you didn't answer his call that you were an enemy. Naturally, he fired on you but just caught the rear end of the transport. Fortunately, you and your wife were blown out by the force of the explosion. I hope there wasn't anyone else with you because that monster Rajak finished off the craft just seconds after you two were thrown clear."

"There . . . was no one . . . else." Merlin was ready to faint from the pain, but he managed to ask how the probing eyes of the dragon had failed to spot him and MaReenie.

"You were lucky," the doctor explained. "You rolled into a ravine behind some rocks concealed under leafy brush. It's the only vegetation in the entire area. That dragon circled for a long time before he was satisfied you'd both been disintegrated with your craft. And another thing, the underground doesn't meet at that field anymore. It just happened that one of our kids was playing out there and witnessed the attack. Otherwise we never would have found you."

Merlin closed his eyes, gritting his teeth against the pain as he asked, "How . . . is my wife?"

"You've both sustained very serious injuries," said the doctor, "but your chances of recovery are fairly good. Right now the best thing for you to do is to sleep and let your body start its healing process. I'm giving you something that will put you out for a while."

When Merlin awoke next morning he still felt racking pains in every part of his body, but somehow they seemed less acute. With an effort, he lifted his head to see where he was; then he remembered the doctor's face looking down at him and telling him he was safe. As he was gently putting his aching head back down on the pillow, two men walked into the room.

"Well, I'm glad to see you are awake," said the short fat one whom they called Gip. "You have some nasty injuries! How do you feel?"

"I'm fine, but how's MaReenie?" Merlin was anxious about his wife. They said nothing, but from the look on their faces, Merlin had his answer.

Gip spoke softly. "We're sorry. We tried everything we could, but her injuries were too severe and they were compounded by her pregnancy. It was too much for her."

Merlin's pain was instantly replaced by grief. "No! No!" he screamed, thrashing his way out of his bed and hurling the men aside. Somehow he would bring her back to life himself. It was only after a violent struggle that the men managed to pin him to the floor. Gip quickly produced a syringe. Before Merlin realized what happened his strength had left his body and he was again dropping into unconsciousness.

Four hours later he was awake again. This time, though, he found three men watching over him — Gip, his companion, and the doctor from the night before who now walked over to the bed. The doctor touched Merlin's shoulder reassuringly.

"You're going to be all right," he said. "But only if you don't try to jump out of bed."

"What's the point?" Merlin's voice was toneless. "She's dead isn't she?" The doctor did not comment. Instead the fat man began probing for answers.

"Look we need some information. What's your name and what were you doing in our old transport?"

Merlin ignored the questions, instead he turned his head to stare at a painting on the wall across the room. "You know she was an artist; as a matter of fact, the most honored and decorated in all of Atlantis." He was weeping quietly. "And now, our young son will never see any of her work."

The men exchanged puzzled glances. "You can't be — you aren't . . . Prince Merlin? We thought all of you had died in the bombing of Lemuria."

But Merlin interrupted. "I'd like to see my wife before . . ." he couldn't bear to say it, " . . . before you bury her."

"Yes, of course," the doctor agreed. "But you cannot be moved. You have suffered some internal bleeding from your broken ribs. I'll have her body brought in here."

The doctor returned in minutes, pushing the hospital bed which held MaReenie's body. Against the doctor's instructions, Merlin forced himself

to sit up. When the doctor rolled the bed next to Merlin's, the torn and broken patient turned over and gently grasped MaReenie's head with his right hand. Miraculously, she was unscarred. A lifetime of memories flooded Merlin's mind as he studied the face so beautiful, even in death. Wanting to memorize every feature, he heaved himself closer to her and kissed her for the final time, then his head dropped to caress her neck. The doctor tried to pull him away, but he stubbornly resisted until, at last, the pain in his body weakened his grip. With help he rolled back over to his bed, overcome by an overwhelming emptiness. Silent and depressed he stared up at the white ceiling.

Merlin no longer even took notice of the men. In a world of his own, he suddenly burst out, aloud. "Kara was right. This revenge has cost me the thing I held most dear." Suddenly his voice became strong, seeming almost to reverberate from the walls.

"Zaran you bastard! You must pay for your evilness!"

Then Merlin's voice fell as he closed his eyes.

"And I . . . I must pay everlastingly for her death."

29
The Die is Cast

Merlin spent the next few months recuperating from his injuries. His left leg, ankle, and arm were broken. So too were six left ribs, while his left shoulder had been dislocated. His entire face and body were scored, swollen, or shriveled by deep cuts, bruises, and burns. A scar like a ravine crossed his forehead. The doctors told him he was lucky to be alive and he agreed, although not on his own account. By surviving, he had been given a second chance — a second chance to destroy the beasts and their creator.

While convalescing, he listened to Atlantian broadcasts as part of his daily routine. The national daily weather forecasts, once a largely overlooked feature, now included up–to–date seismographic reports on volcanic eruptions and earthquakes, not only across the continent but even in all other parts of the earth. When he asked about the sudden changes in the weather patterns he learned that conditions had become volatile just after the bombardment of Lemuria. The newly formed volcanoes and frequent quakes were altering weather systems all over the earth. Now the polar icecaps had begun to melt, causing widespread coastal flooding that added to Atlantis' woes. In an effort to appease the populace Zaran filled the airwaves with lies about the erratic conditions. He told his people that Atlantian scientists soon would have all these tremors under control. To divert their attention from the disaster of crumbled roadways and the personal tragedy of smashed homes, Zaran also began a crusade against purported dissidents within the State who were attempting to undermine his government and its scientific work that would save them from the geological cataclysms. In the wake of the broadcasts came a stream of arrests, but those incarcerated were known to be innocent people. This happened so frequently that the citizenry began to feel paranoid about the police squads that continually patrolled the streets of Alta. In reality the police were attempting to crush the underground movement, which by now had become very strong, but they had very few leads and under pressure from Zaran they saw no choice but to make random arrests. Soon the prisons had become dangerously overcrowded.

While Merlin regained his strength, he remained safely hidden, though in order to allay suspicions he was moved to several different underground facilities. By the time he was able to walk, rumors of Zaran's many corruptions were running rampant throughout Alta. And when Merlin began to plan his trip back to his home city the rumors were compounded by the announcement of plans for new improved dragons. As yet there were no live specimens, only preliminary designs of a prototype, but the news stirred the scientists involved. Merlin became more anxious than ever to put his own plan into action but wisely reconsidered — he would have to wait for Zaran to be in the right place at the right time.

Besides, security was unbelievably tight around Zaran; the doctor was finding it harder than ever to get more information about the ruler's movements. Merlin impatiently waited all the while, though his torn and broken body was visibly mending. The doctor had to keep reminding him that he would need every bit of his strength and more if he was going to tackle Zaran on his own ground; and besides that he would need a clear head, not one addled by revenge and hate. Restoring the strength of his body was easy in comparison to the task of healing his mind, but Merlin set about to clear away the dead mental baggage of the past. He meditated every day, reminding himself that the past was indeed dead, the future, as yet, nonexistent. Only today counted.

One morning the "today" he thought would never arrive finally came. Everything was ready. The underground had done its job. Now it was Merlin's turn to do his.

Rain was falling when he arrived at Alta. Met by a group of uneasy women, he was informed that plans had been changed. Zaran was on his way to Kobbal where he would be much more accessible — the tyrant now had dissidents among his own guards who recently had offered the underground secret help. Though another secret rebel group in Alta had been discovered and all its members executed, and although surveillance had consequently been stepped up, Merlin was still able to receive instructions about which transit tubes would safely take him to his destination. He was also notified of his next contact. At first he was genuinely afraid of being spotted, but on his way to Kobbal he happened to glance at his bearded reflection in a rain–splashed window of the elevated vehicle; for the first time he realized how much his appearance had altered since leaving his native land. MaReenie had been right. Not only had his looks changed completely but he thought differently since those innocent days in Alta.

Hours later he arrived at Kobbal. It was late at night. The rain had stopped but the ground was soaked. In the clear air his shoes clicked loudly as he walked on the wet pavement that led to his contact. He entered a group of clustered buildings and a uniformed man suddenly appeared in front of him.

"There's a curfew in this city, stranger," he announced. "Let me see your travel pass."

The underground had been thorough. Merlin produced his papers. The uniformed man studied them carefully. Merlin put his hands into his pockets, quietly indifferent. His interrogator looked him over very carefully, then said, "Prince Merlin, royalty is usually better dressed."

Merlin didn't flinch. He chuckled, "*Merlin*? I'm Covar, farmer from the outskirts of Alta. I'm visiting my cousin here at Unit 7678 on the eleventh floor."

"Very good," the man laughed. "You stay cool in a crisis. You'll need that when you meet your old childhood friend." He seized Merlin's arm and marched him to the lift, where he pressed the eleventh-floor button. "You've changed a great deal. I wasn't sure you were the right person but that's good — perhaps Zaran won't be so quick to recognize you, either."

Now Merlin realized that he was still among friends and let out a great sigh of relief. The quiet family fed him and gave him a bed, but did not offer much in the way of conversation; they sensibly preferred to know only what was absolutely necessary. By now Merlin had come to understand these precautions. He too kept his own counsel, except to thank the family.

Next morning he found the uniform of Zaran's personal guard on the chair beside the bed. He washed, shaved — leaving only a mustache — and then dressed. The scars on his face momentarily frightened him. His beard, newly grown to hide the effects of the accident, had covered them so completely that he had already forgotten about them. Then he grinned and told the mirror, "I think I've seen you before — in a horror story." Then he walked out into the next room for final approval. "Here's your helmet," said his host. "You look like a pretty tough customer with that face full of scars."

"Yes, it's as though I've been in a war!"

"Well, in a few minutes you'll be getting yourself into one, that's for sure," the man's wife observed.

Merlin stood there looking at his two hosts and their children. He had so many things he wanted to tell them, but he knew better. "Thank you very much," was all he said. They smiled back at him, replying, "Take care of yourself."

Then he departed, to meet the uniformed contact who was waiting outside the building. Quickly the two boarded an idling hovercraft. It was a new military model — with long-range travel capabilities as well as heavy firepower. En route to the scientific complex from which he had escaped almost two and a half years before, Merlin was briefed on the plan and Zaran's movements. When they arrived Merlin and his guide entered the security area. Their falsified documents got them through without difficulty: the guards were told that Merlin was a new highly trained replacement for Zaran's personal protection. This checked out immediately through the security equipment. Finally they arrived at the door that would lead Merlin into Zaran's missile laboratory. Here, his guide gripped Merlin's arm, smiled, winked "good hunting," and was gone. Merlin hesitated for a moment, then took a breath and stepped across the threshold into a destiny he was now powerless to alter.

30
Merlin's Bittersweet Revenge

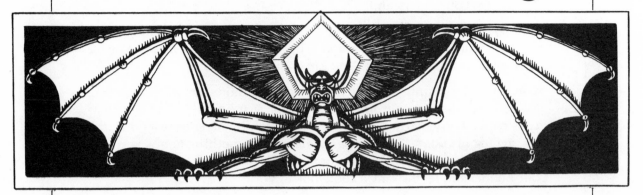

On entering the vast control room the nervous Merlin was immediately met by a guard, to whom he confidently presented his pass and all the other necessary documents that had been supplied by his allies. The stern–faced guard carefully examined the pass, then looked Merlin up and down several times, missing nothing.

During all this, Merlin remained impassive. It was only when he caught sight of the familiar figure across the room that he began to feel unnerved. Facing away from Merlin, intent on the floor–to–ceiling panel of lights, screens and controls, the angry Zaran was loudly rebuking a technician. He did not notice the two men who approached him.

"Excuse me, sire." The guard came rigidly to attention. Zaran spun on him, his face a hurricane of angry impatience.

"What do you want? Can't you see I'm busy?"

The guard swallowed. "I must beg your forgiveness, but I have your orders to bring you the replacement immediately upon his arrival." Half smiling, the guard handed Zaran the documents and backed off, bowing, as Zaran and Merlin faced each other again.

Haughtily Zaran took a cursory look at the replacement, glanced at his qualifications, and said, with a note of sarcasm, "Well, I see you come highly recommended. Further, you're trained in all the new fighting techniques and you're also a pilot. Good! You'll need even the smallest item of that knowledge for this job."

"Yes, sire," Merlin replied, in a North Atlantean accent.

"Well . . ." Zaran paused. "What's your name?"

"Covar, sire."

"Yes, yes, Covar. I must tell you that some of your predecessors haven't fared very well. I don't tolerate incompetence, and at this level of service any failure to do your duty will result in the forfeiture of your life." Zaran smiled. "Do you understand?"

"I understand completely," Merlin looked straight ahead. "But I assure you that I will do my duty no matter what sacrifices I must make in order to complete my assigned task. You can count on that, sire!"

"You certainly sound determined." Zaran's humor seemed to improve. "I see here in the report from your superior that he recommends you as my personal bodyguard." Zaran was now looking Merlin straight in the face, eyeing his scars. Then he said, "There's something about you that looks familiar." Merlin's heart stopped. "Perhaps you should take off your helmet and let me take a good look at you."

Merlin began unlatching his helmet strap. And at that moment an alarm went off — accompanied by a voice on the broadcast system, warning of an ensuing riot outside the building. Explosives were being thrown and the rioters were well armed. All personnel were directed to report to their stations. Within a matter of minutes the area was closed and almost completely vacated except for Zaran and ten personal guards, including Merlin. By now Merlin had drawn his weapon and was listening to another announcement over the speaker: apparently the riot was more widespread than first reported. Zaran ordered the others to go and see what help they could be; only Covar, he said, would stand by him. Merlin smiled to himself; Zaran could not have played into his hands more perfectly.

As soon as the others had left the area, Merlin went to the door and secured it from within so no one could enter without proper authorization. Then he turned and faced his former friend — who now had drawn his own weapon. The time had come. Without warning Merlin fired at the unsuspecting Zaran with his Excalibur. His blast missed the astonished ruler but struck the light-control panel, touching off a cascade of brilliant sparks as it damaged some of the controls. This in turn caused the lights all over the city to dim. But Merlin and Zaran were aware only of the sudden darkening in the control room. Zaran leaped to cover behind a heavy desk.

"What in damnation are you doing, you stupid son of a whore!" he screamed as he aimed his weapon at Merlin. "It's the last thing you'll ever do on this planet! I'm your ruler!"

Quickly Merlin ducked behind the main console in the center of the room. "You're not my ruler. Zaran, you evil bastard," he called out as he let off another blast. "You didn't recognize me, did you. Well, you're not to blame. After all, you've never seen a dead man come to life before, have you, you murdering reptile." Repeatedly Merlin fired off three more shots, exchanging rounds with Zaran while both men zigzagged around the room, seeking the right opportunity.

"Merlin, you snivelling wimp! You're alive!" Zaran smiled at the prospect of personally punishing his adversary. But when Zaran attempted to reach the controls in order to call for help, Merlin fired at his hand but shot away the panel instead. Zaran responded to this with a string of high–pitched yells of uncontrolled, insane rage. Merlin knew he was gaining the upper hand. Simply by mocking Zaran, he would drive his adversary to a fatal mistake.

"You keep missing me, you imbecile," Merlin called back casually. "You've annihilated a whole race but you can't seem to hit your main target. You were talking about incompetence a few minutes ago. You said, 'I don't tolerate incompetence; failure to do your job will result in forfeiture of your life.' Well, you mindless excuse for a man, I'm still here. Therefore, *you're* going to forfeit *your* life for being such a feeble minded, arrogant murderer."

"I'll show you who's feeble minded!" Zaran shrieked back. By now he was literally foaming at the mouth as he crawled along the floor to get a better shot at Merlin. "You'll never leave this room alive!"

Confident in his tactics of taunting, Merlin continued to blast at Zaran's elusive form, all the while stabbing verbally at the ruler's ego. "Listen, you animal, I don't give a damn about escaping. I'm here for one purpose — to destroy your creatures and put you out of your misery. I have the ideal soldier's incentive — nothing to live for. Your damn beasts have killed MaReenie and she was all that ever mattered to me. So you see, you lunatic, you've created an avenging monster."

By now the control room had taken a terrific beating. Both men were missing their targets in the dim light and instead were hitting the levers, switches, dials, panels of buttons, and even some of the few remaining lights. To get into a more advantageous position, Merlin gradually maneuvered himself around the console. But just as he had his former friend in perfect range, the weapon jammed, and Merlin ducked down — barely in time to avoid a perfectly withering barrage from Zaran. The latter's self–control now seemed to return.

"Well, well!" he laughed. "A defective weapon — what a pity! Do you have any last words?"

"Don't fret, my 'friend', I'm still here," Merlin replied, laughing. "And you can be sure I'm not going anywhere till I step over your carcass."

Meanwhile, the diversionary battle outside the complex continued to rage, as the underground factions consolidated their positions against the government troops. The well–organized rebels were too well armed and commanded to retreat — and too much was at stake for them to fail. Thus they had gotten Merlin into the control room that controlled the fire of the government's heavy attack weapons. And now, that very room was being destroyed by a pair of excalibur weapons in a personal duel to the death. It would be the decisive factor in the battle that raged outside.

And for Merlin, the duel had taken a turn for the worse. Without a weapon, he was a duck in a shooting gallery, and he had to keep himself continuously hidden from Zaran's fire. He knew his only hope of surviving would be to keep Zaran's temper out of control, and hope that the ruler would finally drop over the edge of sanity. So Merlin continued to laugh, jeer, and mock, and presently he could perceive that his work was bearing fruit as Zaran literally began to sob with rage.

"Calm down, little man," Merlin called out. "Crying like a baby won't improve your bad aim. I assure you that if the tables were turned, your cadaver would already be starting to stink. Besides, my friend, remember that you're wrecking all your fancy new warmaking equipment. That hardly makes sense — don't you agree?"

Merlin's last barb brought Zaran back to his senses. Realizing that his troops ourside might well be facing defeat, he raced for the door. It would not open. Merlin knew that the combination code had been changed by the underground people, but Zaran did not.

Merlin now hurled his malfunctioning excalibur at Zaran's arm. Zaran screamed and dropped his own weapon. Instantly Merlin was on him, sending him stunned to the floor with a single blow of his fist. As Merlin leaped on him to make the kill, Zaran's outstretched hand felt a weapon. He seized it and took aim, only to have his arm pulled almost out of its socket by Merlin. But in a surge of strength Zaran rolled free, leaped up, and struck Merlin with the weapon, gashing his head badly. Now it was Merlin's turn to roll over as Zaran got off a shot at him. This time Zaran's aim was true — or would have been had his blaster not misfired. Zaran dove to grab the other weapon but Merlin beat him to it. Now both men faced each other with jammed weapons — which they could use only to lunge at one another, parrying with the Excalibur blade, slashing and wrecking the whole room as well as themselves.

Presently Merlin could see that Zaran was losing. But Merlin too was tired of the fight, for he had completely vented all his anger. At one point he felt almost sorry for the pathetically injured creature before him. He even thought of breaking off his attack. However, when Zaran sensed Merlin's softening, he drove in even harder. Just then, a terrible blow bounced off the hilt of Merlin's weapon. It struck one of the discharge buttons — and a fiery blast smashed Zaran to the floor. Stunned by the surprise explosion, Merlin stared dully at Zaran's twitching, blood–spouting, shattered near–corpse. A second later Zaran's body was completely still.

Merlin's feet were glued to the floor. He could not believe what he was feeling. After all that had happened he felt sick at having killed Zaran. How could that be? Zaran was everything evil that had ever crawled on the earth, yet Merlin felt he should mourn not for a dead murderer but for the childhood friend that was lost somewhere inside that insidiously deranged mind. Somehow, a moment later, however, he found himself outside in the empty corridor and heading towards the craft.

Back in the control room, Zaran slowly opened his eyes. Lying on the floor, he took an account of his injuries. He was a dead man. His blood was pouring in torrents from the wounds received by the slashes of Excalibur. But the blaster, which should have killed him outright when it blew a great hole in his stomach, had also given him a brief lease on life by sealing the hole with heat from its shot. However, what little sanity he had left was completely wiped away by his hatred for Merlin. Slowly he began the arduous task of pulling himself toward the main console — despite the bellowing pain in his torn body. In one agonizing effort he reached his goal and, miraculously, with all the destruction around him, found that the controls he needed were still intact. Nearly fainting, he dragged himself up to the console and lifted the lid that protected the sequenced number controls. Then he made careful mental calculations and adjusted each number in the correct order. This done, he managed to push the master lever and place his hand over the screen for identification. Then he waited and watched as the lights clicked into sequence. But when the announcement came over the system, Zaran did not hear it. His mind had drifted out of consciousness; it was trying to alleviate the torture of his body. Yet deep within his subconscious he found the strength to force himself out of his faint. He had one more task to complete before he died.

While Merlin raced to find an exit from the secured building, he heard a different type of alarm go off. Frantically he found an information screen and saw the reason for the alarm. The main crystal system, controlling every power station in Atlantis, was on overload. He had twenty minutes to get out of the building and off Atlantis before the whole power system would detonate. As he finally reached the exit he found a colossal nest of frenzied Atlantians, desperately fighting each other in their attempt to get out the door. Merlin was among those who managed to break clear of the melee.

And now he saw another battlefield before him. The underground forces were holding off hordes of attackers who sought to board the flying craft. Merlin's allies shouted at him to hurry. He had to duck barrages of blasters as he made his way toward the vehicle. He even had to blast — and bandy with — his enemies until he and his companions were aboard. Then the craft pulled up and away while its four passengers watched the shouting, undulating masses disappear from view. Relief at their escape was instantly smothered by sorrow and depression as they heard the announcements on their communicator and watched the chaos below.

"What do you think caused the power overload?" Orlo asked Merlin.

"I don't know," Merlin said "The only thing I can assume is that with all the shooting we must have accidentally blasted something that set it off."

"What do you think's going to happen to Atlantis?" Krella asked.

"Nothing good. With all the tremors and earthquakes, I suspect the continent will go the way of Lemuria. But more than that, I'm afraid the rest of the world is also in for it. Why couldn't Zaran just have left well enough alone?"

Someone clicked on the communicator and an announcement came over the system. "Attention all dragons, this is your master, Zaran."

Everyone in the craft gasped, "He's alive!" Merlin whispered in disbelief. "He can't be. Half of his midsection was blown away."

The message continued in a halting voice. Zaran was obviously struggling to speak. "Your orders are to seek out and destroy any craft attempting to leave Atlantis. Merlin may be on one. You are to destroy him. Do not rest until you have completed your mission." There was a long pause.

Merlin put his face in his hands. "By the power of Atlantis," he said, in a near whisper, "when is it going to end?"

The voice again broke in. "This installation will detonate in two minutes taking with it . . ." There was a pause . . . "all of my dominion. I am dying; so too will my people . . ." Now a fit of coughing was heard. Then, "Rajak, carry out the . . . orders!"

The craft sped off at maximum speed, then shuddered and bucked as the exploding inferno began its destruction. Gone would be a people, a civilization and a technology that the world would have to wait many thousands of years to see again.

31
Nature Rebels Against Atlantis

From the speeding craft, the fugitives viewed the devastation. First the luminous explosion of white and yellow light burst into a mushroom cloud as if reaching for the sun. It ballooned out, blinding all who stood transfixed by its unimaginable brightness. Below the explosion, the earth trembled and rumbled with hatred at having been awakened — she would strike back with eruptions of her own. Volcanos rose where there had been peaceful meadows. The ground cracked and opened to swallow those who had dared to disturb her sanctity. Born of the explosions, hurricanes and tidal waves swept vast chunks of land into the ocean, and engulfed the rest in mile–high waves. The blackened sky was packed with ashes and smoke while the heavens poured out an unending residue of rain, snow, and hail. Ruin was king and death the emperor. The world's land masses would never look the same and much of life would be extinct forever.

Though Merlin's craft was well equipped to withstand the escape flight, those on board could think only of their loved ones, caught in the earth's turmoil below. They hoped against hope that theirs were among the survivors — but some would never know. And for now they had their own battle to fight. They had to withstand not only the elements but also the relentless beasts that sought them.

As previously planned, the group headed towards the Sumerian Valley. At first, they could see nothing but clouds and tidal waves. Though their instruments indicated that the land should be under the craft, they found only water and more water. At one point the continual fierce winds buffeted the craft with such great force that Merlin feared it would break apart. Somehow, the crew landed on the high peak of a mountain range — only to be struck at once by a crippling cold that was intensified by relentless gale–force winds. To survive, the group rapidly packed snow around and over the craft, then dug in themselves, to wait until the worst of it was over, whenever that might be.

After a few days, Merlin ventured out toward the valley. Although the snow continued to fall, the cold air had warmed slightly — but surf still broke at the mountain's foothills. Presently, the others joined Merlin, to gaze at the devastation all around them. Half buried in the snow and mud, the dead could be seen everywhere. Merlin and his friends buried whatever humans they found, and kept some animals for food. Many weeks had to pass before Merlin could fly the craft down toward the valley again, in the hope of seeing what was left of his family's house. All he learned, however, was that the once lovely village had been completely washed away. Nonetheless he landed, and searched for miles around the area, only to find decomposing corpses lying everywhere. On the second day of his grim quest, Merlin located Kara and Arthur. He was wrenched by grief as he looked at what remained of the two lovers, locked in their death embrace. At that moment he lost hope for the other two remaining family members — little Arak and Mupi. And, yet something drove him on — and after laying his parents' bodies to rest, the grieving Merlin began a frenzied campaign to find the two. He even enlisted the help of his friends, though they had long given up hope of finding anyone alive. Still, Merlin persevered, flying high in the hills outside the river valley. Then one day, hovering close to the sides of the high ground, he at last spotted the familiar shape of a feathered mass. Excitedly he landed, almost crashing into the hill, and he ran to the body of the creature.

Poor, battered Mupi, barely alive, was half frozen from exposure. Still strapped on his back was the body of a child. The child was dead. Merlin cried out in hopelessness. Kara's words again came back to haunt him. His revenge had cost him MaReenie, his parents, his homeland, and now his only link to the future — his son. But Mupi's barely audible whine brought him back to reality. He quickly removed the body from the animal's back, then gently set it down on the ground. Next he unstrapped the saddle from Mupi's back and began to examine the extent of the creature's injuries. There was little hope — yet Merlin carried his friend back to the craft. He took out what medical supplies were on board and hurriedly attended the only living remnant of his mangled life.

"Mupi, you mustn't die!" Merlin cried out. "Please don't leave me." The creature whined softly, barely audibly and Merlin realized that Mupi was trying to communicate to him what had happened.

"No, Mupi! Don't try to say anything about that now," Merlin ordered gently but firmly. "Just tell me where you're injured so I can help you." Racing against the clock, Merlin now began the Herculean task of patching Mupi back together. Under the most primitive conditions, practically without medical equipment, he worked diligently for hours, swiftly and calmly using every trick possible — including his Lemurian mind techniques. Yet Mupi was still just barely holding on to life. Then Merlin remembered his serum. It was on board among his things. Instantly he prepared the injection.

"Well, my friend, now you and I will at last see what kind of scientist I really am!" Merlin smiled as he forced the liquid into Mupi's vein. "If you live, I will be an eternally grateful genius. If you don't, I'll consider myself a complete failure — at everything."

Mupi winced at the shot, then lapsed into unconsciousness. After Merlin gently covered the creature, he leaned back against the side of the ship where he would keep a vigil while monitoring Mupi's vital signs. Hours passed. Night fell. The next day dawned and Mupi was still alive, though not yet conscious.

Because his pet had survived the long night, with vital signs now encouraging, the exhausted and grief–ridden Merlin took time out to bury the body of his young son. He marked the grave with one of his last remaining monuments of Atlantis — the head of his Platinum Hawk award. And then, in the cold of the hillside, Merlin talked to his child.

"My son." His voice quivered while tears froze on his face. "How great you could have been. You know you came from a great legacy. Your loving grandmothers were distinguished Lemurian women gifted with great talents and brilliant minds. And your grandfathers — they were Atlantians of the old line, filled with honor and goodness. They could have taught you much." Now Merlin's voice almost broke. "Your mother . . . Oh, my son! . . . She was so wonderful." He fell to his knees and sobbed. "She was a magnificent woman, a consummate artist of incomparable talent, a beauty — and my best friend . . . As for your father . . ." Merlin hesitated. "Well, he was a preoccupied, though well–meaning scientist. I know I could have been better — I hope to be something better." At that precise moment, however, Merlin could not see any future for himself except unhappiness, so he said, "First, though I must cure your playmate, Mupi, and then . . . and then, my handsome son, I have to take care of Zaran's plague on humanity."

As he knelt at the gravesite, Merlin felt totally defeated by his future. At last, however, he rose to his feet and returned to Mupi.

On the other side of the mountains the three underground survivors remained at the camp, growing steadily worried by Merlin's long absence. The dark sky continued to spew mixed torrents of rain, sleet, and snow. The days were not much brighter than the nights and the bitter freezing weather was becoming even colder. The two men and the woman huddled together for warmth, but even their fire seemed frozen. Finally they sealed the entrance to their ice igloo and waited either for Merlin's return or for the weather to change. They could do little else without any means of transportation although — fortunately — they were well supplied with provisions.

Yet back in the hills, Merlin remained with his charge. For five days he saw no change. On the sixth day, he was awakened by the flutter of Mupi's feathers and his weak but happy whining. Almost overcome with gratitude, Merlin wept tears of joy. Now he felt confident that he could endure what ever else life would bring. After all, he still had his loyal friend.

32

The Final Battle

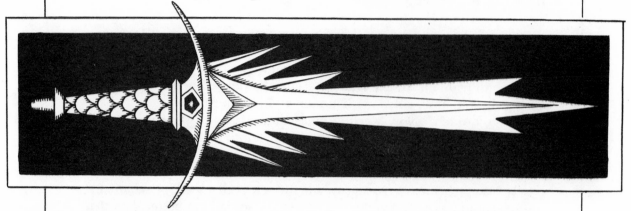

The dream seemed so real that the sleeping Merlin stirred in his secret tomb. Deep within the earth, he lay restlessly on his bier, desperate that his mind release him from his haunting dream. But it persisted.

"Has it been that long ago?" The Great One wondered, as his consciousness came back to his present state of rest. "I remember it as if it were yesterday, but I pray not to relive it. The past is dead." Slowly he attempted to relax again, to maintain a clear mind. Yet the dreams pursued him, images flashing in multiple scenes, jumbled and out of sequence. Now the present, then back in Lemuria, his childhood past, then among primitives in the world's southern continents — his uneasy thoughts cut in and out of history as if it all had happened in the twinkling of an eye. He didn't want to dream. He longed for an empty mind, free from any thoughts, happy or sad. He struggled for oblivion but it would not come. Reluctantly he went back . . . back to that remaining, pitiful pocket of civilization that waited for nature to relent in her rage at Atlantis for having raped her peace.

As he dreamed, Merlin watched himself gathering up Mupi and the others, then heading southward to the area once known as Port Quae; of course it too had been washed away from the earth's map. However, by heading inland beyond the coastal mountains, the group discovered a small settlement composed of refugees from Port Quae, Lemuria, and Atlantis. The tiny settlement, like the rest of the world, still suffered from nature's wrath. The quakes continued to rend the earth while torrents of rain steadily crashed down from the dark sky. However, to the newcomers the winds seemed warmer and softer than those in the north. The fugitives decided to stay and begin anew.

Suddenly Merlin could see, in his dream, one of Zaran's hunters coming in fast. He did not wish to risk the lives of the few ragged settlers, besides which he and Mupi had the rest of the world in which to hide from searching beasts. The two dashed for the craft, and in a moment they were up and away — with just seconds to evade the blasts from the oncoming killer. As Merlin looked back to see the dragon in hot pursuit, he realized that trying to out fly the beast was impossible. He must stay and fight.

Merlin's heart commenced pounding rapidly as he slept — and relived the manuvering and weaving in the clouds. He and the beast both missed many shots, but ultimately Merlin kept his head and took a few calculated risks that paid off. He smiled in his slumber at the sight of his victory over the creature. And then all memory of the dogfight vanished as Merlin's mind took him among the Egyptians. He could see his arrival with Mupi — and hear his own words: "Oh! What a wonderful creature! Everywhere we've been he's treated like a god and venerated as good luck." Amused now, he continued his slumber–visit to Egypt: "Those bright people took to the pyramid as if it were their own. And what fun teaching them medicine, science, and art." Merlin laughed as he remembered waking after one hundred years of sleep to find that the Egyptians were imitating his ritual in the hope of finding rebirth.

"Reborn? . . . Who can truly be reborn?" Merlin pondered once again as the tone of his fancies changed and he thought of his endless pilgrimages to evade the killers, the savage battles to destroy the beasts. In all his centuries of struggling, still two dragons remained — the first of Zaran's most perfected creations: "Where could they be, I wonder?" The passing centuries had made the beasts more resolute in their savage quest. Hatred and vengeance consumed them as they and their network of willing and unwilling spies watched for any signs of Merlin and his companion. In the end, few betrayed the Atlantian, and even those who did perished by the dragon's own fire.

The nightmare of those images made Merlin cry out — but not wake up. Again he concentrated, directing his brain to change the pictures. And presently he could settle back to another unfolding scene. These were different pyramids, embellished with the images of gods and their teachings. "There's Mupi's face!" Merlin laughed. "I told them not to do it . . . Oh no — not me! I'm just a teacher." He fondly remembered, then lamented their passing. Because it was there in the jungles, among those peaceful people, that he felt most at home. And here was another scene from another time. And the voices that kept saying it wouldn't work. "You'll see. There will never be another hanging garden like this one." Oh, how Merlin wished to see it again . . .

But now the pictures picked up speed and zoomed forward in a blur — for many centuries — to the day of his crash landing of the fighter. He called out. "Are you hurt, Mupi? Well, there go our wings. I hope we like it here — because it's going to be hard to leave." Merlin looked at the foggy coastline of the land now known as the British Isles, and he wondered what this place would bring. He considered the mysterious lieu lines and their use as mental enhancers. Then as if his mind were a camera, it pulled back and out into the universe; instantly his whole life flashed before him. With wide-angle overview his thoughts became pessimistic. Everywhere he had encountered humanity, Merlin had taught the principles of peace and unity with the natural order. He had not only given freely of his vast knowledge of all areas of civilization; he had also taught how to develop one's mental capacities, to tap the best energies of the natural world, and to give positive energy to the world in return. Some kept faith with the teachings, while others inevitably fell into corruption and used the power to enslave their fellow men and women. Each time this happened, Merlin retreated further into his sense of failure and inadequacy. Often, he looked homeward toward Lemuria and mourned her passing. Nowhere on earth had a people attained such perfection. He longed for that life . . . but it was no more.

Again, in the tomb, he sighed deeply, as ever impatient. His mind wandered to the life-extension process he had invented — and its consequences. Through each new experience the teacher had certainly gained more understanding and wisdom, and yet, sadly, with every sleep, each much longer than the last, more of his acquired knowledge was lost.

Slowly Merlin began to sense a warning to awake. At first he ignored it. Here was proof that he was no longer the great scientist of Atlantis; rather, more and more, he was relying on his Lemurian mind techniques to gain new understanding. He himself was reaching a high state of spirituality, but whenever he awoke he entered a world that was turning away — more and more — from such powers, to seek technology and material wealth. Now in his sleepy state, he felt as if the same Atlantis had risen again and again, a new Zaran emerging with every age.

Then the tomb rumbled and shook as if in an earthquake. Shocked, he staggered to his feet just as a boulder toppled from the cavern wall onto his resting place.

"What's happening?" He said aloud. But in truth, he knew. Quickly he gave the still-sleeping Mupi a vigorous shake, took hold of his weapon, and left the tomb by a side exit. "Yes, they're here. Mupi, be careful. This may be our last shot."

By the time he and Mupi were outside, they saw what had happened to the village and how the resting place had been desecrated. Even Mupi cringed as Merlin raised his weapon to the sky and roared. "Those damn things won't quit! By Lemuria and Atlantis this is the last of it!" He then stepped out from where he was hiding and shot Xax at point–blank range with his blaster. Taken by surprise the small dragon was mortally wounded.

Merlin and Mupi now fled from the scene. Rajak also took to the air, stunned at what had happened but instinctively stalking his prey. Unexpectedly it was not Merlin he sought, instead Rajak fired at Mupi. This brought an enraged Merlin from behind a pile of rocks. He took careful aim at Rajak squeezed the trigger four times, and leaped back to shelter.

Now bolts of fire began striking the rocks as Rajak fired back. With steely precision the beast shriveled the surrounding ground, but carefully avoided any direct attack as he sought to bring Merlin back into the open. However, he saw nothing move, not even Merlin's creature. Inside the beast was burning to taste his victroy, but he did not, at the moment, wish to destroy the place. He could only circle and circle, probing every corner, keeping his eyes and sensors sharp.

Yet despite his armaments, Rajak was at a distinct disadvantage. Merlin and Mupi were in their own territory, and because Merlin had lived there for such a long time, he knew its every hiding place — and so did Mupi. With only his tail feathers singed, Mupi dove through the hidden opening of a cave where Merlin already waited.

"Are you all right?" asked Merlin. Mupi whined and showed his smoking tail.

"You were very lucky. Now you stay in here — I'm going to finish off that monster for once and for all!" In reply, Mupi rubbed against Merlin's crouching figure and conveyed a thought.

"What do you mean, I won't be able to destroy Rajak by myself?" Then he looked at the weapon in his hand and smiled. "I guess you're right. This thing isn't much good at long range, especially with Rajak. He's as well protected as he is powerful. I'll either have to be at point–blank range or somehow find a way to expose one of his vital areas. But I didn't see any obvious deterioration. Damn you, Zaran, why did you have to be so brilliant?"

Rajak was becoming increasingly impatient. In his old age, the dragon's temperament was growing more and more like his creator's — his ability to keep a cool head was quickly diminishing. But more important, he was also beginning to show some signs of failing strength. Throughout the thousands of years of pursuit, the dragon's sinews had gradually become less powerful, and just now the super–beast was feeling every bit his age. He had been the prize in Zaran's awful stable, and despite the fact that he was now the last of his kind, his monumental pride could not allow defeat. Over the centuries of pursuit, there was only one thing he wanted more than Merlin's death — the serum. The serum that would not only restore his diminishing strength but would bring him the ultimate power — life everlasting.

"Prince — Merlin" he called out in his iron, mechanical voice. Stunned, Merlin sat perfectly still. Even his thoughts came to a halt. "Prince — Merlin, you — are — alive. Give — me — the — serum."

Now Merlin's mind clicked: "So, it's the serum he wants. That means he *must* be weakening."

Mupi knew what Merlin was thinking. Again he warned his master of the danger, but Merlin refused to pay any attention. He was planning his kill.

"I — only — want — the — serum" Rajak loudly repeated, "Not — your — death."

Merlin muttered to himself sarcastically, "So all is forgotten if I hand over the serum." He huddled at the cave's opening and checked his weapon. "Well, *I* won't forget. I can *never* forget what that serum has cost me and the world."

This time Rajak's voice was a warning. "You — cannot — destroy — me — Prince — Merlin — Your — weapon — is — too — weak."

Cautiously Merlin peered out of the cave's entrance. Rajak was circling and hovering above. The area around the cave was flaming, and there was a great deal of turbulance as the monster swept close to the ground. Merlin now decided that before either one of them died he wanted to know how long he had been asleep, and what made Rajak and Xax come back.

"Rajak," he called out, "before I give you life everlasting, I want some answers." He began asking the questions that had baffled him for so long.

"You — were — very — clever — I — believed — you — dead — but — there — was — no — body — of — Mupi — and — Excalibur — was — not — in — the — tomb — I — have — answered — your — questions — now — give - me — the — serum."

Now the ancient Atlantian sucked in a deep breath, took up the blaster, and started out of the cave. Just then he was knocked to the side by a flurry of feathered wings as Mupi flew out and attacked the dragon's underside. Merlin desperately screamed wildly. "NO! NO! Mupi — *don't!*"

It was too late. The creature was at the dragon's underbelly, ripping at the protective plates with his beak and claws. Valiantly he held on while Merlin blasted at the beast's face, but the demon clutched Mupi in his claws, and ripped away his own plate while the courageously battling creature tenaciously held tight. Then, with a single flick of his claw, Rajak flung Mupi to the ground in a deadening thud.

All the while, Merlin's continual blasting of the green–black beast had done nothing to save Mupi, but when Merlin saw the dragon's exposed area, he reactivated the force of the blaster — aiming directly at the unprotected spot. Rajak was temporarily paralyzed by the blast; the next shot would finish him. And at that moment Excalibur only clicked. Paling, Merlin looked at his weapon. It was drained. But so was Rajak. Weakened and unable to spew forth his own fire, the beast lurched at Merlin — to slay him with bare talons. Merlin stood up, facing Rajak, waiting for him to come close enough. Then at last, with all his might, he drove the point of Excalibur into the exposed area of Rajak's body. The dragon's scream could be heard miles away as he attemped to rise in the air. He could not — the blow had been fatal. The last dragon of Atlantis fell from the sky, then slid soundlessly into the waters of a lake near the cave.

Merlin had not watched the dragon's death–fall, as he was rushing instead to Mupi's side. Gently he removed the dragon's plate from the creature's grip. Mupi whined softly as he told Merlin the unthinkable: he was dying. Merlin reached for the serum but Mupi shook his head, saying it was too late. Merlin knelt over his companion's body, allowing tears of angry, despairing, grief to overtake him.

"Oh, Mupi, why?" he finally asked. "Why did you do it?" The creature looked up and softly whined. Merlin felt the love that passed between them. "What am I going to do without you?" But Mupi no longer heard him.

Now Merlin felt totally alone. He was a living relic from another time and world. In his gloom, he laid face–down on the ground, crying not only for Mupi but for his destiny. Looking at the destruction around him, he agonizingly contemplated his life, his worth, and his possibilities. Why was it that death seemed so simple an answer? He recalled finding Kara and Arthur locked in their last embrace — peaceful in the ruins of Sumeria. But Merlin also remembered what he had said that day so long ago at his son's grave site. "Yes, yes," he resolved, "I must do better. After all I too come from that same great heritage." Reverently and sadly he buried

Mupi's body within the demolished stone circle.

When he had completed the task, he deliberately went over to the lake to look at the calm waters that had long stopped bubbling above the last dragon's body. How quickly the lake regained its placidity! Merlin took a long, hard look at the lake's still surface, its clear water. He could barely make out the vague silhouette of the beast, the weapon still jutting from its body.

With leaden feet he turned away from the sight and slowly returned to the cave. Pensively he sat at the opening for a long time. Where should he go? He was already beginning to feel the effects of being prematurely awakened from his hibernation. His ancient body was telling him to return to his sleep. All of a sudden, he felt a swift weakening of his body. He picked up his belongings, and looked toward the smoldering village, but turned and went deeper into the cave. There he lit his portable light and absentmindedly looked around at the rocky walls, their crystalline ceiling, set twinkling by the light's reflections. It was so like the cave at Lawal — the cave where his father and mother had told him of his heritage. "Yes" he said out loud. "This is where I'll stay." He reached for the closely guarded serum. Having injected the final dose, Merlin covered the opening of the cave with a large stone. He turned off his light and at last he slowly fell into a peaceful sleep.

But before long he was thinking of the future, and what his role would be, now that there were no more dragons, now that everyone he loved was gone.

"At last I'll be free . . . liberated from the beast's pursuit . . ." He sighed in relief, and began to formulate a plan. "Perhaps I should take on an apprentice . . . one to whom I would devote my full attention" . . . He visualized it happening. "But it should be a child . . . a small child, like my little Arak. No! Better, a baby." His mind continued to wander in and out of his scheme. "I must rebuild the circle . . . need more strength for a way of life . . . dignity for men and women . . . Lemuria was . . . no injustice . . . no greed . . . no . . ." gradually Merlin started slipping away from reality . . . "How long will it last . . . how much of my knowledge will be gone . . . when I awake . . ."

He was into the peaceful oblivion he had sought for so long.

Epilogue

*T*his time the Atlantian's sleep would continue for many hundreds of years. As his longest hibernation, it was perhaps his last, certainly his most peaceful. His task, which had commenced so long before, was finally completed. Now alone, he would find a new life, a rebirth. In the solitude of his twinkling cave he would gain new powers, new wisdom for his world ahead. In his never–ending quest to find what he had lost in Lemuria, Merlin had brought civilization and order to a suffering world. Though he grieved when the peoples he touched did not keep faith with his teachings, even with his tragic losses and in his great despairs, he continued to hope for a better world. This was his greatest gift to us.

Thus Merlin was a superior being, again born into a primitive world. Though those who knew him in centuries past, who saw his advanced technology, wondered in awe, when at last again he ventured forth with renewed wisdom and renewed strength, what else could he be called but magical?

Merlin rebuilt his stone circle, this time even greater. He found his child and taught him well. The child grew with wisdom and knowledge into manhood. Thus for a brief second in history, Merlin saw Arthur have his Camelot.